Isabel grimaced.

"I feel terrible about forgetting you. I was so self-involved back then. I don't even know what to say."

"It's okay," James said gruffly. "So, how are you?"

"I'm fine. Just working in the store, and—" How was she supposed to ask for a favor now? "I—I was wondering if you might be free to help me move something this morning. Feel free to charge the time to my father."

He was silent. She wondered if she'd just made an even bigger fool of herself.

"Sure," he said at last. "And no need to charge your father." There was a smile in his voice. "See you in a bit."

Was that forgiveness she heard in his tone? James struck her as a man who didn't talk about his feelings too often. Call it gut instinct—she knew men, if nothing else. She had a feeling that while James seemed to fight it tooth and nail, he was becoming her friend.

Whether he liked it or not.

Dear Reader,

When you're twenty-two, you have it. Youth has a beauty and allure all its own, and when you look back on photos of your twenty-two-year-old self, you wonder what you were agonizing over back then. Then you get into the business of life, and you get married, have kids, start going gray... Your body changes, your perspective changes, and the other women who are in the same boat start reassuring you—perhaps a little too ardently—that you've still got it. You're a "hot mama."

Whoever first told us that it's our job to be "hot"? And why on earth did we accept the position? "The successful candidate will be a visual stimulus for males within her general vicinity."

There's nothing wrong with being attractive. I am beautiful—my husband reminds me of it all the time. But I'm a woman—not a trophy. I'm a partner, a cheerleader, a warrior, a defender. Let's start with the assumption that we're all beautiful—because you are!—then let's go forward from there. What else are you? And what are you going to do with the wealth of skill, insight and passion that you bring to the party?

It isn't my job to be "hot." My job includes being intelligent, thoughtful and caring. Being well-read is an advantage, and when it comes to protecting the women around me, I'm a force to be reckoned with. When men see me coming, I don't want appraising glances. My body isn't their business, and if this brain intimidates them, then they can call me "ma'am." I prefer it that way, anyway. Ladies, we're so much more than what society asks of us. I will never call you hot, but I will most certainly call you magnificent!

If you'd like to connect with me, you can find me on Facebook, or at my website, patriciajohnsromance.com.

Patricia Johns

HEARTWARMING

A Baxter's Redemption

Patricia Johns

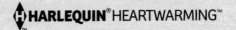

HARLEQUIN® HEARTWARMING™

Recycling programs
for this product may
not exist in your area.

ISBN-13: 978-0-373-36821-1

A Baxter's Redemption

Copyright © 2017 by Patty Froese Ntihemuka

All rights reserved. Except for use in any review, the reproduction or utilization of this work in whole or in part in any form by any electronic, mechanical or other means, now known or hereinafter invented, including xerography, photocopying and recording, or in any information storage or retrieval system, is forbidden without the written permission of the publisher, Harlequin Enterprises Limited, 225 Duncan Mill Road, Don Mills, Ontario M3B 3K9, Canada.

This is a work of fiction. Names, characters, places and incidents are either the product of the author's imagination or are used fictitiously, and any resemblance to actual persons, living or dead, business establishments, events or locales is entirely coincidental.

This edition published by arrangement with Harlequin Books S.A.

For questions and comments about the quality of this book, please contact us at CustomerService@Harlequin.com.

® and TM are trademarks of Harlequin Enterprises Limited or its corporate affiliates. Trademarks indicated with ® are registered in the United States Patent and Trademark Office, the Canadian Intellectual Property Office and in other countries.

Printed in U.S.A.

Patricia Johns has her honors BA in English literature. She lives in Alberta, Canada, with her husband and son where she writes full-time. Her first Harlequin novel came out in 2013, and you can find her books in the Love Inspired, Western Romance and Heartwarming lines.

Books by Patricia Johns

American Romance

Hope, Montana

Safe in the Lawman's Arms
Her Stubborn Cowboy
The Cowboy's Christmas Bride

Love Inspired

His Unexpected Family
The Rancher's City Girl
A Firefighter's Promise
The Lawman's Surprise Family

To my mom, the businesswoman.
She's five-two and tough as they come.
Give her a goal and she sinks her teeth into it,
then shakes the stuffing out of it. "Almost" isn't
good enough for her. I love you, Mom.
You taught me well!

CHAPTER ONE

ISABEL BAXTER'S STOMACH curdled as she glanced around the sunny living room of her childhood home—a rambling, three-story house just outside Haggerston, Montana. Coming home wasn't the same since her father's second marriage, the thought of which still left her angry. The house itself had stood the test of time, but the interior had not. The portrait of her parents was gone, replaced by a jarring abstract painting over the stone fireplace. The removal of that portrait was to be expected, of course, but it still felt like a betrayal to the family they used to be. The antique rocking chair that had belonged to Isabel's maternal grandmother had also been removed, replaced by a modern monstrosity that looked like a dried orange peel, a cup waiting to embrace the hindquarters of unsuspecting visitors.

Her father, George Baxter, was balding and portly, and he sat in his same old spot in the leather armchair. The family lawyer loomed behind him—a young man with a steely gaze. She knew he was the lawyer the minute she stepped into the room, although she'd never met him. Lawyers all had the same look: well ironed and expressionless. Isabel eyed him for a moment, taking in his broad shoulders, his suit jacket tugging ever so slightly around a muscled chest. She sighed. This was the kind of family reunion she'd expected—the kind that required a lawyer. Baxters were nothing if not prepared.

"Do we really need a lawyer here?" she asked.

A slight smile flickered around the corners of the lawyer's lips, and she met his gaze. He was muscular with chiseled features and an easy way of standing that made her suddenly more aware of her own appearance. There had been a time when Isabel would have flirted with him, just to see if she could get his attention, but those days were past. She knew better than to flirt since the accident.

"I'm glad you're here, Princess," her father replied, ignoring her tartness. "How are you feeling?" Was it her imagination, or was he trying not to look too closely at her face?

She knew what he was getting at. She

wasn't the same daughter that George Baxter had sent off to New York six years earlier. A year ago, she'd been hit by a car, leaving her severely scarred. After a bad reaction to anesthetic where she nearly died on the operating table, she declined further cosmetic surgery. She'd just have to carry on as she was. It wasn't a decision her father had ever fully embraced.

"I'm fine, Dad. I assume you asked me here to talk business."

"Yes." Her father heaved himself to his feet with a grunt. "It's about the money."

"What money, specifically?" she asked.

"Your money." He shoved his hands into his pockets. "The doctor says I've got to slow down with my heart acting up this way, and I've decided to sign over your trust fund now, instead of when you turn thirty."

"Why?" She pulled her hair away from her face. "What did the doctor say, exactly?"

"I'm not dying, if that's what you're getting at," her father retorted.

"But what did he say?" she pressed.

"Hardening of the arteries. Some fibrillation. Nothing earth-shattering. Your grandfather lived to be ninety-five eating nothing but bacon and eggs, so I'm sure I'll be just fine. All the same, I'm slowing down."

"And you're finally ready for me to run Baxter Land Holdings?" Isabel guessed, her pulse speeding up at the prospect. She'd been angling for this—preparing for it—since she went to college, not that her father had encouraged it. He'd suggested she take a degree in art history. She'd been the one to choose a degree in business, with a minor in marketing.

"Take over?" George shot her an alarmed look. "Heavens, no. But with your accident, and all that, I thought you could use some cheering up—"

Isabel pressed her lips together. Her father had a stranglehold on the family business, and in his eyes, she'd always be his princess—an endearment that came with as many strings as a spider's web.

"I love you, too, but you know money won't fix this, right?" she asked blandly.

George gestured to the younger man. She glanced uneasily toward the lawyer, and he smiled, then crossed the room. He wore a nicely tailored suit, but it wasn't expensive. She knew suits, and this one was store brand.

"Hi, I'm Isabel Baxter," she said. "George's daughter, in case you weren't up to speed there."

"James Hunter." He shook her hand, his grasp strong and warm. "Nice to see you again."

Again? Isabel squinted at him. *Have I met him before?*

"So come take a look." Her father went on, ignoring their personal introductions. He held a folder, which he opened. "I've requested that your funds be taken out of the investments. There was some good growth, so you'll be comfortable." He came to his daughter's side and pointed to a dollar amount. "It takes a few days for the funds to be released, but I'll give you the paperwork as soon as it is."

"Sure." She nodded. "That would be fine."

There was movement in the doorway, and Isabel glanced up to see her young stepmother, Britney Baxter. Britney was two years younger than Isabel, and she wore yoga pants and a midriff-baring top, with a towel tossed around her neck as if she'd just finished a workout. If she had, she hadn't worked up a sweat. To Isabel, Britney's outfit spoke volumes about her maturity. Technically, this was Britney's home and she could wander around it dressed as she pleased, but she still looked more like a high school cheerleader than a married woman. It was that tanned midriff that drew Isabel's eye—a gently domed belly. Reality took a moment to sink in, then her gaze whipped back to her father in shock.

"You're—" She cleared her throat. "You two are having a baby?"

When her father had married a woman forty years younger than himself, Isabel had considered the possibility of siblings, but somehow she still wasn't prepared for this.

"Yes." Her father shrugged. "I wasn't sure how to tell you, so—"

So they thought they'd announce it with a sports bra and yoga pants? There were better ways to announce these things, and she was uncomfortably aware that this awkward family moment was being played out in front of James Hunter. She glanced in his direction irritably.

"Congratulations," she said, her throat constricted. "That's wonderful news."

It didn't feel like wonderful news, but she wasn't going to confess her true feelings at the moment. Any lawyer would be pleased with that.

Her father smiled widely. He gestured toward his young wife. "Come on in, beautiful. We're done with the business talk."

Britney padded into the room on bare feet and slid into her husband's embrace. She eyed Isabel cautiously.

"Well, I should be off," Isabel said, sucking in a breath. She'd had enough surprises on her first day back in town.

"No, no. You'll stay here, of course." George patted Britney's hip, then released her.

"No, Dad, that's not a great idea."

"Why?" her father demanded, glancing between his young wife and his daughter. "There is plenty of space. This is your home. You grew up in this house." Britney and Isabel had exchanged heated words after the wedding, and they'd never actually made up afterward. But they were expected to forget about all that and act like one big, happy family. Not likely. Britney looked away, her cheeks pink.

"And I'm fully grown now." Isabel shot her father a smile. "Thanks all the same, Dad, but I need a bit of privacy, too."

"Fine, fine," he muttered gruffly. "Suit yourself. You're staying for supper at least, aren't you? I asked James here so he could go over a few of the legalities with you. He's got papers for you to sign, and we could start all of that now—"

"I have a hundred things to do still, so no. Next time. The legalities can wait until the money is transferred, I'm sure." She smiled—not from happiness but from habit, an automatic coping mechanism she hadn't stopped using now that her smile lost its power. "I'd better get going."

Her father shrugged, then stepped forward and enclosed Isabel in a strong hug. "It's good to see you, Princess."

"I missed you, too," she whispered, squeezing him back.

Turning toward the door, she heaved a sigh of relief. She'd been dreading this first visit home after her move back, and now she could tick that off her list of uncomfortable obligations. All she wanted right now was to get as far from this house as possible.

Dad's having another child.

She knew things were different, but seeing Britney's pregnant belly had hammered that fact home. Everything—absolutely everything—had changed.

JAMES WATCHED AS Isabel left the room, her low-heeled pumps tapping against the hardwood floor. Her long dark hair swung half-way down her back, a few inches above her close-fitting blue jeans. She hadn't lost her ability to dress for her figure over the last decade, and James was reminded of the Isabel from high school—the girl with whom a hundred teenage boys fell in love from afar. He had, too, but she hadn't been a terribly compassionate person back then. She'd known how much power she wielded over the male population, and she'd used it regularly. Sweet smiles or scathing criticism—she'd use whatever helped get her way. He'd recognized that smile she'd shot her father—he could still see Haggerston's exploitive beauty queen beneath the scars.

The front door opened and shut, leaving the room in awkward silence.

"It looks like you won't be needing me, after all," James said, glancing toward Mr. Baxter. The older man shrugged.

"Actually, there is something you can do for me," Mr. Baxter replied. He patted Britney's shoulder, and the young woman hesitated for a moment.

"I'll leave you boys to the business chatter," she quipped, and headed for the door. "I thought I'd go shopping this morning, Georgie…"

"Good girl." Mr. Baxter smiled fondly in his wife's direction, but he waited until the door was shut before he spoke again. "I need you to keep an eye on my daughter."

"Isabel?" James couldn't hide his surprise. "Why?"

"She's—" Mr. Baxter stopped, frowned. "How to say this… She takes after her mother more than me. She's not exactly business minded."

James swallowed a laugh. "Doesn't she have a bachelor's degree in business from Yale?"

That constituted some business sense in James's mind.

Mr. Baxter batted his hand through the air in dismissal. "A degree and an actual instinct for business are two different things. She tried to start up a line of natural soaps and creams a couple of years ago, and it tanked. I'd told her that the market was saturated, but she wouldn't listen. Hers would be better, she said. Even if they were, it didn't matter. There was no more interest in skin-care start-ups by fashionistas. Before that, it was a line of scarves, I think—those wispy things women accessorize with. She insisted that all the girls wanted to be like her, and now they could—for the low, low price of thirty-five bucks. She spent a few weeks in front of a sewing machine until she realized she hated sewing, and apparently no one outside this town wanted to be just like her. I could have told her that much, but would she listen to me? Never. She needs guidance with the money I'm signing over to her, and she might not be willing to accept it from me—directly, that is."

"So you want me to give her your advice?" James clarified.

"And keep me informed."

This was very quickly inching beyond the scope of his job description, and James glanced around the room while he gathered his thoughts.

"I won't follow her," he said, bringing his attention back to Mr. Baxter. "I'm your lawyer, not a private eye."

"I thought you'd be willing to be somewhat flexible."

James smiled grimly. He'd never been described as flexible in anything, least of all matters of conscience. "Not that flexible, sir."

Anger simmered in Mr. Baxter's eyes, but

he nodded and turned away for a moment. "Fine. But give her advice so that she doesn't do anything stupid, would you?"

"That I can do," James agreed.

"She wasn't raised to survive in this world without that pretty face, James. I spoiled her, and I let her think that she was doing things on her own when she never was. I had friends buy two thousand dollars' worth of scarves with my money. She needs more help than she realizes."

James was more familiar with his boss's daughter than the older man even realized. He'd been in her graduating class, and his cousin had dated her. Everyone knew Isabel Baxter.

"Understood, sir." He glanced at his watch. "Now, unless you wanted to move into another billable hour, I'd best be on my way."

Mr. Baxter shot him a grin. "All right then. I'll be in touch."

The housekeeper showed James to the door, and as he stepped out onto the spacious veranda, he was mildly surprised to see Isabel sitting in a shiny black sedan, the windows down and her head leaning against the headrest. She glanced toward him as he trotted down the stairs. He grimaced inwardly.

While he was curious to see if Isabel had changed at all since her disfiguring accident, she still wasn't high on his list of favorite people. He couldn't just walk by, though, so he angled his steps toward her car.

"Is there a problem?" he asked.

"My car won't start." She glanced toward the house. "And I can't go back in there."

He nodded. He could understand that, at least. The tension in there had been unmistakable.

"Want me to take a look?" he asked, jutting his chin toward the hood of the car.

She arched a brow—a look she'd perfected years ago, but when she did it now, it tugged at the damaged skin along her temple. "You fix cars, too?" she asked incredulously. "I thought you were the lawyer."

"I am, but my dad's a mechanic. I picked up a few tricks." She really didn't seem to recognize him, and he wondered why that even surprised him. She'd flirted her way into having him fix her car after a fender bender back in high school, too. But that was when she was "secretly" dating his cousin, Andrew. Of course, she couldn't tell anyone about their relationship, but she could cash in on James's skills to hide her bad driving from her father.

She leaned forward from the driver's seat, stretching to reach something, then the hood clicked and released. She opened the door and got out, meeting him at the front of the car. A waft of vanilla perfume tickled his senses as he took off his suit jacket and rolled up his sleeves. He tossed the jacket over the side mirror and lifted the hood.

"So you're a Yale grad," he said.

"Hmm." She leaned closer, watching as his fingers moved over the engine, looking for the issue. He spotted the loose wires almost immediately.

"How long are you back in town?" he asked.

"For as long as I need to. I don't have a leaving date yet, if that's what you're asking."

James raised an eyebrow but didn't say anything as he tightened the connections. So the prodigal daughter had returned—for now. He doubted that many people in this town would be happy to hear that. Isabel had been a beauty, but she'd also left her mark, Andrew being just one of her casualties. Andrew claimed they were dating for months, but there was no outward sign of it. James had thought his cousin was making it all up until he actually spotted them together one evening. Andrew was a math whiz, and Isabel had needed some tutoring. Apparently, it panned out, because she'd gotten into Yale. James had always suspected she got more than just the tutoring out of Andrew, because she'd continued with the relationship for a few months after the SATs. It was when her friends found out she was dating a poor boy from the raggedy side of town that she'd dumped him and told the school that it was nothing more than tutoring—that Andrew had made it all up. Andrew had been heartbroken and left for boot camp before prom. He was sent to Afghanistan and never did make it home.

We'll take that road trip together before I go, his cousin had promised... It hadn't happened.

"Your father hired me as the family's legal counsel," James said, dropping the hood back down with a bang. "That includes you."

"I might be better off getting my own lawyer," she said. "To protect my interests."

"Against Britney, you mean," he clarified.

"Yes." A spot of color appeared in her cheeks. "You have to admit that things are complicated. I'm not entirely sure that my father has my best interests at heart right now."

"My job is to offer you legal advice," James said. "I'm not interested in playing sides. I'm a lawyer, and a good one. Your father is footing the bill. I'll never tell you his private business and I'll never tell him yours. If you hire another firm, legal fees will cut into that nest egg your father is signing over to you, but it's up to you." He straightened and nodded toward the driver's seat. "Try again."

Isabel got back into the car and turned the key. The engine coughed to life.

"Thank you," she said, the old smooth voice again, a cool mixture of sweetness and indifference. She paused, cleared her throat and changed her tone. "What did you do?"

"Reconnected loose wires on the starter. It happens sometimes."

"Well…" She smiled. "I'm grateful."

"No problem."

She eyed him for a moment. "What are they like?"

"Who?"

"My father and… Britney."

"Happy," he said with a shrug.

"You have to say that, don't you?" Bitterness laced her tone.

"I don't have to say anything," he replied. "And I can't say more than that. Like I said, discretion is part of the job."

"Of course it is." She smiled tightly. "Well, thanks again."

She put the car into gear and pulled away, her tires crunching along the drive.

James was no longer a smitten teen. He'd never acted on his crush on Isabel because Andrew was dating her, but her cruelty was what doused his feelings for her. She was heartless and self-centered.

Would it have been different if she'd had the compassion to sit down and talk to Andrew instead of publicly mocking him? People broke up all the time, and it didn't end their lives. Would Andrew have made different choices, maybe been more careful over there in the war zone, if her cruelty hadn't pushed him out of town early? She hadn't remembered him—and it made him wonder if Andrew had slipped from her memory, as well.

He'd do his job. He'd give her the advice

her father wanted her to have, and he'd provide legal counsel should she require it. But after that, Isabel Baxter was on her own.

CHAPTER TWO

HAGGERSTON WAS A TOWN that landed like a splatter in the middle of open prairie, cut through by a highway, and left on its own in the patchwork of Montana's fields and pastures. It was large enough to have the main amenities—a supermarket, a hardware store, a veterinarian clinic—but small enough that everyone still knew each other.

Isabel had been born here, and when she left home to go to college, she never thought she'd return. Not like this. She'd always imagined her homecoming to be a triumphal entry—a successful, beautiful woman come back for a quick weekend where she showed off her husband and kids. She'd be the topic of local gossip, word of her arrival spreading faster than the flu.

She had the gossip part down, she realized wryly, but not the way she'd hoped. Life had a way of turning full circle and swallowing a person whole.

When she'd graduated from Yale and moved to New York for her first job—a desk job in a marketing company—life had seemed shiny and exciting. And it was. For a young woman with family money, New York had a lot to offer.

One rainy evening after work last year, Isabel had headed out to catch a cab home. As she'd stepped out into the street to hail one, a bike had swerved around her and pushed her into oncoming traffic. She didn't remember the car hitting her at all, but she did recall waking up in the hospital, in agony from head to toe. Her face had been badly cut, and from that moment on, she knew that her life would never be what she'd imagined.

After that first surgery, she could remember feeling like a heavy weight was on her chest, refusing to let her inhale. It was like being smothered from the inside, and when the doctors told her that she'd nearly died on the table, she knew she wouldn't have another surgery. Vanity wasn't worth dying for, but the adjustment to becoming ordinary when she'd been used to being stunningly beautiful was a difficult one. No one jumped to open doors for her anymore. No one checked her out in the street—unless one

wanted to count the double takes from pass-
ersby when they saw the scars. They weren't
looking with admiration. They stared in pity,
then dropped their gazes.

So when her father suggested that she
might come back to Haggerston for a while,
that old yearning to finally be a part of the
family business—maybe even take it over—
resurfaced. New York was a big and scary
place for a woman who'd lost her beauty, and
she'd already been passed over twice for a
promotion at her marketing job. She'd gotten
her education, had four years of work experience under her belt, and she was no longer
the beauty queen who'd left town eight years
ago. Perhaps a shot at Baxter Land Holdings
wasn't as out of the question anymore. So
she packed up her things to make the move.

It was then that she'd seen the ad for a tiny
house for sale. It was beautiful—a minia-
ture home on wheels like a trailer, but built
to look exactly like a house, complete with
sloped roof and a small porch on the front.
Inside, it was arranged with artistic precision.
The front door opened onto the wee sitting
room, behind which were the kitchen and
bathroom. Overhead was a sleeping loft, with
long, narrow windows spilling light under

the sloping roof. The entire inside was made of natural wood, softened by wax, and was at its most beautiful in the afternoon light.

Everything had to be carefully arranged so that not an inch was wasted, and that was part of what made Isabel fall in love with the tiny house. It forced her to reexamine her life and the items that she'd collected along the way and pare them down to the essentials.

Who was she underneath the makeup, the fashion, the money… What mattered most?

So she'd bought the house, hooked it up behind her SUV and began the long drive from New York to Montana.

Within a week after her visit with her dad, she'd been set up. Finding a place to park her little house had been easier than she'd imagined. Outside Haggerston, a local man had a piece of property with electricity and water all ready to hook up, and he charged her a miniscule rent for the pleasure of living on his land. It had a view of green pasture where horses grazed on one side, and on the other, the foothills sloped lazily toward jagged mountains. Just standing there, breathing in the pristine summer air made everything seem possible again.

Isabel pulled two grocery bags full of fresh

produce out of the trunk of her car and was heading back to the house when the sound of an engine rumbled into the drive. She turned back, squinting against the afternoon sun. A black pickup truck pulled in, dusty from the road. It came to a stop next to her white SUV, and her father's lawyer—James? Was that it?—grinned down at her out the open window.

"Hi," he said with an easy smile. "This isn't what I expected."

She glanced back at the little house. No, she doubted that her living arrangements were what anyone expected from her, but at this point, she didn't care. Life hadn't been what she'd expected, either, so she figured they could all be mildly surprised together and then get on with things.

"How did you find me, exactly?" she asked. She hadn't given him her address— she hadn't given it to her father, either, for that matter.

"In Haggerston? Nothing's as secret as you think," he replied with a shrug. "I asked around a little. Didn't take much."

She didn't doubt that for a minute. Haggerston was nothing if not efficient in its gossip. James opened the truck door and hopped out.

"What can I do for you?" she asked. She turned and climbed the three steps up to the tiny porch and opened the front door. Inside, she had everything arranged already—two wood-framed leather chairs on one side, an oval table between them that doubled as a place to eat and a place to visit. Across from the little table was another compact chair, this one upholstered in gold and burgundy, with a Tiffany lamp perched on a plant stand next to it. Afternoon sunlight slanted through a window, brightening everything into a cheery glow.

James ambled after her, pausing on the porch to peer inside. "Does your father know about this?"

She turned to eye him curiously. "Do I need his permission?"

He smiled wryly. "Sorry, that was just curiosity." His gaze moved around slowly. "It's kind of neat."

"Thanks." She moved toward the kitchen space. "Make yourself comfortable."

"I take it you don't remember me."

"You're my father's lawyer," she said, giving him a funny look.

"I mean from before."

"No. Should I?" Her parents had always had a hundred business contacts, and she'd never been able to keep them straight. Perhaps James was the son of one of them. Although he didn't come from money if his suits were anything to go by, so maybe a nephew. She pulled open the small fridge under the counter and began to unpack her groceries into it—peaches, pears, nectarines.

"I'm James Hunter." He paused. "Jim Hunter. They called me Jim. We went to high school together."

"Oh—" She stopped herself before she could pretend to remember. She certainly hadn't been friends with a Jim Hunter, and she'd remember a guy as good-looking as this lawyer was. He was tall, broad and muscular, with green eyes and the faintest hint of freckles across his cheekbones as if he'd stepped off the farm and into a suit. His jaw was strong, and he met her gaze with easy directness. She shut the fridge and rose to her feet.

"It's okay. We didn't run in the same circles." He smiled wanly, and for the life of her she wished she could remember him, put him into context.

"I'm really sorry," she said with a sigh. "I stayed pretty busy in high school."

"I know." He cleared his throat. "I came to bring by those documents your father mentioned. I have a check for you here, and a few pages for you to sign."

He put a folder onto the tabletop.

"Have a seat," Isabel said, sinking into the chair opposite him.

"Thanks." He sat down and opened the folder. He slid a check toward her, and she scanned the amount. It was the contents of her trust fund, enough to invest in a small business of her own. She folded it in half. "I just need you to sign here stating that you've received the money, then here and here and initial here."

Isabel looked over the papers, then signed in the designated spots. She put down the pen with a click and looked at James speculatively. "Why are you really here?"

James didn't appear surprised at the question, and he met her gaze easily. "What do you mean?"

"You could have called me into your office," she replied. "You were holding the check. If I wanted the money, I'd have come to you."

"I'm the family lawyer, remember?" he replied. "This is my job."

"You're my father's lawyer. There is a difference."

"No, I'm here for you, too. If you need any legal advice, I'm here to help. Everything will be billed to your father."

Isabel laughed softly. "The one thing my father taught me was that nothing in life is free. There are always strings attached. What are the strings here?"

James shrugged. "He's your dad. He worries."

"So you're the official spy?" she clarified. "He's just signed over a large chunk of cash, and you're here to make sure I don't do anything silly?"

James dropped his gaze. She'd hit the nail on the head, and on her first try, at that. She would have been more impressed with herself if she weren't so annoyed with the situation.

"I'm not interested in spying on you," James said after a momentary silence. "I'm a lawyer, and contrary to family opinion, I do have a few limits on what I'll do. I'll tell you what I told your father—I'm happy to give you some legal advice. I'll even pass along any advice your father has for you, if you're willing to hear it. But after that, my duties are complete, and the rest is none of my business."

He rose to his feet and collected the papers together once more.

"Look, James—" Had she offended him? "I don't mean to take this out on you. We've got a complicated family dynamic."

"Tell me about it." His tone was grim, but he shot her a wry smile. "Don't worry about me, Ms. Baxter. I've got a hide like an elephant."

"And a memory to match," she replied with a low laugh.

"It doesn't take a stellar memory to remember you," he replied, pausing at the door. "Everyone knew Isabel Baxter."

Isabel smiled wanly. "Well, as you can see, those days are gone. I'll have to face life just like everyone else now."

James regarded her thoughtfully. "You'll do okay," he said. Then he pulled the door open and stepped out onto the small porch, then he paused and took a business card out of his pocket. "That's my contact information. If you need anything, give me a call."

Isabel watched as James made his way back

to his truck and slid into the seat. He raised his hand in a wave, then slammed the door.

James Hunter—Jim, he'd been—had done well for himself. And in a way that no one could dismiss. He'd worked hard, become a lawyer, and if he weren't one of the best, her father would never have put him on retainer. No one would brush off his success as a by-product of his good looks. Isabel had worked hard for her degree, too, but she still felt like her self-confidence had been pulled out from under her. She knew how to face these challenges as a beautiful woman, but how was she supposed to get over the hurdles without a brilliant smile, a flirtatious laugh or a lingering look that would leave the men weak-kneed? Those had been her tricks, because under that surface confidence, she hadn't really believed that she could succeed based on her intelligence alone. She'd wanted to, of course—she'd desperately wanted people to take her seriously—but she'd never really believed they would. Somehow, the patronizing smiles and pats on her hand were more believable than the whisper inside her that said, "I could do this…"

"How do women manage?" she asked herself aloud, and her fingers fluttered up to the scars along her left cheek.

She'd never felt more powerless in her life. JAMES DROPPED HIS briefcase on his desk and pulled off his suit jacket. Jackson, Hobbs and Hunter was a small law firm, consisting of James, Ted Jackson, who made a habit of doing far too much pro bono work, and a transplanted lawyer from another town west of Haggerston named Eugene Hobbs. Eugene was tall, gangly and looked like a fourteen-year-old, but his thirty-five-year-old brain was a steel trap.

The office building was on the corner of Preston Street and Main, a three-story building that overlooked Saint Mary's Catholic Church's parking lot on one side and a string of little shops along Main Street on the other. James enjoyed the view of the parking lot, as strange as that seemed to his law partners. He watched kids learn how to ride their bikes in that parking lot, people come and go from the church, teenagers get their first driving lessons with white-knuckled parents. Looking over that parking lot helped him to think and put his mind onto different paths. This afternoon, the church parking lot was empty, except for one small hatchback car that belonged to the priest. It wasn't helpful.

James turned on his computer and checked his email. A smile twitched at the corners of his lips when he saw a forward from his younger sister, Jenny. She was always sending him little jokes—this one about driving in England. He was about to reply when Eugene stuck his head around the door.

"Hey, you're back," the gangly man said. "Did you get Ted's email about billable hours?"

"Yeah, I got it."

Eugene came into the office and looked out the wide window at the parking lot. "So how've you been? I haven't seen much of you the last few days."

"I've been busy with the Baxters," James replied.

"They keep you hopping."

"It's called a retainer," James quipped.

"I heard that Mr. Baxter's daughter is back in town."

James shrugged, unwilling to say too much. "Yeah, she's back."

"I've seen the pictures of her during her beauty queen days, but I haven't seen her in person yet. Are the scars as bad as they say?"

James considered for a moment, thinking back to Isabel and the white lines that tugged at the left side of her face. But it wasn't just the scars that had altered Isabel—there was something else that he couldn't quite put his finger on, but she'd changed. "Yes," he admitted. "She looks a lot different."

"The gossip has been fierce," Eugene said. "It doesn't seem like people around town liked her much."

James shrugged noncommittally. He had his own grudge with the Baxter beauty, not that it mattered. Life went on, and people who held on to their anger only punished themselves. According to Gandhi, at least.

"So what was the deal with her?" Eugene pressed.

"Oh, just that she was gorgeous and wealthy, and relied on her looks a lot."

"I know the feeling. I rely on mine, too."

"It's because you look like Opie," James said with a laugh. "Everyone opens up to you."

"That's what I mean." Eugene's face broke open into a wolfish grin. "It works for me."

James laughed. Eugene wasn't as young, or as simple, as he looked. At thirty-five, he still looked like a teen, a cowlick making the hair at the back of his head stand up straight, no matter how much product he applied to flatten it. The tiny lines forming around his eyes were incongruous.

"But you liked her?" Eugene asked.

James barked out a bitter laugh. "I can't say that any of us liked her much. She used people—men, mostly. She knew how to get her way. But I'm not willing to carry a grudge from high school. If you saw her—what the accident did to her—you'd see what I mean. That's punishment enough."

Eugene's phone blipped, and he pulled it out of his pocket, raised a finger and picked up the call. "Eugene Hobbs here." He listened for a moment, then covered the mouthpiece and said to James, "Talk later, okay?"

James gave a thumbs-up, and Eugene headed back out into the hallway, leaving James in quiet. Isabel had left her mark all over this town—from being Miss Haggers ton three years running to breaking hearts. And though she hadn't done much to James himself, she'd broken his cousin's spirit, just before he left for war.

His office phone rang, and James answered on the second ring.

"James Hunter," he intoned.

"Mr. Hunter? This is Bob over at Family Cheese."

James closed his eyes and suppressed a sigh. What was wrong now?

"What can I do for you, Bob?"

"I'm afraid we have to let Jenny go."

"You're firing her?" James clarified, his stomach sinking. This wasn't exactly a surprise—he'd dealt with this before. "What happened?"

"I'm sorry. We did our best, but she just lost it on a customer. Screaming, yelling. It isn't working out. Can you come pick her up?"

Jenny had Down syndrome, and he'd become her legal guardian after their mother's death in a car crash three years earlier. It had been hard enough to find a job again after the last time she'd "lost it on a customer" at a local diner. There was more to the story, of course. There always was, but no one wanted to hear it.

"Why did she get upset?" James asked.

"No reason that I could see," Bob replied. "Look, I've got customers, so I've got to go. But you'll need to come pick her up. She's waiting outside on the bench."

"I'll be there in five minutes," he replied. "Thanks, Bob."

Hanging up the phone, he pushed himself to his feet. Jenny was his only sibling, and he'd always been protective of her. In school, she'd never been picked on because everyone knew that if they messed with Jenny, they were taking on Jim Hunter, too. With Jenny's big blue eyes and wide, laughing mouth, it was hard to imagine her getting angry, but she'd been having trouble keeping a job for the past year. He clicked his computer into sleep mode and rose to his feet. His jaw was tense, his gaze drilling into the wall ahead of him.

"Oh, James—" Eugene poked his head back into James's office, then froze. "Okay. Sorry. Not a good time."

James didn't even bother reassuring his colleague. Right now, he had something else to do, and that old protective instinct was kicking in. No matter how many years slipped by, his role remained the same—Jenny's big brother. He'd be the brick wall between her and an unkind world.

CHAPTER THREE

ISABEL TURNED IN a circle, taking in the large kitchen. It was more than she needed, but a full, professional bakery was hard to resist. For the last couple of years, she'd been mulling over a new idea for a small business—a chocolate shop. She'd call it Baxter's Chocolates, and her father would be enraged at her use of the family name for another one of her business schemes, but it was her name, too. He wasn't the only one with claim to it.

Gleaming ovens, a ceramic stove top with a huge stainless steel hood hovering above it, vast counter space and everything tiled in brilliant white. A double refrigerator loomed next to the owner, Roger Varga, who stood near the door, arms crossed over his chest as she poked through cupboards and into corners.

"What happened to the business that used to be here?" Isabel asked, glancing over her shoulder.

Roger stroked his fingers over a graying mustache. "Times are tough. They weren't able to make the money they thought they could."

She nodded, hiding the worry that built up inside her. That was her fear, too, that her chocolate business wouldn't take off and she'd be left with another failed business on her hands. Of course, her father could always bail her out—he always had in the past—but this time, it was a matter of pride. This time, she wanted to make it on her own.

"I think the lease is a little high," she said, angling her steps back over to where he stood. "It doesn't do you any good to lease the place out for three months, then have it stand empty for another eight if I go under, does it?"

He paused, seemed to be considering her words. "What did you have in mind?"

"Half of the asking price."

"I can't do that." He shook his head. "I'd rather have it stand empty. But I could go down to this—" He jotted a number on the corner of the lease papers.

Isabel considered for a moment. The number was fair, but she had a feeling she could get him lower. She shot him a smile, and only after she pulled the smile-brilliantly-at-your-rival routine, did she remember that she no longer had that card in her deck. She wasn't going to dazzle him, and she sucked in a deep breath, covering her momentary discomfort by looking down. Could she even negotiate without her go-to feminine wiles?

Do I have a choice?

"How about this—" She jotted another number below his. "And I'll make you something amazing for your next anniversary with your wife."

"How amazing?" A smile twitched at the corners of his lips.

"Trust me. I know what impresses a woman. It will be chocolate, and it will melt her heart. Just be sure to tell everyone who made it."

He laughed and shook his head and scratched the new number into the lease. "You drive a hard bargain, Ms. Baxter, but you have yourself a deal. Care to sign now?"

"Not yet," she said with a shake of her head. "I just need to have my lawyer look over the fine print, and then I'll drop it by your office."

"Fair enough." He shook her hand, and they walked together through the echoing shop and out the front door. The bell tinkled overhead, and Isabel glanced up at it. This was it—she could feel it in her bones—her shop. She'd mentioned this chocolate shop idea to her father before the accident and he'd liked the idea—in New York, at least. He'd suggested that it might keep her entertained until she got married and started having babies. That had been insulting, but he'd paid for her trips to France for chocolate-making classes. It had been a victory, of sorts. His one repeated warning had been, "But you don't seem to have the sixth sense, Izzy. Entrepreneurs need to have that tingle that tells them where the money is, and you haven't really got that…"

Was he right? Was this a dumb idea, or was her instinct better than either of them imagined? Well, this wasn't his business. He bought and sold land with Baxter Land Holdings, but she wanted something different—Baxter's Chocolates. Truffles, bars, nuggets and cream-centered confections. She'd perfected the art in her own kitchen—polishing up her skills on those vacations to Paris. Her friends thought she'd gone to France to shop, and she had done a fair bit of that, too, but her main reason had been for the private chocolatier classes she took from the best in the world. And after all that personal research and now her trust fund money, the time was ripe.

"Thanks so much," Isabel said, shaking Roger's hand firmly. "I'll be in touch."

This side street was quiet this time of day. A block away, Main Street was bedecked with hanging planters of fragrant hydrangeas, but Nicholson Avenue was bare. It ran from Main with some businesses on either side of the street—a little bistro across from the closed bakery—and then melted into a residential area of tiny houses from the fifties. Isabel sucked in a breath of fresh air and smiled to herself. This felt right. It was coming together, and after all the changes to her family, after her accident, she needed this.

"Is that you, Isabel?"

Isabel blinked and turned to see Britney teetering across the street toward her, one hand on her belly, the other outstretched to stop a pickup truck as she made a great show of pretending to run across the road, taking tiny steps and laughing at herself. Isabel smiled wanly. Had she ever acted like that? She wasn't sure she'd like the honest answer.

Roger gave a final wave and headed off in

the other direction, leaving Isabel alone on the sidewalk, waiting for Britney to make it across. When Britney stepped up onto the curb, she laughed and shook her head.

"I just can't run like I used to! My goodness. Babies are heavier than you think." She flipped her hair over her shoulder and looked around, wide-eyed. "Oh, my…are you doing what I think you're doing?"

"That depends," Isabel replied drily. "What do you think I'm up to?"

"Something…" She waved her hands in the air as if she were drying a manicure. "I don't know—something expensive."

Isabel shrugged. "Does it matter?"

"Of course it matters," she replied. "That's why we have Jimmy."

Isabel raised a brow. "You mean James Hunter?"

"I call him Jimmy. It just suits him. He's such a teddy bear."

Isabel knew that Britney's gushing shouldn't bother her, but on some level it did. "Jimmy" wasn't a teddy bear, he was a lawyer, and she had the feeling that he'd rather have respect than diminutive nicknames. Or was that just her right now?

"So what are you up to?" Isabel asked, changing the subject.

"Oh, just out for some brunch. Eating for two!" She hunched her shoulders and gave a girlish giggle, rubbing a hand over her belly. "I'm just starving these days. Do you want to go find something to nibble?"

"No thanks." She attempted to infuse some warmth into her tone, but she had a feeling she failed when she saw Britney's face. "I'm not hungry."

"So…" Britney leaned to the side to look around Isabel. "What *are* you doing here? Didn't this used to be Gordie's Bakery? I don't think it lasted long."

Gordie. Georgie. Jimmy. Did any man who Britney came across have a full name?

She doubted it would even matter if she told Britney about her plans. The money was hers, after all. It was snuggly stashed away in her very own bank account, and nothing Britney or her father said would change anything.

"I'm looking into leasing a storefront," she replied.

"What for?" Britney's eyes widened again, but Isabel caught the slight twitch at the corners of her mouth. Britney wasn't as childish as she put on.

"I'm opening my own business. A chocolate shop."

"Oh…" Britney squinted. "Where do you buy the chocolate?"

"I make it."

"Oh!" She pulled her hand through her hair and pursed her lips—Isabel was willing to bet that she'd just caught sight of her own reflection somewhere. "Well, Georgie says—" She blushed and shrugged apologetically. "*Your dad* says that you're better off talking this stuff over with Jimmy. He's good with these things, and we girls don't even know where to start, you know?"

Isabel cocked her head to one side, regarding her young stepmother. There had been a time when Isabel had used the same tactics. Pretty girls got their way, but pretty and intelligent girls were too intimidating and put men off. She'd learned quickly how to "dumb it down" in order to make people do what she needed, but seeing this same manipulation in Britney was mildly annoying.

"I have a degree in business," she replied coolly. "I'm pretty sure I know where to begin."

"Just saying." Britney shrugged. She pulled a necklace out from under her blouse and ran it idly through her fingers. Isabel's gaze locked onto the pendant—a princess-cut yellow diamond, surrounded by white diamonds nestled in white gold. Isabel knew this necklace well—it had been her mother's.

"Where did you get that?" she demanded.

"This?" Britney shrugged. "Your dad gave it to me. Isn't it pretty? I love it."

Isabel shot Britney a tight smile. "I see."

It looked like a lot of things were changing around here, and Isabel didn't have to like it.

"Well, anyway, I'm meeting up with Carmella, so I'd better go." The younger woman beamed at Isabel once more. "Baby's hungry!"

With a flutter of her fingers, Britney pranced away in her two-inch heels, leaving Isabel on the curb with a white-hot feeling searing through her middle. She didn't use the word *hate* lightly, but right now, she truly hated Britney Baxter.

Pulling her phone out of her pocket, she fired off a text to James Hunter: I need your advice on a lease contract. Can we meet?

She dropped the phone back into her purse. If there was one thing her father had taught her, it was that feelings might get hurt, but business wasn't about feelings. It was about money, and it was about building something bigger than yourself.

And right now, she'd stick to business. Feelings were a little too volatile to be trusted.

Britney met a woman on the opposite side of the street who paused, shaded her eyes and peered in Isabel's direction. Isabel knew her well—Carmella, a high school friend. She'd been running into old acquaintances a lot the last few days, and their first reactions had never been very warm. There had been some sympathy over her scars that barely concealed their satisfaction at seeing her brought down a peg or two. Some didn't bother saying anything—just stared. And a couple of old classmates had crossed the street to avoid her, which made their feelings about her pretty clear. So far, she hadn't come across people from the wealthier circles she'd used to move in, and they were the ones who intimidated her the most right now.

"Isabel Baxter, is that you?" Carmella hooted across the street. "Get over here, girl!"

Isabel pasted a smile on her face, hoping

it didn't look like a grimace. "Carmella Biggins?" she called back, and headed across the road.

Sometimes, there was no way around it, and all a woman could do was face it head-on. Like a firing squad.

JAMES PULLED UP to the curb next to Family Cheese and turned off the engine. Jenny sat on a wooden bench, squinting in the morning sun. Her shoulders were hunched, her plump legs dangling, not quite reaching the ground. A slanted triangle of shade from the building behind her just missed her shoulders, and her blond hair shone like gold in the sunlight. Her eyes, small in her round face, followed the truck as he parked, but she didn't move.

Every time this happened, Jenny was crushed.

Pushing open his door, James got out and headed over to where she sat. Another car drove past, tooting a horn in hello. James raised his hand in a distracted wave, not even bothering to check to see who it was. He stopped in front of his sister and looked down at her. She looked girlish from a distance, but up close she looked like the adult she was.

"Hey," he said quietly. "You okay?"

"Nope." She heaved a sigh. "No one wants me, Jimmy." She had a slight lisp, and it still reminded him of when she was a little girl. His heart welled with love.

"I do," he said.

"You don't count." She looked away.

"Ouch," he said, sinking down to the seat next to her. "I like to think I count a little bit."

"Sorry," she retorted.

"So what happened?" he asked. Jenny didn't answer right away, tears misting her eyes, then she turned toward him, her lips quivering with anger.

"He called me retarded."

James blinked. "Bob did?"

"No, not Bob." She shook her head, eyes flashing in exasperation. She put her fingers up to make air quotes. "The customer." She still wasn't clear about how to use air quotes, and she tended to use them when she was upset.

"And Bob didn't stand up for you?" Images of lawsuits danced through his head, but he sucked in a breath to try to calm his anger. "So tell me what happened. Exactly."

"This little boy was pointing at me and

laughing," Jenny said. "So the boy's dad said, 'Don't do that. It's not nice. It's not her fault she's retarded.' So I threw cheese at him."

An image of his sister launching Gouda at a customer's head struck him as funny, and James stifled a laugh. "You had to know that wasn't a good idea," he said.

She shrugged, not looking the least bit apologetic.

James attempted to control the smile that tickled the corners of his lips, but he had a burning question. "How was your aim?"

"I have great aim. I hit him in the face. With a nice, old, gooey brie."

James laughed out loud and shook his head. "Jenny, you're a nut."

"Yeah, well, I'm a nut with good aim!" she shot back, but a smile toyed at the corners of her lips. "It was expensive, too."

"I don't think we have a leg to stand on to argue this one, Jenny," he said apologetically. "You can't throw cheese at people."

"I know."

"We'll find you a different job." The words came easily enough because he wanted them to be true, but Jenny already had a reputation around this town. She stood up for herself, but she had her own method that didn't always suit customer service. And what other jobs were there for her?

"Really, Jimmy?" she asked hopefully.

James paused. "I actually don't know. But we'll sort something out."

"I'm not *retarded*," she said, her voice low. "I'm a person."

"I know, Jenny. And you're a good person, too."

The problem was that people didn't understand Jenny the way he did. He'd gotten her a job in his office stuffing envelopes and doing some photocopies, but the pace was too quick for her and he'd felt terrible when he saw how frustrated she was. It would have been perfect to have her close, but what could he do?

His phone blipped and he glanced down at the text message. It was from Isabel. She wanted to meet up.

"Who's that?" Jenny asked.

"A client," he replied.

"Do you have to go back to work now?"

He sighed. "No, it's okay. I'll take you home first."

He paused to text Isabel back, his thumbs hopping over the keys: I can meet you around 2, if that works. Let me know where.

Jenny scooted forward until her running

shoes hit the ground and glanced up at James. "I wasn't ladylike."

James shot her grin. "So? I'm not lady-like, either."

It was a long-standing joke between them. Jenny grinned and rose to her feet.

"Do you want to stop for a milk shake on the way home?" James asked.

Jenny cocked her head to one side coyly. "I wouldn't object."

He chuckled and opened the truck door for her to get in. As he shut the door after her, he wondered what he could do to find a place for Jenny to belong. She'd always be his sister, and this would always be her town, but she needed more than that—she needed the equivalent of what his legal practice was to him. It seemed so simple, but it wasn't. She needed more than a job. She needed someone who would understand her, and that was one tall order.

His phone blipped again, and he glanced down at the text. It was from Isabel again.

Ruby's Diner. 2 pm is perfect. Thank you, James.

There was something about the words that struck him as sweet, and he pushed any softening feelings firmly away. For the moment, he had an important appointment with his sister and the ice-cream parlor.

CHAPTER FOUR

"How long has it been, Izzy?" Carmella asked, hitching her apple-green Coach bag higher up onto her shoulder. She looked away from Isabel's face uncomfortably and shot a smile at a passing waiter instead. They stood inside the foyer of the little bistro with Britney, the tinkle of cutlery and the clink of glasses melting into the murmur of chatting customers.

"Only a couple of years," Isabel said with a chuckle. "Remember, I was here when you got married."

"Feels like longer, doesn't it?" Carmella cast Isabel a tired smile, then lowered her voice. "Are you and Britney okay being in the same room together?"

"Perfectly," Isabel replied. It was mostly true. She could be polite. Carmella and Isabel had been friends in high school, and with Isabel gone, Britney and Carmella had gotten chummy. Girlfriend loyalty went only so far in a town this size, where there weren't many people to choose from.

Isabel glanced around the little restaurant. She remembered this place well. This was where her father used to take her to celebrate her birthday every year. It hadn't changed since she'd been gone. The same watercolor art hung on the walls, and even the smell of the place was the same. A server approached them—a young man with a mane of dark hair and dark, smoldering eyes. His smolder didn't seem to be very discerning, however, since he gave each of them the same sultry look, including a woman in her seventies behind them. He knew how to get tips, that much was obvious.

"Hi, Carlo," Carmella said. "Just us girls. Are you going to be serving us?"

"Of course," Carlo replied with a smile. "Women as lovely as yourselves need the best service."

Isabel winced. Carlo was probably barely out of high school, and if she'd been the babysitting type as a teenager, she probably would have babysat him. Britney pursed her lips into an oval mirror in her hand and dabbed at her lipstick, looking up only when

Carlo led them into the dining room and over to a table by a window.

"I hate to intrude on your brunch," Isabel said as they sat down.

"You aren't intruding, right, Brit?" Carmella rolled on without waiting for a response. "Carlo, let's start with some mimosas. What do you say, girls?"

"Make mine virgin," Britney sighed. "You want one, too, Izzy?"

"Sure."

Carlo winked, mostly for Carmella's benefit, it seemed, and disappeared once more, leaving them in quiet.

"Britney said you were back in town," Carmella said, "but you didn't call."

"I'm sorry," Isabel replied. "I meant to. I've been busy getting things set up."

"Set up for what?" Carmella's brows rose.

"I'm moving back. For good."

This didn't seem to be news to Carmella, and she and Britney exchanged a look. Then Carmella leaned closer. "I see there's no ring on your finger, but is there a guy in your life at all…?" She let the question hang there.

They didn't have much else to talk about. That was the problem with leaving town for several years—you were no longer part of the same rumor mill. Carmella was trying to make conversation, but the question still grated.

"No. Not at the moment," Isabel replied.

"Well, Britney and I could take care of that," Carmella suggested. Her gaze went to Isabel's scars once more and she cleared her throat. It was a friendly offer that Carmella couldn't make good on. Not anymore, at least. Besides, the implication that the kind thing was to "get her a man," chafed.

"Let's just get this out into the open," Isabel said. "I'm badly scarred. Things are different now. And I'm not looking for a boyfriend."

Just as the words came out of her mouth, Carlo returned with three champagne glasses filled with mimosas—just orange juice for Britney—and set them in front of each woman at the table. They all smiled weakly up at him, and when he'd left, stared at each other in uncomfortable silence.

"What about plastic surgery?" Carmella asked at last.

"I'm not doing any more of that. I had one reconstructive surgery done after the accident and I had a bad reaction to the anesthetic. I just about died. So this is me. I'll just have to get used to it."

The table went silent, and Isabel glanced at the tables around them. Most people were engrossed in their own conversation, but an older woman across the dining room was looking at Isabel, an expression of pity on her face. She dropped her gaze when she was spotted.

"Maybe some good makeup?" Britney asked weakly.

Isabel wasn't pleasantly disposed toward Britney on a good day, and she held back her desire to snap in response.

"It would take a pound of foundation to cover this up," she replied with a wry smile. "And the men that we're talking about wouldn't be interested anyway."

"That's not true," Carmella protested, but her tone said even she didn't believe it.

"Sure it is," Isabel replied. "These guys can get any woman they want, and they want a beautiful wife. That boat has sailed."

Britney's cheeks blushed pink, but Carmella shrugged coolly.

"They aren't all that shallow," Carmella replied. "Besides, you're still a Baxter. Don't lower your standards now. If you want a comfortable life, you'd better marry a man who knows how to provide it."

Isabel understood Carmella's sentiments perfectly. She'd been the same up until the accident, expecting to "marry well" so that her lifestyle wouldn't change. That meant marrying money that could match her own. She used to look down on plain girls, pitying them because she knew that she had something they could only dream of. Well, now she'd joined their ranks, and she was intimidated.

"You both still have your looks, and you're married to wealthy men," Isabel replied evenly. "I'm playing in a different game now."

"I didn't marry for money." Britney's voice was low, and she was clearly offended.

Isabel regarded her young stepmother evenly.

"I didn't!"

"My dad is old enough to be your father," Isabel retorted. "There was a teeny, tiny incentive there."

"I love him."

"Would you have married him if he had no money at all?" Isabel asked.

The atmosphere around the table got uncomfortably silent again. This had been a bad idea. If she couldn't make nice, she shouldn't be sitting around drinking mimosas.

"What about Greg Cranken?" Carmella asked. "He comes from a good family."

Greg Cranken was short, balding and narrow-shouldered. He was the pariah of dinner parties since none of the women wanted to be stuck sitting next to him. His father was in the beef business, but even all that family money hadn't been enough to entice a woman to marry him. Isabel shook her head.

"I'm not looking."

"So what *are* you doing," Carmella asked, lifting her drink to her lips, "if you aren't looking?"

"Starting a business."

Carmella choked on her mimosa and coughed delicately into her napkin. "You're what?"

Carmella had been privy to a couple of her past business schemes, and Isabel felt a wave of mild embarrassment rising. Friends from her youth weren't going to see her any differently now than they'd seen her then. But then again, she hadn't exactly done anything to change their view, either.

"Starting my own business," Isabel repeated. "A chocolate shop."

"And having someone else run it, of course…"

"No, running it myself." Isabel chuckled. "Is it so shocking?"

"That's just wrong." Carmella leaned back and shook her head. "I mean, if you really like running a business, do it. But don't let it take over your life. That's what men do, and they drop dead from the stress. Look at it this way—" Carmella put her glass down onto the tablecloth and leaned forward again. "You could work your fingers to the bone, or you could marry a nice but boring guy like Greg Cranken, and live a comfortable life. I mean, starting a business might be fun at first, but before you know it, it turns into actual work. Do you remember those scarves? *Actual work.* Trust me. I tried making purses and selling them online. I don't like to speak of it. You'd think I'd have learned from your scarf debacle." She shuddered. "I made, like, three purses before I couldn't do it anymore."

"I'm not husband hunting," Isabel replied with a shrug.

Britney cleared her throat. "She knows what she wants to do, Carmella. Let her be."

"Thanks, Britney." It wasn't often that they were on the same side.

"Fine, fine." Carmella heaved a sigh.

"So how are you and Brad?" Isabel asked, changing the subject.

"We're good. He's in New York for a couple of weeks on business, and when he gets back, I'm going to London for a bit of shopping. You should totally come."

"Thanks, but I'll be busy," Isabel replied.

"With the business. See?" Carmella shot her an annoyed glance. "Your sudden interest in making money instead of spending it is already getting in the way of a perfectly good shopping trip."

Isabel laughed. "I love how you just say what you're thinking."

"Someone has to," Carmella muttered.

Carlo came by their table once more, a pad of paper in hand and a smile on his lips. "What can I get you ladies today?"

Carmella sucked in a deep breath and half closed her eyes in thought. "I'll take a green salad with goat cheese and olives, quiche and a side of quinoa."

"And for you?" He turned to Isabel. His smile flickered, his adoring attention slightly more difficult to maintain when it came to her. This was the way it would be from now on. While she'd been used to the fawning attention of every man within a mile's radius, she was now no more than a plain woman with pretty friends.

"Actually, I've got to get going, girls," she said, hoping she sounded more apologetic than she felt. "I have another appointment."

It wasn't entirely true. She wasn't meeting James for another two hours, but she felt stifled, and she desperately needed to get out into the fresh air. Britney pulled out a mirror and checked her eyeliner, batting her lashes as she inspected herself yet again.

"What appointment?" Carmella demanded. "Don't tell me this has to do with business, because I'll scream."

Isabel laughed. "You'll survive. I'll call you, okay?"

"You'd better."

"I will," Isabel insisted. "And I'll see you later, I'm sure, Britney."

Britney fluttered her fingers in farewell, snapping her compact mirror shut. Isabel slid from her spot and dodged around the waiter. She beelined out of the bistro and into the welcoming air. Then she directed her steps toward her SUV across the street.

She wasn't the same woman she used to be—her beauty queen crown had been hung up for good. Beneath her irritation with her scarred appearance and her annoyance that she was no longer the prettiest one at the table was a certainty that she wanted more than the life she'd taken for granted.

Much more.

She wanted the people who knew her to look at her with respect. Not jealousy. Not attraction. Not even admiration. She wanted someone to respect her for her mind.

JAMES GLANCED AT his watch, then took a sip of coffee. Ruby's Diner was a low-key place, located just outside town along the highway. It was an old-fashioned diner with a striped awning over the front door and red, plastic-covered stools along the counter. It catered to travelers and truckers, but the Haggerston locals also took advantage of the down-home cooking. Ruby had died several years ago from a stroke, but her niece took the place over and kept the name. Ruby was still part of this place, in name and in spirit.

This wasn't a Baxter sort of establishment, and maybe that was why Isabel had chosen it.

It was two o'clock, and Isabel was due anytime now. He sat at a table near the back, assuming that Isabel might appreciate some privacy when it came to her business concerns. He'd been surprised that she texted him to begin with. He had a feeling that she didn't trust him—whether that stemmed from her relationship with her father, or some "first" impression, he had no idea.

After a milk shake at the local ice-cream shop—heavy on the cream—he'd taken Jenny back home and dropped her off. She seemed to be in relatively good spirits, but he always worried. Life wasn't easy for Jenny. People didn't always understand Down syndrome, and they oftentimes expected things from Jenny that she couldn't deliver. She lived in a world that didn't "get" her, and she was always trying to prove that she wasn't any different. Except that she was.

The front door opened and James turned to see Isabel step inside. She wore a white, breezy summer dress that scooped down in the front—not enough to sacrifice modesty—and flowed over her figure in the most flattering way. A broad, pink belt cinched her narrow waist, and she pressed a matching pink purse between her side and her elbow. She glanced around the diner, and a few truckers looked up from their meals admiringly. She still had it—the ability to draw all the attention when she walked into a room. She just didn't seem to realize it.

James stood and she smiled and headed in his direction. James sat when she did, and he gestured for the waitress.

"What can I get you?" he asked.

"Oh, nothing." She shook her head. "I've already eaten."

"Coffee?" he asked.

"Sure. Thanks."

The waitress came by and poured another cup for Isabel.

"Anything else?" the waitress drawled. "We have some specials today—"

"No, thank you." Isabel smiled up at the waitress easily. "Coffee is fine for me."

The waitress retreated, leaving the two of them in relative privacy, and Isabel heaved a sigh. "Thanks for meeting up with me. I have a lease for you to look over."

"Oh?" James accepted the papers that she slid across the table, his trained eye moving down the page, identifying the typical clauses and subclauses of a commercial lease. He raised his eyebrows in interest and looked at her from over the pages.

"You're leasing the old bakery?"

"Yes."

He turned back to the lease and perused the last of it. It looked like she'd negotiated a surprisingly low price for the place, too.

"This looks pretty straightforward," James said. "It's a month-to-month lease—open-ended so that you can get out if your business fails or you want to take down your shingle, for whatever reason."

"No surprises in there?" Isabel asked.

"Not one." James handed the paperwork back and regarded her curiously. "Do you mind me asking what you're planning?"

She arched a brow. "So that you can report back to my father?"

James leaned back in his chair. "If you were afraid of that, why did you ask to meet me?"

She shook her head. "You said before that you were willing to keep my business private. Does that still stand?"

"Of course."

She nodded. "Do you know how difficult it is to be watched all the time?"

"No," he admitted.

"It's hard. People think that money brings freedom, but my father taught me early on that nothing comes without strings, and that money he signed over to me comes with so many strings attached."

"Only if you let it," he said. "It's in your name. You can do what you want with it."

Not exactly the advice Mr. Baxter wants me to give.

"I'm willing to bet that my father wants you to keep an eye on me," she said.

James didn't flinch, but he didn't answer, either. They sat in silence, and he wondered if Isabel would say more. Her dark hair fell past her shoulders, and for a moment, her reserve slipped and he saw conflicted emotions in those big, dark eyes. Men had always fallen for Isabel, and it wasn't only her beauty that drew them to her. She was gentler than she liked to let on, and he felt himself softening toward her despite his best intentions. She was like Helen of Troy—men would go to war for her. Andrew had gone to war early because of her…not quite the same thing, but a woman like Isabel could stir a man's heart and shove him into battle. The end result for Andrew had been the same.

"I've decided to open a chocolate shop," she said finally, breaking the silence. "That's why I'm renting the old bakery."

James pulled his mind back to the job at hand. George had given him a brief description of Isabel's business ventures so far. Did she have what it took to start up a new business like this?

"I didn't know you made chocolate," James said.

"I imagine there is a lot you don't know about me," she said, a smile flickering across her lips. For a moment, he thought she might be flirting, but just as quickly, the playfulness evaporated. "And I have no idea what my father will say about it."

"You should ask him," he said. He'd much rather that father and daughter hashed this one out alone.

"I will." She nodded. "Eventually. I don't really want to listen to his depressing lectures right now."

George's lectures could be a bit tedious—James knew this firsthand—but the man did have a great deal of business experience that his daughter could benefit from.

"So you don't think he'll approve…" he guessed.

Isabel sucked in a slow breath and held it. "He liked my chocolatier classes because he saw it as a hobby. I let him believe that. It was easier. He was more supportive that way."

"What did he want you to do instead?"

James asked. "You're his only child, right? The logical one to take over the business eventually."

He was fishing here—he knew his boss's opinions about his daughter's business abilities, but maybe she didn't.

"I'll pry the reins out of his cold, dead fingers. He's never been one to actually think about his own mortality. As far as my dad's concerned, he'll live forever."

James smiled at her imagery, then took a sip of his coffee. "So in the meantime, you open your own business."

"You make it sound like I'm killing time until my dad dies," she retorted. "First of all, he'll live to be ninety-five, and probably have another wife after Britney. And secondly, this isn't a hobby. I intend to prove to him that I can start a business, build it and make it flourish. I'm going to come out of this with a profit. He did it with Baxter Land Holdings, and so can I."

"Fair enough." He eyed her with grudging respect.

"So I have one more question," she said. "Is there any legal reason why I couldn't use the Baxter name for my business?"

"No legal reason," he said. "As long as

the company name is different from your father's."

"I'm calling it Baxter's Chocolates," she said. "And my father is going to hate that."

James was inclined to agree. "So why not call it something else?"

"Because I don't want to. My father is a Baxter and so am I. I'm no less a Baxter because I'm a woman, and I have every right to use my own name."

James laughed softly. "Miss Baxter, you are a force to be reckoned with."

For the first time, a smile lit Isabel's eyes. "I certainly hope so."

"So here is the issue." James pushed his coffee cup aside. "Your father would like me to give you legal advice about using your money. Do you want it?"

She was silent for a moment, then she shrugged. "James, I'd be an idiot to turn down legal advice when I'm starting up a business. As long as you don't try to talk me out of my dream, I'm grateful for all the advice I can get."

"Great." He smiled. "You have my number. Contact me anytime."

She gathered her purse and folded the

lease. Then she held out her hand and shook his firmly. "Thank you."

"You're welcome."

Isabel walked briskly out of the café, every eye following her. She either didn't notice, or was accustomed to ignoring the attention.

Her father hadn't given her enough credit, but neither had James, for that matter. He knew it went against his better instincts, but he was curious to see what Isabel did with herself now that she was back in town. Would she stay? Would she prove her father wrong and actually make some money off this venture?

He wasn't the type of man who wished anybody ill, but he didn't trust her, either. While beauty was a great factor in her ability to manipulate men, so was pity. The minute she discovered that she had a whole new kind of power, she'd be back to her old tricks. She just hadn't figured that out yet. His bet wasn't on Isabel having changed.

CHAPTER FIVE

FAMILY SUNDAY DINNERS had been of paramount importance when Isabel's mother was alive. Her fight with breast cancer had been fierce, but after she passed away, George Baxter had insisted on continuing the tradition, claiming she would have wanted it that way. After Isabel left for college and George married the young second Mrs. Baxter, family dinners evaporated along with half the furniture and the painted portrait of his first wife. So when her father called on Sunday morning, asking if she'd come for a family dinner, Isabel felt torn between nostalgia and misgiving.

Isabel stood in her miniscule kitchen, eating a bowl of strawberry yogurt with chopped banana. It was a favorite snack.

"Family dinner?" she asked incredulously, her cell phone pinched between her shoulder and cheek. "Do we still do that?"

"Yes, we still do that," he retorted. "Be here at six. On the dot."

"And Britney is okay with it?" she asked, entertaining some images of her young step-mother pouting through the whole thing. She licked off her spoon and gave her yogurt another stir.

"She's fine. She likes the idea now that she's pregnant."

Isabel resisted the urge to roll her eyes. "Okay. I'll be there. Should I bring anything?"

"Like what?" he asked.

"Jell-O salad?" she asked teasingly. They had an aunt who used to bring Jell-O salad to every family gathering—wedding, funeral, picnic. It was a standing joke between father and daughter.

"Change that to wine, and you have yourself a deal."

"Britney drinks while she's pregnant?" Isabel asked.

"No. Shoot." She could almost see her father's discomfiture. He was as smooth as ice in anything business related, but when it came to family affairs, he fell apart. "Whatever. You and I will drink it. Just come."

Isabel laughed aloud. "See you at six, Dad."

Hanging up, she stood still for a full minute, staring down at her cell phone. A family dinner with Britney. She'd endured a mimosa at lunch, and that was about as far as she cared to push things, but her father seemed to want something more... And what could he really expect? If he'd at least married someone older than Isabel, she'd have a better idea of what to do.

It might not be as bad as it seemed, she thought wryly. She'd always liked family dinners—before Britney, at least. They were a good start to repairing her damaged relationship with her father. She turned back to her yogurt, determined to simply let the evening unfold without too much worry...if that was possible.

AT SIX O'CLOCK SHARP, Isabel stood on her father's doorstep, a bottle of sparkling apple juice in hand. She'd had a moment of generosity in the grocery store and had decided to get something they could all share, something she was seriously regretting now that she was faced with a wine-free evening with her stepmother. Isabel wore a pink summer dress with a full skirt and a cinched waist. She wore her dark waves up in a messy bun at the back of her head, and she tucked up a stray tendril as she rang the doorbell. There had been a time when she would have just opened the door and gone in, but that was back when this old house had been her home. Perhaps it was her new, tiny accommodations, but the house seemed ominously large these days. Too big. Too sprawling. Too empty.

The door swung open to reveal her father, a surprise, since she'd expected to see the housekeeper. He ushered her in. He wore a pair of khaki pants paired with a dress shirt, open at the neck. His hair rose up in tufts on top of his head, and she smiled fondly.

"It's good to have you home, Princess," he said, leading the way into the sitting room.

"It feels different now," she admitted quietly. "Where is Britney?"

"Upstairs. On the phone with her mother."

Isabel attempted to hide her relief. It wasn't often that she had time alone with her dad anymore. They sank into their old seats— her father in his leather armchair, and she took the end of the couch closest to him as she always had. They stared together at the mantel and the abstract print hanging above it, discordant colors splashed together.

"Is that awkward?" Isabel asked after a moment.

"What?" He glanced over, bushy eyebrows raised.

"Britney's parents are your age. Isn't that uncomfortable?"

He shrugged. "Sometimes. But it doesn't matter how they see me. Only how Britney sees me."

The comment was quietly honest, and Isabel felt her face heat. Did she really want to discuss this part of her father's life? But they'd started, and she'd been wondering ever since the wedding...

"Does she make you feel young?" Isabel asked.

"She makes me feel *loved*."

"I love you, Dad."

"In a much different way." He shot her a pointed look. "Can't argue with that one, can you?"

Isabel chuckled. "No, I can't."

"So." Her father pushed himself forward and leaned his forearms on his knees. "I heard that you're thinking of starting a business with that money."

So this was the reason for the visit. Maybe

the nostalgia she'd been nursing was wasted, after all.

"Yes, I am," she admitted. "I've just signed the papers for a lease."

He winced. "I'm sure James can find you a loophole to get out of that."

"Why?" she demanded. She'd known that he might disapprove, but it didn't take the sting out of the unfairness.

"It's not a good idea, Princess. Trust me."

"You don't even know what the idea is," she retorted.

"The chocolate shop. Britney told me."

A twist of distaste settled into her stomach. Of course Britney told him. She hadn't expected her stepmother to keep a secret exactly, but she could only imagine the tattling kind of tone that would have dominated the conversation.

"Dad, you signed the money over to me. Would you rather I used it to travel for a few months?"

"I would rather you used it for plastic surgery."

His words were sharp, and she froze. She'd momentarily forgotten about the scars. His words were crueler than he probably intended, but she wouldn't be put off that easily.

"I'm sorry to disappoint you, Dad, but I told you before—I'm not going under the knife again."

"Okay, okay." He heaved a sigh. "But still, it isn't a good investment, Sweet Pea."

Isabel sighed. He did this when he wanted to cajole her into doing things his way. She became Princess and Sweet Pea, and he expected her to bow to his superior wisdom.

"I've wanted to do this for years now," she said.

"It doesn't make it commercially viable," he shot back. "Wanting something and making money off of it are two different things. You're so much like your mother…"

"I'm actually a lot like you," she snapped. "I only look like Mom."

Her mother had been a beauty queen, too. She'd been gorgeous, bright, cheerful and the envy of her father's friends. Her mother had been the Audrey Hepburn from *Breakfast at Tiffany's* when her parents married, and she'd aged with equal grace and ease.

"Sweet Pea, you don't understand these things. A chocolate shop is very romantic, and it sounds like a pleasant place to spend your days, but—"

"Dad, I'm not an idiot," she snapped. "And stop calling me Sweet Pea."

He looked ready to say something, then clamped his mouth shut. He leaned back into his chair.

"And quit putting up that offended act," she added. "I've watched you negotiate business deals for as long as I can remember, so I know your tricks."

"Money is a tool, Izzy," he said. "It's a tool to make more money. Without money—well, you don't know what it's like to be without money." He smiled sadly. "Trust me when I tell you that this is a bad idea. I've been at this game longer than you've been alive, and a bachelor's degree at Yale doesn't make up for that."

He'd successfully swiped her one argument off the table with that last comment. She was proud of her degree at Yale. She'd wanted to get into a top school so badly that she'd even found her own tutor to get her math grades up in high school. It had gotten messy—she'd fallen for her tutor, and she wasn't exactly proud of how she'd handled it—but she wasn't the idiot everyone seemed to take her for. She'd had plans, goals, and she'd worked hard to achieve them. She'd earned that degree, gotten top grades and studied hard. Her father had paid for it, of course, but she'd worked for every A she got.

Britney came into the room just then, and she slid onto the arm of the chair, Isabel's father slipping his arm around her hips.

"Dinner's ready," Britney announced, rubbing her belly. She glanced around. "Is Jimmy here yet?"

Isabel shot her father an incredulous look. "Why did you invite the lawyer, Dad?"

"The lawyer." He eyed her with exaggerated disappointment. "He's got a name, you know."

Was he really going to lecture her about recognizing the household workers as people with names and lives? She was no longer a self-centered teenager, and if James was coming to dinner, then that meant that he had some business planned.

"His name is *James*." She emphasized his first name, irritated with Britney's insistence on calling him Jimmy. "I'm well aware. The question is, why invite him to a family dinner?"

She had a suspicion of why her father would want James Hunter here this evening. She already knew that this dinner was about her chocolate shop, and her father was bringing in some reinforcements. He wasn't about to let her spend her money without his input, that much was obvious. Had James been part of the ploy all along? Was he stringing her along, reporting back to her father?

"I didn't invite him, but he'd be welcome to stay," her father retorted. "He's dropping off some papers for me, not that it's any of your business."

She didn't believe that for a second. The doorbell rang and Britney smiled brilliantly.

"Well, speak of the devil. I'm sure that's him."

GEORGE BAXTER WAS the patriarch of a very wealthy family. He was a self-made man, and George had volleyed between making money and losing money for a decade before he finally started making more than he lost. Word around town was that George Baxter was hungry to prove himself to the old money of the county. He was now one of the ten most influential men in Montana, and he'd raised his daughter with the expectation that she'd marry well and never experience the hardship that he had. He was giving her a better life on a silver platter.

The big house had the look of old wealth, even though the Baxter dynasty was young, indeed. Mr. Baxter's first wife had been the decorating master, and she'd had a delicate touch. The house was big, but not overly ostentatious. The furnishings were high quality and expensive, but homey, too. The grounds around the house were natural and reminded James of the perfect place for a tire swing and a red-checkered picnic blanket. The original Mrs. Baxter's touch was the foundation of the place, and it couldn't be erased. As James stepped inside, he smiled at the housekeeper who ushered him in. He'd always liked Mrs. Franklin. She was a constant, a regular rock, and under that stony facade, he always suspected there was a sense of humor, although he couldn't quite prove it.

"Here are those documents, sir," James said, passing an envelope to his employer. "It looks like I'm interrupting. Have a good evening, everyone."

"Oh, stay for dinner," Mr. Baxter said. "We have more than enough."

"Thanks, but I've got work—"

"Come on through," Britney called, beckoning him toward the dining room. "You're just on time. I'll be so disappointed if you don't."

"It smells amazing, Mrs. Baxter," he replied with a smile. "Thanks for the invitation."

His gaze landed on Isabel, and he found himself relieved to see her here. She interested him. Professionally, of course. That's what he'd been telling himself all day. Her hair was up, pulled away from her face so that her large, dark eyes were dominant, meeting his with an expression of mild surprise. It was enough to make her scars melt away in the moment, and instead of facing a scarred former beauty, he was facing the beauty herself. She looked less than pleased with his arrival, however, and before he could say a word, she turned and walked into the dining room without a word.

"Never mind her," Mr. Baxter said with a chuckle. "She's just moody. She'll get over it."

Mr. Baxter sounded like a man making excuses for a teenager's petulance, but Isabel was no teen, and he couldn't help but wonder what family drama was about to unfold. Mr. Baxter never invited him to dinner just for the pleasure of his company, and this whole friendly scene wasn't how things normally went. He was willing to bet that this whole display was for Isabel's benefit.

"Not a problem, sir," he replied with an uneasy smile, following the older man into the dining room.

The Baxters dined in relaxed style. A long, farmhouse-style table dominated the room, early evening sunlight streaming in through tall windows. The table was set without a cloth or place mats, gold-edged china placed directly onto the polished wood. Gleaming silverware sparkled on top of napkins. An extra place had already been set, and he got the distinct impression that this was more planned than he thought. Flowers spilled from vases, placed around the table in a way that looked almost meticulously casual— something he couldn't quite put his finger on. A bowl of steaming potatoes sat in the center next to a large, clear jug of lemonade. Another dish of string beans reminded him that he was indeed hungry.

"Oh, you know us," Britney said with a wave of her hand. "Sit wherever you like. We're family, after all."

Family, huh? James didn't actually know them that well, at all, and he had that awkward feeling like anywhere he chose to sit would be wrong. James sat down at the nearest place setting, while Isabel and Britney both moved toward the same chair.

"Except for this one." Britney laughed lightly. "I always sit here, don't I, Georgie?"

"She always does," Mr. Baxter agreed absently. "Never would sit at the foot of the table like a proper wife." He laughed at his own little joke, then kissed Britney's fingertips.

"Of course," Isabel said, moving to the seat next to James. "It's been a long time since I've been here."

Here. Not home. James noted her wording.

"Oh, here comes the ham," Mr. Baxter said.

The dining room doors swung open and Mrs. Franklin wheeled in a cart with a covered serving tray. The savory aroma of ham filled the room, and all eyes turned to Mrs. Franklin, who stood in her gray uniform, sweat on her brow.

After everyone was served, the meal began, and for several minutes, the only sound was silver against china. The food was amazing, and James had to admit that he didn't often eat like this in Haggerston.

He was used to the regular diners that the town had to offer, and his own cooking, of course. He wasn't a bad cook, but he wasn't too proud to admit that Mrs. Franklin's cooking was a treat.

"You'll have to bring us some of your chocolates, Isabel." Britney broke the silence. "I've never tried them, and I've been craving chocolate something fierce with this pregnancy."

"They're good," Mr. Baxter said, around a bite of food. "A nice hobby for her."

Isabel smiled tightly.

"Speaking of business—" Mr. Baxter began.

"We weren't speaking of business," Isabel replied, her tone even, but a look of warning sparkling in her eyes.

"We're always speaking of business," the older man replied. "It's like breathing. But have you done the research, Princess?"

"We've already discussed this," she said, putting down her fork with a clink. "Not now."

"Why not now?" Mr. Baxter looked around the table. "It's family. What's the problem?"

"James isn't family," she replied tersely.

She had a point. James sat back in his seat,

watching the strained expressions around the table. He'd been in courtrooms that were more relaxed.

His employer shrugged. "He's a lawyer. His job is to be discreet. I don't know what you're worried about."

"Fine. Since in this family, all we talk about is business," she replied icily, "what were you going to say?"

"I was going to ask if you know how many small businesses fail after starting up." Mr. Baxter swirled a speared potato through a puddle of gravy and popped it into his mouth.

"You didn't fail," Isabel replied. "You're a raving success, I'd say."

"James?" Mr. Baxter turned his attention toward him, and James heaved a sigh. They were quickly coming to the reason for his invitation. Like Britney's cooking, Mr. Baxter's research was never done personally.

"Forty-seven percent," James replied.

"And in the food industry?"

"More than that." He was doing Isabel a favor by not mentioning the number.

"Chocolate is a niche market," Mr. Baxter said, wiping his lips on a napkin. "It's high cost, low margin. The real estate market has the highest rates of success."

"I'm aware of that, Dad," Isabel replied stiffly.

"Now, James, if you were to advise my little girl about starting up a business, what would you tell her?" Mr. Baxter asked.

Isabel turned her glittering eyes to him, daring him to speak. He could feel the repressed rage radiating from her, and he had to swallow twice before he spoke.

"I'd tell her to ask her father's advice," he replied cautiously.

"Aha! Smart man." Mr. Baxter chuckled. "Pass the green beans, please, Britney."

Britney passed the dish, and he helped himself to another serving.

"And you would tell her to ask my advice because I've made money, right? Because it takes a success to know how to be successful."

"You've also lost money," Isabel countered. "You went bankrupt when you and Mom first got married."

Mr. Baxter's eyes darkened, and he dropped the spoon back into the bowl with a clatter. Red crept up his neck and into his cheeks. James had never seen Mr. Baxter openly challenged before, and he found himself mildly concerned that the older man might pop a blood vessel.

"I paid for this home, for every stitch of clothing you ever wore, for all of your beauty contest coaching, for your vacations, your hobbies, your shiny Yale education…and you dare throw my failures in my face?" He sucked in a breath through his nose. "I'm your father, and you don't have a penny except by what I've earned! Show some respect, young lady!"

"You're throwing your money in my face," Isabel shot back. "You supported me through school, and I appreciate that. But when I got a job of my own in New York, I told you I could support myself. You're the one who insisted that I stay in that overpriced condo so that you wouldn't worry about my safety. So yes, you paid for it, but I *never asked for it.*"

She was shaking, and she closed her fist over a crumpled napkin. "You say that we talk business in this family, but we don't. We talk *money.*"

"I'm trying to spare you a monumental failure!"

"And what if I succeed?" she demanded. "What if I'm actually good at this, after all?"

Mr. Baxter calmed himself, taking a deep

breath and closing his eyes for a moment as he gathered himself once more. The red in his face faded, and he opened his eyes.

"You were always a pretty girl," he said. "I didn't properly prepare you for the shark pool that is the business world."

"Dad, shut up!" Isabel rose to her feet and glared at her father across the table. She leaned forward, her skirt sweeping free as she pushed her chair back. "You know I love you, so when I say this, it's coming from a good place. But Shut. Up."

The room fell into awkward silence, and Mr. Baxter gaped up at his furious daughter. Her lips quivered and a tendril of hair slipped down from the bun at the back of her head, sliding down her pale neck. She wadded her napkin and tossed it onto the seat of her chair.

"Thanks for the *family dinner*." Her voice dripped disdain. "But I think I'll pass."

She turned and nearly collided with Mrs. Franklin, who was just coming back into the room with a bottle of sparkling cider, uncorked.

"Thank you for the delicious meal, Mrs. Franklin," Isabel said sweetly. "You're an excellent cook, and I'm sorry I can't stay to enjoy it."

And with that she was gone, leaving James at the table.

CHAPTER SIX

"Isabel!"

Isabel stopped next to her SUV and turned to see James in the doorway of the house. He swung the door shut behind him and jogged down the steps, heading in her direction.

"What now?" she demanded, pulling the door open a little harder than necessary, but she needed some way to vent this anger.

"I just wanted you to know that I didn't know that was going to happen," he said as he reached her.

"And how did you think that would go down?" she retorted.

"I came to drop off papers. Nothing else." He met her gaze easily, dark eyes drilling into hers. "That wasn't planned."

"And the extra place at dinner?" she asked with an icy smile.

"Okay, someone planned it," he admitted. "But not me. I was a pawn in that one."

She was tempted to believe it. Her father

was nothing if not dramatic in his attempts to "get through to her" when she wouldn't cooperate with his decisions. It had worked when she was a teenager, but while he admitted that she'd grown up, his tactics hadn't changed.

"So what are you doing out here?" she asked cautiously. "Did he send you out to calm me down?"

"Nope." He shrugged. "Wanted to know if you'd get a coffee with me."

She regarded him for a moment, weighing his words. "You'll annoy my father."

"Who says I'm not annoyed already?" he retorted.

Isabel sighed. "Sure. As long as there is no more talk about my business."

"Understood." He put up his hands and shot her a wry grin. "I told you before that I wasn't going to get in the middle."

"You have noble intentions." She chuckled bitterly. "But my father might have other plans with that one."

"Let's meet up down at that old coffee shop at Main and Spruce—the one we all used to go to during high school," he suggested.

Isabel smiled at the memories and nodded.

They'd felt so grown up frequenting a coffee shop back then. "That sounds good. I'll see you there."

The drive from her father's house to town was short, and as Isabel pulled up and parked in front of the little shop, she heaved a sigh. She'd always known that her father was a force of nature, and it wasn't often that she went against his wishes, but she couldn't back down this time. This decision was her own, and she'd see it through.

She was overdressed for a coffee, and the pretty dress reminded her of times when she'd draw every eye in a place when she stepped through the door. Some days she missed the attention, but today she felt differently. She'd take respect and trust over admiration. She wanted someone to believe she could succeed based on her intelligence and character. Was that so much to ask? Now that she'd lost her flawless face, her father seemed to doubt that she could do much of anything.

Isabel pulled open the door and stepped inside. Soft jazz music played in the background, mingled with the hiss of a milk steamer. A few tables were scattered around the shop, the lowering light outside the window growing softer and more golden as the sun sunk closer to the horizon. James was waiting, standing at the counter. He looked taller than she'd given him credit for, dark eyes moving over her in slow evaluation.

"What'll you have?" he asked, accepting a latte from the barista. He nodded his thanks to the young man.

"I'll get it myself, thanks," she said and he shrugged. She wasn't even in the mood for chivalry tonight. She ordered a latte as well, then headed over to where James sat waiting for her.

"So what was that at your father's place?" James asked.

"That's what happens when my father thinks he knows best." She slid into the seat opposite him. "My father can be a big pussy cat, but the minute he turns his iron will on you, it feels a whole lot different."

"So you have a complicated relationship," he concluded.

"You could say that." She took a sip, letting the sugar soothe her frayed nerves. "You know the really stupid thing? Dad thinks I can't do this because when I was eighteen and twenty, I tried two different business ideas. Now, for most eighteen-year-olds, their stellar ideas get filed away for when they're older, but not for me. I had a dad who financed every business idea I had, and when they flopped—which, of course, they did— he took it as proof that I didn't have what it took to be like him."

"So if he'd done a little less financing..." he suggested.

"I'd have been better off," she agreed. "And I know how dumb that sounds coming from someone who just had her trust fund signed over to her. But I wasn't ready to have someone make my dreams a reality. I needed to dream a little longer."

"Wow." He raised his eyebrows. "I'm surprised to hear you say that."

"I'm full of surprises—" She stopped herself short. That was the old flirtation coming out again, and she really should know better by now. James wasn't flirting, and she had nothing to gain by trying to manipulate him. She sighed. "He's judging my adult abilities by my adolescent attempts."

"Not exactly fair," he agreed, and his confirmation of that simple fact relaxed something inside her. Most of her conversations with men ended much earlier than this—at least back when she still had looks. She'd bat aside serious topics and fix him with her smoldering gaze and enjoy the power. It was fun to get men flustered, to make them forget the matter at hand.

But everything was different now, and she'd opened a vent on thoughts and feelings she hadn't ever put into words, and James's quiet attention was loosening her lips. As she talked, her thoughts came together, making sense of a dynamic she hadn't been able to sort out yet.

"I agree that my ideas back then were pretty stupid, but I couldn't really be blamed. My world was small. I was patterning myself after movie stars who started their own clothing or makeup lines—women who wanted to be taken seriously in the business world, but went about it in a stereotypically girlie way. But that was all I saw. I mean, we're in Montana, and if you aren't in the beef industry, there aren't a lot of role models."

"And your mom?" he asked.

"A beauty queen before me." She felt the bitterness in the words. "Mom was amazing, but she was someone who ran more on heart and less on intellectual examination, you know? There's nothing wrong with that. She was artsy and beautiful and described her feelings with colors. And maybe Dad wants me to take after her more… I don't know. But while I got Mom's face, I got Dad's brain. And he's never really accepted that."

Her father had used pet names with her mother, too: Beautiful, Gorgeous, Sunshine, Lover… The last one had embarrassed Isabel, but that had been what their home was like—two beauties doted on by a proud man.

"Did you notice what he called Britney?" she asked.

"No…" He frowned. "I didn't."

"He called her by her name." She swept her hair away from her face. "Me? I'm Princess, Sweet Pea, Cupcake, Sugar, Sweetie Pie…and do you know why?"

"You're his daughter?" he asked.

"Exactly." She took a sip of her latte, as if to punctuate the point. "I'm his daughter. Britney gets to be Britney. I get dumbed down to the name of a plush toy."

A small part of her was relieved that he hadn't recycled those old endearments that he'd used on her mother the way he had the diamond necklace—that something had remained sacred—but Britney's retention of her name irritated her in a whole new way.

James chuckled. "A little more than a plush toy, but I see what you mean."

Fine, the toy part was dramatic, but she was sick of being patted on the head. She'd kept her distance in New York, putting together a life of her own. Her father may have bankrolled her apartment, but accepting that gift had soothed her father's conscience and he'd given her some space. Her friends from work thought she was silly to be so annoyed with her overprotective father, and they'd joked that they'd gladly take her place, but they didn't understand what that entailed. Those strings were tighter than anyone imagined.

"And it isn't because I want to spend his money," she went on. "Well, *my* money now, since he signed it over. Britney does nothing but spend his money. It's because he knows that I want to do something more, and he honestly doesn't think I've got what it takes. And that's what hurts the most. He uses words like *Princess* and *Sweet Pea*, but underneath all that is his true opinion of me, and it isn't high."

"He's pretty old-fashioned," James agreed. "And his views on women could probably use some updating, but he does love you."

"With a stranglehold." She smiled coldly. "Just like his business."

James was quiet for a moment. "He can't actually stop you, you know."

"I know." Sadness welled up inside her. "But this isn't about having my way. It's about having his respect. I can get the former easily enough, just not the latter."

She was definitely saying too much. She didn't know where all this talkativeness was coming from, but she'd been on her own with these issues for too long. And back in Haggerston, she was more isolated still.

"I should stop talking now," she said, and laughed uncomfortably. "That all just sort of came out, didn't it?"

"I don't mind." James took a sip of his coffee. "There's more to you than I thought."

"Thanks." She smiled wryly. "I think. So enough about me. What about you?"

"What about me?" he asked, raising a brow.

"Why law?"

"I want to help," he replied. "I've seen too any people get tilled under, and I wanted to stand up for the underdog."

"Like me?" she asked, eyebrows raised. He'd seemed to take an interest in her since she'd arrived in town, and if anyone counted as an underdog right now, she was pretty sure that she did.

"You?" He laughed. "No, not you. You're hardly an underdog, Isabel."

"What makes you so sure?" she asked. She certainly felt like she'd lost her glossy position here in town. She'd gone from stunning beauty to ordinary woman, and she had to fight for every ounce of independence she got.

"You're wealthy, Izzy." That was what people had called her in high school—was that how he still saw her? How many times had she been reminded that she was rich? She came from money, so she had no right to complain.

She blinked. "Money isn't everything. I used to be rich and beautiful. Now, I have access to some money, but it isn't as glamorous as it looks. Trust me."

"But it smooths over a whole lot," he replied curtly. "Even after that accident, you're no underdog."

She found herself annoyed with his pronouncement. He hadn't been through the pain that she had. He hadn't been laid up in a hospital for weeks, thankful not to be paralyzed. He hadn't lost what she'd lost.

"I hardly think you can judge that," she said quietly. "I've been through a lot."

"Sure you have. So has everyone else."

She eyed him skeptically. Was there a monopoly of suffering—anyone who'd endured less than a POW didn't count?

"Well, you seem to be doing okay for yourself," she said. "You've climbed enough for my father to notice you and you're under thirty."

"Yeah, maybe," he admitted. "But we all have our pain. I lost my cousin in Afghanistan the year after high school. He was like a brother to me. Do you remember Andrew?"

She froze, the memory of her math tutor coming back. But he'd been more than a tutor... Their romance had surprised her as much as it had him. He'd been lanky with hair like a dust mop and the sweetest smile. She hadn't told anyone because she knew it couldn't last. It was doomed right from the start—he wasn't from the right people. It got ugly at the end.

"Yes," she said. "I do. He died?"

He should have been married with kids by now. And he'd been the type of guy who would have made a good husband to some girl around town. She could imagine him with a couple of little girls and a doe-eyed wife.

"What happened?" she asked, the image of the adult Andrew evaporating.

"Afghanistan happened," he replied bitterly. "He was trying to save a buddy, and he got shot. He never made it back."

"He was a nice guy," she said. That was an understatement—he'd been really special. He'd been smarter than the football players she normally got involved with. It was sad that he'd died so young. "I'm sorry."

"He was a hero. A real hero. You can't replace people, Isabel. You might have lost your looks—and I'm really sorry for how painful that accident was—but you didn't lose as much as you could have. Everyone's lost something."

The muscles in James's clenched jaw rippled. They sat in silence for a moment, and Isabel rolled his words over in her mind. He was angry, that much was clear, but why he should be mad at her, she had no idea. She was used to having men fawn over her, brush aside her weaknesses—at least before. James wasn't like that.

"You think I'm spoiled, don't you?" she concluded.

"A little bit," he agreed.

Anger simmered up inside her and she shook her head. "So because I survived, my hard times don't count?"

"I didn't say that."

She shook her head irritably. Did he blame the wealthy for his cousin's death? Was this a political stance? And how could the death of a soldier in Afghanistan make her own disfiguring accident any less horrible?

"So what are you saying then?" she demanded.

"I'm saying that you're not as hard done by as you think, and while everyone else might be inclined to feel sorry for you, I don't."

"I didn't ask for your pity," she snapped.

It was then that she remembered something that she hadn't thought about in years—sitting in Andrew's basement across from another young man with that same unsympathetic glare. Jimmy Someone…his dad had been a mechanic, and Isabel had just dented her brand-new car.

"What?" James seemed to sense a change in her.

"You fixed my car, didn't you?" she asked quietly. "Back then—in high school. You're the Jimmy who knocked that dent out for me."

The door to the coffee shop opened and closed behind her, though she didn't bother turning until she heard the low rumble of a familiar voice.

"Izzy Baxter, is that you?"

She swallowed her irritation at the interruption and turned to see who'd come in. Mike Gum was an old friend, a friend she'd almost gotten romantically involved with once or twice after breakups, if she had to be utterly honest, and she hadn't seen him since high school graduation. He was now a slightly portly man with a broad smile and a tan.

"I thought that was you!" Mike said, nodding to James. "How about a coffee?"

She looked back toward James. He gave her a tight smile that didn't reach his eyes.

"I've got an early morning tomorrow anyway. Have a good time," James said curtly and picked up his briefcase.

"That was you, wasn't it?" she repeated, unwilling to be put off.

"Yeah. That was me." He gave her a nod and strode out of the coffee shop without a backward glance. She watched him go, hoping he'd turn back, but he didn't.

She *had* met him back in the day—he'd

even done her a favor. She remembered how relieved she'd been that Andrew had a cousin who could make her problem go away, and that had been all she'd cared about. How could she have forgotten? No wonder he thought she was spoiled.

We talked about me the entire time, she realized with a stab of embarrassment. There was a time when that would have been the status quo, but she hadn't wanted to talk about herself tonight. She'd actually wanted to know more about James, and then she'd started blathering on.

"So, Mike," she said. "How are *you*?"

She had to stop monopolizing conversations.

JAMES LOOKED THROUGH the window at Isabel's back, her glossy dark hair coiled up into a bun, and her pink dress blending softly into the creamy skin at the top of her back.

He shouldn't have told her about Andrew. It brought up too many old memories for him, but once he started talking, it all just seemed to spill out of him. He hated that—talking when he should just keep his mouth shut. Professionally, he could keep secrets. In his personal life, he'd always been pretty tight-lipped, too. So what was it about Isabel Baxter that made him talk about things he'd rather keep private?

But she'd remembered him—at the last moment. He'd been wondering if he'd made any impression on her at all back then. Not much of one, apparently. Still, she'd realized who he was, and that was oddly gratifying.

What was I thinking? He got into his truck and slammed the door. He started the motor, the growl of the engine rumbling comfortingly beneath him. Maybe this was what Andrew had felt like in the army—surrendering himself to something bigger, something big enough to swallow his own pain. The rumble of a hemi engine certainly didn't compare to a US Army tank, but it was something.

He put the truck in Reverse, and the wheels crunched over the gravel as he pulled out of the parking lot. Somehow he felt like he owed this to Andrew—to remind the girl who'd so cruelly crushed him that he'd existed, and he'd been worth something. He was a war hero, killed in the line of duty. Andrew had always been the heroic type—taking on more than he had any right to try for, Isabel included. James could recite by heart that last letter that Andrew had sent him:

Hey man, how are things in college? You wouldn't believe the size of the spiders here. I keep finding them in the shower—enough to make a guy avoid bathing for life. I can't even describe what it's like. It's hot—always hot. You breathe in dust constantly. We cough up brown stuff. At least it keeps me from thinking. I think too much over here.

Happy birthday. Hope it's a good one.

Don't take the shade for granted.

The streets of Haggerston were deserted, and he stopped at an empty intersection before easing forward again. He thought he knew what had been taking over his cousin's mind—or did he? Had the war managed to squeeze out the humiliation and heartbreak of his senior year? He wasn't sure if it was kind to hope for that or not. Maybe it was more merciful to have a man's heart broken than put the horrors of war into his soul.

Isabel might think that she was hard done by, but the Baxters rolled over everyone in their paths, and they never seemed to notice the bump in the road. Isabel certainly hadn't seemed to notice what she'd done to Andrew. *He was a nice guy.* That was all she remembered?

He was her legal counsel, nothing more,

and he regretted opening up that part of himself. He hadn't spoken about Andrew to anyone in more than a year. It was easier to just bury all of that deep inside him. Opening up tonight had taken off the pressure, and it all came out. He should have kept his trap shut.

He pulled his truck onto the highway. The gas tank was full. He'd drive out his frustration tonight. It was safer than talking. Pretty much anything was safer than talking right now.

CHAPTER SEVEN

THE NEXT MORNING, Isabel stood in the center of her new store, a to-do list in hand. She'd already spent several hours scrubbing out the kitchen, scouring the oven and stove top and soaking the filter from the exhaust fan in a tub of hot, soapy water. Her muscles ached. Sunlight filtered through the windows, making soft, warm squares on the hardwood floor.

In her mind's eye, she could see the shop fully dressed and ready for customers. There would be ceiling-high shelves in the corners, but along the walls she wanted low counters where she could have different displays at fingertip level. She also wanted to take advantage of the natural light in this shop—a rare luxury in retail spaces, but since this shop was on a corner, she had windows on two sides of the store.

Her mind was still on James this morning, however. She'd forgotten him—used his talent and his father's garage, and then promptly forgotten about his existence. She hadn't been that blind to the people around her, had she? He thought she was spoiled. That irritated her. She'd worked hard to get as far as she had, and just because her father had money didn't make her less human than anyone else. But she hadn't exactly been at her best last night, either. She'd been angry with her father and focused on herself. She hadn't wanted to be like that. She'd wanted to make up for her earlier gaffe of not remembering him, but he hadn't given her the chance.

A shadow stopped at the window and she looked up. It was the science teacher at her old high school, Miss Maitland, looking inside. She looked older, more tired than Isabel remembered. After the woman spent that many years teaching high school, Isabel couldn't blame her. Isabel smiled, waved, and Miss Maitland gave her a quick nod and hurried on. There was no wasted friendliness there, not that anything had changed since she got back. People acknowledged her presence, just didn't look glad to see her. Was that her imagination? It wasn't like Miss Maitland had been a favorite teacher or anything. Maybe she hadn't even remembered Isabel. Still...

She turned back to the work at hand. Her father was right that there was very little room for wasted dollars in this business, so she was doing as much as she could herself. She'd hired a local contractor to make the basic store outfit—shelves, counters, display cases. But there was one piece she wanted to work on herself—an antique sideboard. She wanted the look and feel of Baxter's Chocolates to be a cross between old-world charm and sensual indulgence.

The sideboard—an elegant chest with a marble top—sat under a plastic tarp along one wall. It was a large piece of furniture, about six feet long and two and a half feet deep. Two men had carried it into the shop an hour earlier, and after a quick trip to the hardware store for supplies, she'd promised herself that she'd get the sanding done, at the very least.

She pulled the tarp off and ran her hand affectionately over the smooth, green marble. The wood finish was cracked and peeling on the sides. She'd known the moment she saw it that she'd buy it, and it hadn't taken too much haggling to get it down to a price she could live with.

Isabel tugged on the mammoth piece of furniture, and it didn't budge. She braced herself and tried again, but it moved only a couple of inches. These old pieces were made to last—like boulders.

There was no way she'd be able to work on the base with it sitting against the wall. She attempted to pull the drawers out, but there were stops that kept them from coming out all the way, and she frowned at the sideboard in frustration. There were some days that she sincerely wished she had a few employees to order about instead of having to do everything herself.

She glanced at her watch. It was after eleven. She ran through the people she might be able to call, and there weren't many. Most of her friends had moved to Billings for work, and those who had stayed in town—besides Carmella and Mike Gum—hadn't been her biggest fans. Apparently, Miss Maitland was part of that group. There'd been a time when she would have poked her head out the door and crooked her finger at the first man to walk past, but not anymore. It wasn't only her lost looks, either, that held her back.

Other people had lives and things to do that had nothing to do with her.

"James?" she wondered aloud, looking down at her cell phone. He was the best bet she had at the moment, but even so, she held back. She'd asked him for a favor back in high school, then forgotten him. And now she was going to ask for another one?

She attempted to move the sideboard once more, and when she felt a muscle twinge along her back, she gave up. Her body weight wasn't going to be enough. She'd need some muscle behind this one, even if that muscle came with a bit of judgment attached.

Pulling her phone back out of her pocket, she started to type a text, and then changed her mind. This required an actual call. She dialed his number. He picked up on the second ring.

"James Hunter…wait, is that you, Isabel?"

"It is." She grimaced. "Look, I feel terrible about forgetting you. And about Andrew, too. I was so self-involved back then. I don't even know what to say."

"It's okay," he said gruffly. "It's fine."

"But it isn't." Not by his reaction last night, at least.

"I said it's fine." He sighed and then was

silent for a beat. "Andrew and I were insepa-
rable. Our birthdays were exactly one month
apart, and we did everything together from
going to kindergarten to tux shopping for
the prom. I even fixed his girlfriend's car.
What can I say?"

Obviously, Andrew's cousin would have
known the truth, but the term "girlfriend"
still jolted her a little.

"Then one day, he was gone. His parents
got a visit from an army rep, and I got even
less than that. I miss him. I guess I've been
missing him more than usual lately. It funny
how that happens. I shouldn't have dumped
that on you." He cleared his throat, and the
intimacy of the moment before seemed to
evaporate. "So, how are you?"

"I'm fine. Just working in the store, and—"
How exactly was she supposed to ask for a
favor now? "Never mind. You have a good
day, James."

"You called for a reason," he prompted.

"I know it's obnoxious of me, but I was
wondering if you might be free to help me
move something this morning. It would only
take a couple of minutes, but now that seems
like a really dumb thing to ask."

"What do you have to move?"

"A rather large sideboard," she admitted. "I can't move it alone."

"I'd have to be the most expensive muscle you ever hired."

"Probably," she agreed. "But worth every cent. Feel free to charge the time to my father."

He was silent for a couple of beats, and she stood stock-still, wondering if she'd just made an even bigger fool of herself. If she'd had anyone else to call, she would have.

"Sure, I'll come by," he said at last. "I'm going to be working late tonight, so I can take a bit of time this morning."

"Thanks, I really appreciate it."

"And I won't be charging anyone." There was a smile in his voice. "See you in a bit."

Was that forgiveness she heard in his tone? She tucked her phone back into the back pocket of her jeans and put her rubber gloves back on. She sat on her haunches for a moment, her mind moving over his words. She picked up a scrub brush, and she couldn't help the sad smile that came to her lips. His loss was devastating, but he'd been willing to share that with her, and James struck her as a man who didn't talk about his feelings too often. Call it gut instinct—she knew men, if nothing else. She had a feeling that while James seemed to fight it tooth and nail, he was becoming her friend. Whether he liked it or not.

Her phone rang again, and she peeled off her gloves again and pulled it out. It was Carmella.

"Hello?" she said.

"Girl, I heard you were out with Mike Gum last night!"

"Where did you hear that?"

"Tricia Libbon saw you and called me immediately. So what happened?"

"Nothing." Isabel shook her head. "And I'm busy right now, so you'll just have to believe me."

"I need details!" her friend prodded. "Come on. If you don't fill me in, I'll pass along a rumor of my own making."

"I'll have to take the chance," Isabel replied wryly, and then paused. "Carmella, do you remember that time we tried to parallel-park my brand-new BMW and I put that massive dent in the fender?"

"Vaguely," Carmella replied. "Why?"

Isabel suddenly realized that she hadn't told Carmella how she got the car fixed. Andrew had been a bit of a secret, and explaining his cousin would have let the secret out.

"Nothing. Just remembering old times," she replied, putting more cheer into her voice than she felt. "But I've got to go. I'll call you later."

Isabel disconnected and stood in silence. She'd been oblivious back then. And mean. She couldn't help but wonder how many people she'd stepped on over the years, and never even noticed. And she was trying to open a business here? She might be as stupid as her father thought.

JAMES HAD STARTED EARLY, spent the morning in meetings, and now had some time off before he had another round of meetings in the evening. When he'd gotten the call from Isabel, he'd already been regretting the night before. The war in Afghanistan wasn't her fault, and while her cruelty had pushed his cousin into the army sooner, Andrew had been talking about joining the armed forces since he was sixteen, so it wasn't exactly out of the blue.

He also sensed that she really did need his help in her shop. She used to be able to crook her finger and men would dash to her side, but now—

"I'm not dashing," he muttered aloud.

His office was walking distance from Nicholson Avenue, so he took advantage of the bright June day, left his suit jacket in the office and headed down Main Street toward her store. The afternoon was quiet, and as he passed the familiar shops, he realized how long it had been since he'd taken a break in the middle of the day. Work was his refuge.

Nicholson Avenue came up quickly, and he walked around the corner, then crossed the street to the closed bakery. The windows weren't covered, and he could see inside. Everything looked clean and empty, but Isabel was nowhere to be seen.

He scanned the place. It was a nice location, and he had to admit that she had good taste.

Isabel's head popped up right in front of him, and he startled. She waved sheepishly, a dirty rag in one hand, then pointed toward the front door. She wore a pair of jeans and a fitted white T-shirt—a relaxed look that suited her more than he liked to admit. In high school, Isabel had been the girl always done up to the nines, but this look appealed to him more. It felt more honest, somehow. James met her at the door, and she pushed it open for him.

"I didn't know you were down there," James said with a laugh. "The place looks good."

"Thanks." She stood back to let him in. "I appreciate your coming. I know this isn't exactly in your job description."

She looked worried, a little pent up. This was why he wished he hadn't said anything last night. He didn't want to talk about it— not with her. And he didn't want to make things awkward. His task was difficult enough with this family, without adding to the tension.

"I'm not here as your lawyer," he said.

"No?" She eyed him cautiously.

"Call this a friendly gesture." He inhaled the scent of floor wax and the distant hint of cleaning products. "So when are you going to open?"

"Well, I have to get this place put together first. I'd designed my sign as a project for a class in Yale, so it's just a matter of waiting for it to be made and delivered. I'm sure there are more things to do than I'm even planning for right now—" She stopped and color rose in her cheeks. "Sorry, I guess I'm excited."

"I can tell." He regarded her with a hint of admiration. She was her father's daughter, all right, and he could almost hear that Baxter hunger for business coursing through her veins.

Isabel led the way to a long, narrow table with three sets of drawers beneath it. It looked like solid wood with marble on top, and he could see why she wouldn't be able to move the thing.

"If we can just get it over here—" She pointed to a square of cardboard waiting in the center of the room. "Then I can work on it without making a mess."

"Sure." James tested one end. It was heavy. He unbuttoned his shirtsleeves and rolled them up. Her gaze flickered to his arms, then she cleared her throat and took the other side of the piece of furniture. Was she actually noticing him? That might be a first.

"On three," he said. "One, two—"

She attempted to lift her side, then shook her head. "Wait, wait." She adjusted her grip. "Okay. I'm ready."

"Three."

They both lifted, and while James carried

the bulk of the weight, pulling the sideboard toward the center of the room, Isabel at least kept her side skidding above the ground until they were at the cardboard. When they put it down, she heaved a sigh.

"Thank you. I couldn't have done that alone."

Isabel sounded like she meant that. This was a side to her that James hadn't expected to see—the hardworking entrepreneur—and he was undeniably impressed. She brushed a strand of hair away from her face with the back of her wrist, then smiled.

Crikey, she was still gorgeous.

"Not a problem," he said. "You had good timing. I'm not normally free this time of day."

After last night, he figured he owed her this much, at least.

"Do you want a soda?" she asked.

He should go. He'd done the favor, and broken the ice again. It was better to just head out and see her the next time she needed legal advice. But she stood there with her fingers tucked into her back pocket, brown eyes fixed on him as if she half expected him to turn her down, and he couldn't bring himself to.

"Sure," he said.

She led the way into the kitchen and pulled two bottles of cola out of the fridge, passing him one. He cranked off the lid and took a cold sip.

"Thank you for fixing my car...the fender." Color rose in her cheeks. "I don't believe I ever thanked you for that."

"You're welcome." He nodded, suddenly feeling uncomfortable. "I didn't mean to make you feel bad, you know."

"No, it's okay," she replied. "I have a feeling not many people are happy to see me back. Do you remember Miss Maitland?"

"Yeah. She's still teaching at the high school," he said with a nod.

"I saw her today." Isabel shrugged. "And she didn't seem too pleased to see me. Am I being overly sensitive?"

No, she wasn't. He'd heard some of the gossip around town, as had Eugene at the office, and people weren't overjoyed to see her.

"Maybe just a bad day," James suggested.

"I hope it doesn't affect sales," she said, and he realized that the sentimental side had closed. Business wasn't personal. Wasn't that what people said? With Isabel, that seemed to be an odd balance. She sipped from the bottle and met his gaze. "Why did my father hire you?"

The conversation was taking an unexpected turn, and he frowned. "Because I'm good at my job."

"You're young," she countered.

"And top of my class." He shot her a grin. "I'm a lot more impressive in the courtroom." He paused, then eyed her uncertainly. She wanted to know why her father had chosen him, but he wanted to know something more specific than that. "Why did your father fire Ted Jackson?"

He'd wondered what happened for a long time, but no one knew. All they knew was that Mr. Baxter had a change of heart about Ted Jackson as his legal representation and he'd handpicked James as the replacement. James had been more than curious, but Ted hadn't shed any light on it. All he'd said was, "George is your client. Trust no one but George. You work for him and no one else. Got it?"

"He advised my father against marrying Britney," she replied. "He told him that she was after his money, and that he was foolish to marry a woman younger than his own daughter."

But that didn't really sound like Ted, either. What would he care if an older man married a woman half his age? Lawyers wrote up prenuptial agreements for these situations, they didn't give relationship advice.

"And your father fired him for that?" James asked.

"He said that law has as much to do with a gut instinct as it does with actual legalities, and he no longer trusted that man's gut."

That sounded like George, but right now, James's gut was telling him something different. "Did *you* ask him to talk to your father about it?"

Color rose in her cheeks, and she looked away for a moment. "Yes, I did. I honestly didn't know my father would fire him, though. My dad always said that business wasn't personal. But it got personal there, and he reacted in a way I didn't expect. I thought he'd think about Ted's advice and give it some serious consideration. I was wrong—really wrong."

This explanation made Ted's warning make a whole lot more sense. If James cared about his position with Mr. Baxter, he wouldn't allow himself to be influenced by his persuasive daughter. She seemed to have

a pattern of using men for her own aims.
She seemed to be deeper now since the accident, apologetic even, but obviously Ted had
fallen for her wiles, so how could he trust
that she wasn't doing the same thing to him?
He should be more careful. Business wasn't
personal, and neither was the law. But with
Isabel, all those lines kept blurring.

"I don't trust Britney," Isabel said. "I really don't, and that hasn't changed. But my
dad seems to love her."

"And that counts for something." James
took another sip of cola. "Plenty of men have
married younger women."

"And plenty of women have married older
men," she agreed. "But I always thought my
father deserved a woman who loved him for
himself, not just for his money."

"Maybe she does love him."

Isabel shrugged. "Do you honestly think
she'd stick around if my father lost his last
dime? Without his money, he's no longer a
debonair millionaire—he's just a sagging old
man."

Did she really expect him to badmouth her
father behind his back?

"I can't judge that," James said. "And like

you've said, it isn't in my best interest to judge it, either."

She smiled wanly. "That's true."

"Maybe he's getting exactly what he wants out of his marriage," James said. "I mean, if she really did marry him for his money—and I'm not saying that she did—then maybe he's just as happy with a beautiful, young wife to come home to. Maybe he doesn't want anything more than that."

Her gaze clouded and she shrugged weakly. "You mean maybe my father is no different from any of those other rich men who want a beauty queen without much intelligence?"

James shook his head slowly. "That's dangerous ground, Miss Baxter."

She shrugged. "I felt terrible for getting Mr. Jackson fired. I won't do the same to you. I promise."

James wasn't quite convinced, however, and Ted's warning was ringing in his mind. He worked for George Baxter, and while George had asked him to give his daughter advice, he'd better keep his loyalties in order.

"I have to get that sideboard sanded," she said, pushing herself away from the counter and heading for the door. "I'm sorry. I don't mean to put you in an awkward position."

James glanced down at his cell phone. He'd put it on Silent, and he'd already missed three calls. He watched her walk away from him, and for a moment, he considered asking her to wait—to talk more. But this was already dangerous ground, and he sighed.

"I'd better return a few of these calls," he said.

She turned and took a few steps backward as she moved out of the kitchen and into the store area. "James, are we okay?"

"Sure." He nodded. "We're just fine."

"Okay." She smiled hesitantly, then picked up a piece of sandpaper. James angled his steps to the door, and when he looked back, she was already crouching next to the table, ready to work. She glanced up with a small smile as he pushed open the door.

As he ambled back up the street, he couldn't help but realize that he honestly liked her at this point. That might not be good, because he was still uncertain about her character. He had Jenny to look out for, and a life here in Haggerston. Starting anything with a woman accustomed to using the people around her was dangerous, not only for his career, but also for his sister. Jenny didn't deal with betrayal well. If he had only himself to consider, he might take a chance, but not with Jenny. It took a special woman to take on a man's family—a family that might need his direct support for the rest of their lives. And Izzy? Well, he knew better than to even daydream about anything more with her.

He liked Isabel, was even finding himself attracted to her, and that was going to make his job with her father that much more difficult. Whatever her intention, she'd just given him a warning.

CHAPTER EIGHT

THAT EVENING, ISABEL sat in the center of her bed, a bottle of pearly pink nail polish in one hand as she leaned over her toes and meticulously painted her smallest nail. She liked having her toes painted, even in the winter. It made her feel put together, and it was as far away from her face as possible.

Her face wasn't the only part of her body that bore the scars from the accident. Her arm was scarred from a nasty break, and her leg had been gashed, as well. When the seasons changed, the puckered lines ached again, reminding her of the injuries that never quite went away.

Isabel glanced out the long, narrow windows. The sun was slipping down behind the mountains, crimson light pouring over the rugged foothills and trickling down the flatlands. She paused, absorbing the beauty of the scene. Outside, birds twittered their last calls, and the light grew dimmer and dimmer, until she reached over and clicked on the lamp beside her bed. The peaked ceiling gave her enough room to sit comfortably in the center, and the windows, like long gables, opened up the rest of the world around her.

This tiny house felt like a cocoon, and right now, she needed that. She needed somewhere to lick her wounds and figure out who she was now with these scars. More important, perhaps, she had to decide who she wanted to be.

She stretched her leg out to admire her toes, shining softly in the light of the lamp and the last of the sunset. It was ironic that the only part of her body that hadn't been changed by the accident was her feet. Her short toes, the half-moons of her nails, the pale skin—her feet were the last part of her that remained from her beauty queen days—and they were the part that people cared about the least.

There were countless times that Isabel wished she still had her mother—like whenever she had a question during puberty, or before she went to dances in the school gym, or when the other girls snubbed her. That had happened more often than she cared to

admit. The girls were always waiting for her
to tumble from her pedestal.

And right now. When the whole world saw
you at your worst, your mother would still
see her little girl...just like her father did, except she hoped that her mother would have
been able to recognize the woman in her, too.

Isabel reached for a small photo that she
kept by her bed. The frame was silver, black-
ened with age in the corners. It was a picture
of her parents when they were first married.
Her mother sat on a sofa, her legs crossed,
looking down at her wedding ring. Her father
sat next to her, gazing adoringly at his young
wife. Her mother had been a rare beauty—
dark hair framing her face and long lashes
brushing her cheekbones. The colors in the
photo were faded—though not even the or-
anges and browns from the late seventies
could diminish her mother's good looks.
Stella Baxter had been a timeless beauty, and
she'd passed those magnificent looks down
to her daughter.

Thinking about it now, Isabel realized that
she'd never heard anything else about her
mother. Her mother was beautiful, and that
was what mattered most. Her father always
told her that she had her mother's good looks,

but no one ever mentioned her mother's intelligence or talent of any kind. It wasn't that Stella hadn't been both intelligent and talented, because she had maintained a massive garden, designed all of the landscaping around their home and even grew a vast array of herbs along the kitchen windowsill. Isabel remembered her mother's penchant for green things well. But nobody else did. To everyone else, Stella Baxter was a rare beauty, and that was where she stopped.

Isabel had looked just like her mother, so she got the same attention focused on her looks. And if Isabel were honest with herself, she hadn't minded so terribly before the accident. Before, she was still the prettiest girl in the room and she could get her way easily enough. Did she want her father to recognize her abilities? Of course, but she hadn't lost sleep over it. After the accident, however, those views that failed to take her mind into account chafed a whole lot more. She didn't have the looks to offset it anymore.

Isabel looked down at the photo of her mother. Had she cared about the excessive focus on her looks? She'd died young, so she'd never lost that beauty. Isabel had taken this picture from her parents' bedroom after her mother's death. Isabel had been only eleven at the time, and the cancer that claimed her mother had been swift, leaving Isabel with only her father to help her to navigate the world.

The cardboard back of the frame jiggled now, and Isabel looked closer. It was an old frame, and the stand had been getting looser and looser over the years, but this wasn't just the stand. The clasp that held the frame together was also weakening. She leaned toward the light, and as the backing came off, something fluttered free.

Isabel picked it up. It was a black-and-white picture of a newborn baby in a woman's arms. The baby wore one of the tiny caps that hospitals gave out, and there was a tube running from the baby's nose and out of sight. Next to the tiny face was the diamond pendant that Isabel knew so well.

"Is this me?" she asked aloud, but when she looked closer, it couldn't be her. She'd been born with a full head of black, spiky hair, but this baby was bald. As far as she knew, there hadn't been any complications when she was born, either. There was no explanation. No writing on the back to indicate who this baby had belonged to... Just a photo of a newborn sleeping in Stella Baxter's arms secreted away behind a photo of her parents.

Isabel frowned. A cousin, perhaps? A friend's baby? But why keep it hidden? Unless it was put back there by accident, somehow. She turned the picture around in her fingers, her mind working over the problem, until she sighed and put it back where she found it.

She'd ask her father about it the next time she saw him. There was probably some silly explanation.

"Oh, that's your mother's cousin's baby," she could hear him saying in that slightly distracted way he had when talking about anything other than business. "I think we were godparents, but then the parents got divorced and we never heard from them again."

Most of the family history she knew had been told in backhanded comments.

"Oh, your grandmother? She was from Poland and agreed to marry your grandfather sight unseen."

"Who, Uncle Neville? No, he's not actually a relative. He was my father's best friend, and my father liked him better than family."

Her father didn't like history. He liked the promising glow of the future better, and he answered her questions in only two sentences or less.

That was another reason that she wished she had her mother back. She needed an interpreter…someone to tell her the bigger stories that her father avoided.

Isabel put the frame back together again and put it gently on the floor next to the lamp. Then she lay down on her pillow and let the memories wash over her until her eyes drooped and finally closed in slumber.

THE NEXT DAY, James stood by the reception desk, drinking a mug of coffee. It helped to change his scenery a little bit when clearing his head, and he glanced up as the main door opened and Mr. Baxter stepped inside.

"Good morning, sir," James said with a smile. "Looking for me?"

"I am." Mr. Baxter nodded briskly. "Let's do this in your office, shall we?"

George Baxter strode off down the hallway toward James's office, and James exchanged a look with the receptionist. He followed his client inside, then shut the door behind him. Mr. Baxter shoved his hands into his pockets.

"Have a seat," James said, gesturing to a

chair opposite his desk before going around to his own. "What can I do for you?"

"How are we doing with that lawsuit over the land with the tainted water supply?" the older man asked, still standing. This lawsuit was serious—and Mr. Baxter's company would be liable. The question was how much would Baxter Land Holdings owe, and while James didn't get to see into the bank accounts, there was a lot of tension surrounding this lawsuit, more tension than seemed necessary. Mr. Baxter had been sued several times before and had settled out of court every time. It was cheaper, and it kept the story out of the papers. But George was nervous about this lawsuit.

"We're close to a settlement that should be acceptable to them."

"How close are we talking?" George's gaze drilled into him.

"Well, let me show you what they faxed us this morning."

Mr. Baxter took a seat and they talked for a few minutes about legal issues and liabilities, all of which were important but didn't require a personal visit. This could have been taken care of with a simple phone call, which made James suspicious. George always said that he liked to look a man in the face when he talked to him, and James respected that. A man didn't rise as far as Mr. Baxter had without developing a unique wisdom along the way. But this was still a bit much.

When they'd exhausted any legal updates, Mr. Baxter fell silent but didn't look inclined to stand up again, either.

"Is there anything else, sir?" James asked.

"I want to redo my will," Mr. Baxter said at last.

It seemed like they had finally gotten to the real purpose of this visit. James had seen his client's current will, and it appeared fair, stipulating that the bulk of his business was to be run by a hired general manager with a generous percentage of profits paid out to his daughter quarterly. The house and a chunk of investments were left to his wife. It was relatively straightforward, as far as wills went.

"If there are any changes you want to make, just let me know and I'll adjust it for you—"

"No, I mean I want to completely redo my will," Mr. Baxter said. "Things are changing. I have a child on the way. I want to start from the floor up. I'll make an appointment for next week."

Change his will completely? Change it *how*? James swallowed his surprise and nodded. "Sure. Not a problem."

They were silent for another few beats, but Mr. Baxter still made no move to go. James leaned back in his chair, determined to wait him out. His client had something else on his mind, he could tell, and Mr. Baxter was not a man who allowed himself to be rushed.

"I like you, James," Mr. Baxter said, breaking the silence.

"Thank you. The feeling is mutual."

"So I'm going to ask a favor of you," Mr. Baxter continued slowly. "I want you to ask my daughter out."

James nearly choked. "Excuse me, sir?"

This was far from professional—it was a blatant abuse of Mr. Baxter's position. James was working for him, and any kind of personal relationship he might have with Isabel should have nothing to do with her father. It felt seedy.

"Ask out Isabel. On a date."

James stared at Mr. Baxter, wondering if he were joking, or perhaps testing him to see if he were attracted to Isabel, but Mr. Baxter simply stared back, his expression deadpan.

"Are you sure that's wise, sir?" James

asked carefully. "I don't like to mix business and pleasure."

"Oh, this wouldn't be pleasure," Mr. Baxter replied. "Trust me on that."

A smile tickled the corners of James's lips. "You don't have a very high opinion of your daughter, then, sir."

"No, no." Mr. Baxter batted his hand through the air. "The thing is, she's not doing well."

"How so?"

"That accident... You know how gorgeous she was before. And now, she's—" Mr. Baxter swallowed "—she's lost something, her sparkle. She's not the same girl she was."

"That kind of thing would definitely change a person," James agreed. "But I don't understand how my asking her out would help."

"Because she's been single ever since," Mr. Baxter explained. "That isn't like her. She always had a boyfriend and several men in line waiting for a chance to take her out, and now, she's just...alone."

"Being alone for a little while isn't the worst thing in the world," James said. "I've been single for a couple of years now, and it's not a tragedy."

"We aren't talking about you, James," Mr. Baxter replied curtly, and James chuckled.

"Understood, sir."

"We're talking about my daughter. I don't expect you to get serious. She just needs to get her feet wet again."

"Because of Britney," James concluded. With Mr. Baxter remarried, perhaps he felt a bit guilty seeing Isabel dealing with her struggles on her own. Did he think that a man in her life would set things right?

"I didn't ask you to psychoanalyze me," Mr. Baxter snapped. "I asked you to take my daughter out for dinner. Something civilized. Something chaste. Nothing too intimate… just remind her that she's still a woman."

That's a tall order, James thought wryly. *Keep it simple, somewhat formal, don't get too close, but remind her that she's a woman. That's quite the tightrope.*

Aloud, he said, "I see her quite often as it is, sir. And if you don't mind me saying, I don't think you have to worry. She's doing well. She's strong, confident. She's got it together."

Mr. Baxter raised a brow. "You seem to like her."

James grinned. "You want me to take her out, but you don't want me to like her? You don't have to worry about me, sir. I'm not interested in crossing that line."

"So it's agreed, then." Mr. Baxter rose to his feet. "Thank you, James. I knew I could count on you."

"Wait a minute." James felt a surge of panic. "I'm not agreeing to this. This could really complicate things. I'm your lawyer, not—"

Mr. Baxter shot him an annoyed look. "She's my little girl, James. I need to make sure that she's okay, and no offense, but I know her better than you do. I'm asking you to do me a personal favor. Personal. This isn't about business."

James nodded. Mr. Baxter was his client, but he'd also been kind to Jenny, allowing her to live in one of his rental houses free of charge. It was a strange balance between professional reserve and generous offers like that one that made turning down a request for a personal favor so difficult.

"Okay," he agreed grudgingly. "I'll see what I can do."

"Thank you." Mr. Baxter moved toward the door, then turned back. "And make sure you toe the line, James. No breaking hearts, you understand?"

"Completely, sir."

As Mr. Baxter shut the door behind him, James glared at it from across the room, daring it to open again.

This was a terrible idea. It wasn't that he didn't find Isabel appealing, because he did—a whole lot more appealing than Mr. Baxter would be comfortable with, he was sure. He had no intention of dating Isabel. He didn't get involved with women he couldn't see a future with, and Isabel wasn't the kind of woman who could help him take care of Jenny. He'd just agreed to something very stupid. Chances were, this whole thing would blow up in his face.

CHAPTER NINE

THAT EVENING, ISABEL sauntered down the aisle of Haggerston's small grocery store. It was a brick building with a too-small parking lot with signs that said Grocery Customers Only in front of each spot. It was right next to the town's second hardware store, and the stores battled over parking with rare aggression. Haggerston had a cheese shop and a bakery on Main Street, but the grocery store provided all the other essentials, and while it wasn't a large store—having exactly fourteen carts and three checkouts—it tended to be busy.

Living in her tiny house had changed the way Isabel shopped for food. She bought enough food for two days, and then she shopped again. There was a time when she would have gone through the store with a cartload of groceries intended to last, but with cupboard space the size of a playhouse, and a fridge that fit under the counter, planning was more important than stocking up.

Planning. She'd been trying to plan for her life, too, but she couldn't foresee the pitfalls ahead—a little piece of wisdom that her accident had made painfully obvious. She used to plan for sunny skies, but over the past year she'd become more pragmatic. She planned for aching scars when it rained. She planned for lonely evenings when everything caught up to her. She planned for steak dinners for one—a small luxury she could enjoy whether she had a special occasion or not.

She already had a tub of yogurt, some tomatoes and a bag of fresh green beans in her basket. She headed in the direction of the meat fridge, gliding past the cereal aisle.

As she came around the corner, she stopped short. Standing with his back to her, James perused the cuts of local beef. His shirtsleeves were rolled up to his elbows, his tie and jacket missing. His shoulders, wide and strong, sagged ever so slightly, broadcasting his tiredness.

"James? Is that you?"

He turned, and when he saw her, a smile flickered at the corners of his lips. "Fancy seeing you here."

"Well, a girl's got to eat."

"True enough." He shot her a grin and stepped aside to give her space.

Isabel turned her attention to the packaged meat. "Long day?"

"Very long," he agreed. "How about you?"

"I finished that sideboard. I've got the blisters to prove it." She held up a hand with a few bandages covering the worst of her blisters.

"Ouch." He took her hand in his for a closer look, and she felt her cheeks warm at the gentleness of his touch. "I hope the end result was worth it." He released her, and she pulled her hand back quickly.

"Absolutely. You'll have to come see it." A smile flashed across her face at the memory of the sideboard, gleaming in its new coat of varnish. Granted, it would need to dry for a few days, but the bulk of the work was finished, and she'd moved on to an antique bookshelf that would display her wares.

"Although, I have to say," she added, "I've moved on to an electric sander. It's that much faster."

She'd gone to the hardware store next door and picked one up. She'd gone to school with the store manager, and they'd stopped to talk for a few minutes. He was one person who didn't seem entirely antagonistic toward her, and she'd bought the more expensive sander as a result. Funny—she used to be the one who manipulated with kindness.

James nodded, eyeing her as if he were pondering his options, and she smiled uncomfortably.

"What?" she asked.

"I'm impressed."

She turned back to the meat again. "Thanks." She dropped a steak into her basket.

"Are you free tonight?" he asked.

"Why do you ask?" She shot him a quirky smile. Were her purchases so obvious?

"Why don't we go out for dinner? I could use a friendly face."

Isabel looked down at her basket, considering. She'd been thinking about a mouthwatering steak since midafternoon. "I'm in the mood for home-cooked steak."

He chuckled and grabbed two steaks from the refrigerator. "You drive a hard bargain. I happen to make a pretty spectacular steak, myself. What do you say? My place?"

It had been a long time since a man had asked her out, and Isabel regarded him thoughtfully. It was a terrible idea to get involved with the family lawyer, but it would be equally pleasant to have dinner with someone other than her father and Britney for a change—or alone. Still, the complications could be endless, and the last thing she needed right now was more of those in her life.

"I'm not sure this is a good idea," she finally admitted. "I mean, you're the family lawyer, and—"

"As friends." He held up a hand in retreat. "That's all. More than that would be hard to juggle, I agree. But if that makes you uncomfortable, don't worry about it."

She smiled ruefully. She kept forgetting that she wasn't the stunning beauty anymore with men clambering after her. In a way, it had been harder then. She'd never really known who she could trust—who cared about her as a person and who just wanted a chance to brag that they'd been with a beauty queen. But those days were behind her now, and James eyed her uncertainly.

"Actually, that sounds really nice," she said. "Sorry, I'm still getting used to—" She stopped. How to explain without sounding conceited?

James's cell phone rang and he glanced down at it, then shot her an apologetic look.

"It's my sister," he said. "I'd better get this."

It took the pressure off Isabel to explain herself any further, and she breathed a sigh of relief. She moved a few feet away to give him some privacy.

She had to admit that things had been awkward in the dating department ever since the accident. First of all, men weren't interested in her now that she was no longer a piece of arm candy. Second, she didn't know how to act anymore. She knew how to brush off unwanted advances. She knew how to play coy. She knew how to meet a man's eye and then wait a couple of beats for him to realize that he might actually have a chance with her. But this—this world of ordinariness—was confusing. How did a woman get a man's attention when she didn't naturally draw every eye in the room?

"No, Jenny, you don't have to pay anything... I'm sure of it... Okay, read me the letter... Wait—see? Right there. It isn't even addressed to you..."

Isabel glanced over to see James talking earnestly into the phone. His head was down so she could see his profile, the stubble on his chin catching the backlight of the refrigerator. His features were angular, and the way he held his phone up to his ear accentuated the bulge of his biceps. He was a good-looking man, but his attractiveness wasn't the kind that stood out. It took a moment of observation to notice his latent strength, or the defiant set to his jawline.

Or maybe it's obvious to everyone else, and I was just too self-centered to notice, she thought wryly.

Not that it mattered. James was still the family lawyer, and therefore out of the question romantically. Isabel wasn't stupid—he had her father's interests at heart, not hers. But in spite of all of those very logical reasons to steer clear, she was looking forward to an evening with him. It had been a long time since she'd had the opportunity to see the subtler attractions in a man. She sighed. This had better not be because she was lonely. She used to think that men could smell desperation, and she wondered if she was giving off a whiff of it, too.

Her phone blipped, and she looked down at an incoming text. It was Carmella.

What are you up to tonight? Want to do a movie?

She smiled to herself before she typed her reply: Sorry, can't. Have dinner plans with a man.

That would give Carmella something to chew over until they talked next. If she was going to pass on some rumors, let a few of them be in her favor. It was a bit mean, since Isabel knew as well as James did that nothing would come of this dinner. But still, it was nice to at least pretend she still had it. She grinned to herself and pressed Send.

"… Okay, okay. I'm on my way." James ended his call, then glanced at Isabel. "That was my sister."

"Is something wrong?" Isabel asked.

"She got a letter delivered to the house saying that she owes money. It's all a mistake, but she's freaking out over there, so I need to pop by and take care of that. It won't take long." He paused. "Did you want to come?"

"Wouldn't I be in the way?" she asked.

He looked like he was about to agree, then he shrugged.

"Not at all. This will be quick. I promise."

She could have bowed out, but she realized that she didn't want to sit alone tonight, after all. She wanted company, and Carmella's shallow prattle wasn't going to cut it. "Sure. Why not?"

JAMES PUT THE car into gear and slid his emotions behind a granite mask.

What were you thinking?

He hadn't planned on asking Isabel out like this. He'd hoped for something halfway between a business meeting and a friendly chat—something to cover the bases for Mr. Baxter without letting things get personal, but there had been something about seeing her in the grocery store that threw all his plans out the window.

She'd just seemed so…lonesome. Or had he been imagining that? It was a male thing to want to be the conquering hero—the rescuer. Chances were, he was falling into the same old trap that men always fell into with Isabel Baxter—thinking that she needed them. Andrew had been the same way. He'd been the tutor in her time of need, and he'd believed that she felt more for him than she had. Granted, she'd done her part in convincing him of that.

James glanced over at Isabel, seated next to him in his car. They'd just dropped her SUV off at her place and were now headed back into town toward Jenny's house. She leaned her head back against the headrest, her dark hair falling in glossy waves around her shoulders. She looked the same—except for the scars angling down her temple and cheek. Perhaps it was the scars that made her seem so much more vulnerable now. He couldn't fall into that trap, though. Her gaze flickered in his direction.

James cleared his throat. "Jenny's place isn't far. She's in Raven's Glen—that residential area that was built up on the hill when we were in high school. Remember it?"

She smiled. "I do. My dad owns a few houses up there."

He wasn't sure if Isabel knew every piece of real estate that her father owned, but she probably wasn't aware that his sister was living in one of her father's houses. Would this be awkward? Maybe he should have taken her up on her offer to do this errand on his own, but he'd been half-afraid that if he let her off the hook, he'd lose his chance at having her over for dinner, too. Obviously, he hadn't thought this one through.

James slowed for an intersection and signaled a turn. "It's a nice area—safe. Jenny really likes it."

James took the last few turns that led up to Raven's Glen. This area had been too rich for his blood when he was a teen, but as an adult, he could see what everyone else had seen. It was a good neighborhood, well designed and safe. The houses were attractive—unified in appearance, but not identical. Jenny's home was nestled at the end of a cul-de-sac. As he parked in front of her little yellow house, he noticed the curtain flick.

"Why don't you come say hello?" James said, then pushed open his door and got out. Isabel followed suit, and he met her on the other side of the car.

"This is your sister's place?" Isabel frowned toward the house.

"Yeah, this is it."

There was something in her eyes that told him she recognized the place, and he sighed. He might as well be open about the situation.

"Your father owns it. Jenny has two other friends with special needs, and they live here together. Your father allows them to live here rent-free. He's very generous."

"Hmm." She nodded. "He really is."

James caught the tightness in her tone, but just then the front door opened, revealing Jenny, a letter in her hands.

"Jimmy, you're here!" she said loudly. "Come see it. Come look at this." Jenny looked frantically from James to Isabel, not even bothering to say hello to his friend. "I don't have money, James. Not enough."

"It's okay, Jenny. Let me see."

They walked inside together, James perusing the letter. According to the letter, property taxes hadn't been paid all year. That didn't seem right. Mr. Baxter didn't let these things slide as a rule.

"Jenny, look." He pointed to the greeting. "This is addressed to George Baxter, not to you."

"But I live here." Her blue eyes widened, trying to make her point.

"I know. But you don't own the house. It belongs to Mr. Baxter." He sighed. His sister had also lived here for the past three years without paying a cent. "Look, Jenny, I'm going to pay the taxes myself, okay? I'll take care of it."

"Why would you do that?" Isabel spoke up for the first time. "My father will pay it.

I'm sure it was just an accounting error. You don't need to use your own money, James."

She made it sound ridiculous, but she didn't understand exactly how embarrassed he was about this, either.

"I said I'll take care of it." His tone was gruffer than he intended, but this whole situation frustrated him. He wasn't a charity case, and neither was his sister. When Mr. Baxter refused to accept any rent from the women, James had been amazed at his generosity, and they'd accepted his gift because it benefited all of them, none of whom could afford much at the time. James was still paying off some expensive student loans, and a small-town lawyer didn't exactly roll in money. It had been a tough time all around, but things were improving now. That student loan was paid off and James could take care of this. In fact, he'd already written the checks to start paying rent on his sister's behalf.

Isabel cast him a mildly confused look, which he ignored. He folded the letter and put it into his pocket. "It's going to be fine, Jenny."

"You sure?" she asked uncertainly.

"Positive. I'll take care of it. Now, what do you ladies have planned for the evening?"

"We're watching *You've Got Mail* and making sundaes."

"Well, don't let me intrude." He nudged his sister's shoulder. "I've got to get going, but I'll talk to you later, okay, Jen?"

"Sure. Thanks, Jimmy."

Jenny was the only one who could get away with calling him Jimmy now, at least with his permission. Britney Baxter had picked up on the nickname and used it, too, and he'd let it slide. A wise lawyer didn't annoy his biggest client's wife. As he and Isabel made their way back out to the car, he caught the strange look that Isabel shot toward the house.

"It was a really kind gesture from your father," James said after they were settled in their seats. "Jenny and her roommates were in a trailer park before this. It wasn't safe for them. Every other day, the cops were going out there for a domestic violence call for their neighbors, or some fight between drunk guys. I was afraid something would happen to her."

"Why doesn't she live with you?" Isabel asked.

"She won't. She says she's an adult, and she wants her own space."

Isabel nodded. "Fair enough. Can't say I blame her."

"Your father is tough," James said. "He wants things done his way right away, and I respect that. But under that tough shell is a very kind man. I'm sure you know that."

Isabel smiled wanly. "I do, but James, I can't let you pay those taxes. This house…" She glanced back as they pulled away from the curb and headed down the road. "I've got a personal connection to this house."

"Oh?" James had been afraid that things were about to get complicated. He signaled a turn down the main Raven's Glen road that led out of the community.

"Don't worry about it, but I'll talk to my father. Jenny will never be bothered by this again, I promise."

Silence stretched out between them while James rolled this new information over in his mind. He'd never been completely comfortable with her father's generosity, and this raised new concerns.

"Do you mind if I ask what your connection is?" he asked.

"Oh, it doesn't matter that much." She

smiled quickly. "Now, what about this steak you promised me?"

Not every piece of her history was his business, and for the time being, he let the topic drop. He had a nagging suspicion, however, that things were about to get incredibly awkward. His plan was to keep everything professional, but with Isabel, he kept sliding past that and into the personal without even thinking. He didn't want to end up as one of her casualties, one of her offhanded apologies later on. *Oops. Sorry. Didn't mean to ruin your life, James.*

CHAPTER TEN

JAMES LIVED IN A little farmhouse outside town, a squat, single-level, two-bedroom house that sat on three acres of land. It had been the center of a large farm about sixty years ago, but the land had been sold off as the town expanded until his little plot was all that was left.

James normally made decisions logically, but when he bought this house, it was a purely emotional purchase. There was something about the tiny rooms, the warped glass in the windows and the ruggedness of the surrounding land that tugged at him until he made an offer. A low offer. The owners took it, and he moved in.

There had been times in the past year that he'd wondered if he'd made a mistake. Old houses might have history, but they also had wear and tear, and this one was no exception. It seemed like everything was on its last legs in that house, and every evening and weekend was spent driving to the hardware store and watching online how-to videos on everything from plumbing to roofing. He'd never been a terribly handy guy—he was more of the book-smart type—but by the end of his first year of home ownership, he could fix pretty much anything, and there was a certain satisfaction in that.

"Make yourself at home," James said as they came inside. He flicked on a light and moved through the little sitting room toward the kitchen. "I don't know about you, but I'm starving. I'm going to start cooking."

"Me, too." Isabel followed him into the kitchen, letting her eyes roam around the petite space. The counters were all originals, gold-flecked Formica. The cupboards were small, the counter space narrow and the sink gigantic. It suited him just fine.

"You like small spaces, too," she said.

"Not quite as small as yours." He chuckled as he deposited the grocery bag onto the counter and began to unpack. "These old places were definitely smaller."

"People didn't expect as much," she said.

"Yeah, I guess so," he agreed. "People worked for what they got, and they worked hard."

"Hmm." She leaned against the counter and crossed her arms. "I never did have to work too hard for anything."

He glanced over. "I didn't mean it as a criticism."

"I know," she replied. "But it's true. My father had money, and I had—" She sucked in a breath and didn't finish the thought. "I didn't have to work for it. Everything landed in my lap."

He was surprised that she'd admit to that, especially after he'd accused her of being spoiled. Neither was he sure how to respond, so he turned his attention to opening the meat packages and flicking on the gas burner on the stove. After a moment, he glanced over to find her watching him.

"The money isn't the problem," he said. It was her tendency to take advantage of people and use them for her own gain.

"But there is definitely something wrong with taking it for granted," she conceded.

He felt a smile tug at his lips. "All right. I'll give you that."

She eyed him skeptically. "My father obviously likes you a lot, and he isn't a cuddly kind of guy. He's rather brash. He doesn't tend to get along with—"

"Regular Joes?" James asked, amused. He couldn't help but wonder how a woman like Isabel saw a man like him. Did she even notice him as a man, or was that swallowed up in his social station?

"I always say the wrong thing." She blushed and gestured to the steaks. "Can I help?"

"Chop these." He slid a knife and some mushrooms in her direction, and her flingers slid softly over his as she took the knife from him. Their eyes met and James felt that old longing from high school rising up inside him again. He'd always felt a surge of longing when he looked at her. His mind had been stronger than his heart, unlike his cousin's, but he was surprised at how little had changed. She was still out of his league, and he was still attracted to her. He pulled his mind back to the conversation.

"You're right," he said, reaching for the pepper. "Your father isn't cuddly, but he's honest and fair. I'm not exactly a teddy bear, either. I'm a lawyer. I'm at home in a courtroom, duking it out."

"You sound like the son he always wanted." She chuckled wryly.

There was something in her tone that drew

his gaze, and he found her focused grimly on the mushrooms, chopping more forcefully than necessary.

"He doted on you," he countered. "Everyone knew it."

She raised her eyebrows and glanced back at him. "Doting on and respecting are two different things." She paused, then sighed. "I'm well aware that I'll have to convince him that I'm capable or he won't leave me the company."

James knew this, too, but this was a side of Isabel Baxter he'd never seen—the excluded heiress. All those years when she'd pranced around town with designer jeans and purses, freezing out some girls and warmly accepting others, he'd never imagined that she'd felt frozen out in her own family.

"Well, you're a grown woman now," he pointed out.

"Sure am." She grinned, and he felt the heat rise in his face. She was certainly a woman—something he'd been uncomfortably aware of for some time now. Her slender fingers moved fluidly as she reached for the next mushroom, and he turned his attention back to the food in front of him.

"You know what I mean." He swirled the

oil around in the iron skillet, then gently laid the steaks in the pan to sear. "He might have thought of you as his little girl when you *were* a little girl, but a lot has changed. Maybe he'll see reason yet."

"Not as much has changed as you'd think," she replied. "He's still waiting for me to get married."

"Are you going to oblige him?"

Isabel laughed, her eyes lighting up with humor. "Absolutely not!"

"No?" He grabbed a towel to wipe his hands. "Out of spite?"

"Maybe a little." She laughed softly. "It's complicated."

"How so?" The pan spattered and sizzled as the steaks cooked, and he planted a lid on top. "It seems pretty simple, really. Meet a nice guy. Fall in love. Get married. Lots of people do it. In fact, I'll probably be the one to hammer out your prenuptial agreement."

"The prenup." She smiled wanly. "That's the problem. Whoever marries me is probably going to be angling for my father's money."

"So you don't know who to trust?" he summarized.

"Partly. When you come from privilege,

you tend to marry privilege. That's just how it works. That way, you know that the man isn't just after the money. It's an emotional safety net. My mom's family was the one with money. My dad had nothing when he married her, and her family was furious. They had to elope. Ironically, my dad warned me not to do it their way—too risky."

"So that means that regular Joes are out of the running."

"Yes." She arched a brow, looking every bit the society woman. He shot her a teasing look.

"Yeah, but if you only have a pool of, say, a dozen men to choose from, how do you know he isn't just marrying you because of your family? He's still marrying you for money, even though he's got it, too. It doesn't leave a lot of latitude for falling in love."

"You prove my point," she replied. "It's complicated. I come with enough money to doubt the honest feelings of guys who don't have any, but at the same time look at me. I'm not going to be anyone's trophy wife."

"So what do you want?" he asked. "You've been talking about what everyone else wants. What about you?"

"To press Rewind…" Her tone was wistful, and for a moment, he pitied her.

"And without the rewind button?" he asked.

She smiled. "I want my chocolate shop."

"A consolation prize?"

"Hardly." She slid the board of chopped mushrooms down the counter to James. "I've wanted this for years. I'm just finally doing it."

The cooking was a relatively quick process. James was never a gourmet cook. He cooked for results, and he tended to start the cooking when he was hungry, which meant that he wanted those results sooner rather than later.

It didn't take long to get both steaks on the table with a fresh salad. As Isabel took her first bite of steak, she rolled her eyes toward the ceiling and sighed happily.

"Oh, this is good," she said, and James felt a surge of satisfaction.

"Don't get your hopes up. I only cook about three things well, and steak is one of them."

"Good enough for me," she murmured past another bite. "I could live on this…"

Her appreciation of his cooking was rewarding in itself, and for a moment, he wondered what it would be like to do this more often. But this was her father's idea, and Mr. Baxter had made it clear that James wasn't to cross any lines. Still, he had to admit that he didn't exactly regret that paternal nudge. This was nice…maybe too nice. He wasn't supposed to get attached.

"What would your dad think of this?" James asked carefully, wiping his lips with a napkin.

"This?" She raised a brow and swallowed. "As in the two of us eating together?"

"Exactly."

She was silent for a beat, and their eyes met. She shrugged weakly.

"I thought this might be his idea," she said. "I doubt you'd be going out of your way to have dinner out with me."

"Why not?" he asked.

"Come on, James. You've already told me what you think of me. Besides, when you asked what my father would think, you tipped your hand." She smiled wryly. "It's okay. I appreciate the gesture."

James felt the heat rise in his neck. "It's not entirely your dad," he countered. He was enjoying this on a personal level, too.

"No?" She didn't sound convinced.

"Don't we count as friends at this point?"

"Friends don't get manipulated into dinners by my father." She rolled her eyes. "But don't worry. This was worth it for the steak. You're a good cook."

This hadn't exactly gone according to plan, but part of him was relieved that she knew about her father's requests. It was better than deceiving her and wondering if he was leading her on. She was smarter than he'd given her credit for, and he found that he liked her that much more.

She glanced at her watch. "But I've got to get going. I have to catch my dad before he goes to bed."

"Oh?"

She rose to her feet, dropping her napkin next to her plate. "I refuse to have you paying our bills. I'm going to get that property tax taken care of tonight. I'll feel better."

James stood up, head and shoulders taller than she was, and for a moment, he had a crazy idea that he might like to dip his head down and kiss her. Not that he should—he knew better. Starting a fling with a Baxter, knowing it could go nowhere, was a bad idea. He needed a woman who could share the burdens with him, have Jenny's back, too. This—this was attraction and nothing else. Wanting to slide his hand behind her neck and tug her in closer...

Don't be a fool. As if she'd let you!

She caught his eye, and for a split second, he thought he saw embarrassment in that look. "Thanks for dinner. Would you mind driving me back to my place?"

Had he embarrassed her? It hadn't been his intention.

"Sure," he said. "Let's go."

It was probably best to end the evening now, anyway, before he said something too revealing. Even now, Isabel had a strange way of making him want to talk too much.

She headed toward the door, and as she reached it, she glanced back.

"Next time, though, tell my father no, okay? I'm just fine. I don't need rescuing."

He didn't doubt it for a second.

THE DRIVE BACK to Isabel's house was quiet, but the silence was the palpable kind. The rustle of his shirt, the whisper of his hand against the steering wheel as it spun back to center under his palm...it all seemed louder, more meaningful. She'd almost spoken a couple of times, willing to be the first to break that silence, but then she changed her mind. She'd lose the upper hand—that impression of cool indifference she'd managed to set inside the house. It wasn't as easy to maintain anymore, and it wasn't just her loss of manipulative power. She cared more, somehow. She cared what James thought of her, and having him see her as a charity case stung.

Her father had set this whole thing up. Somehow that didn't shock her in the least, but it disappointed her. She'd honestly thought that James wanted to spend the evening with her before he'd mentioned her dad. She'd been blissfully ignorant, and it had felt good to be desired in some small way. She wasn't naive enough to think that she could stir his blood like she used to do with men, but to be appreciated for herself… A small part of her wished she could have stayed in the dark about the true state of affairs, believing that James was feeling something more for her than simple professional interest. Just for the evening. Of course, she'd want to know before she saw him again, but to find out in front of him—that had hurt. She felt like those people who thought that servers and customer service agents were flirting with them. Some people were paid to be nice.

He looked over at her a couple of times, and she did her best to keep up that appearance of indifference, but she wasn't sure that she managed it considering the regret written all over his face. Did he pity her now? Not if she had any choice in the matter! What she needed was to get home, crawl into her bed and cry this out. She'd be fine by morning, but this kind of humiliation didn't need an audience.

As they crunched up her driveway, she felt a strange combination of relief and sadness. So this was how it felt to be toyed with. She'd done enough of it in her day with the many men she'd sweet-talked. Back then, she'd taken a perverse pride in seeing their hearts on their sleeves, sadness in their eyes when they realized she hadn't been serious. She'd pretended not to see their emotions, because she thought that the nicer thing to do—to pretend they hadn't taken it seriously, either. She thought it was respectful, but looking back on it now, it was only cruel. This was karma, all right.

"Thanks for the ride," she said, and she felt

the tightness in her throat. Her voice sounded different. She pushed open the door and got out. The shorter this goodbye, the better.

"Hey." He'd gotten out of the truck, and they both slammed their doors. What did he want—to rub this in?

"Hey," he repeated, and she sighed and turned toward him. He stepped closer, looking down into her face. He was illuminated by the silvery moonlight, nothing else, and looking up into his face, she found her careful reserve begin to crack. Cool indifference wasn't as easy to maintain when gentle brown eyes were drilling down into hers.

"Thanks again," she said, but she felt tears mist her eyes. Blast it. She wasn't going to cry in front of him.

"I'm sorry." His tone was low, and he reached forward, moving her hair away from her eyes. "I think I hurt your feelings."

"No, I'm fine." She attempted to smile and wasn't sure how successful she was. "I'm used to my father, trust me."

George Baxter was heavy-handed in everything he did, and she'd been at the receiving end of his well-intentioned but ill-timed parenting for her entire life.

"I didn't want to do it," James said. "It was highly inappropriate, and unprofessional—"

"Thanks, that makes it better." Sarcasm might be easier to pull off than honesty at the moment. So he'd been strong-armed into spending an evening with her, not just asked. How low had she really fallen? She hadn't realized it was this bad until her father's intervention here. If her dad thought he was helping matters, he was sadly mistaken.

"That's not what I meant," he said. "I wanted to make you dinner. I didn't want your dad to be part of the equation."

"Oh…" That did make it better…a little. A gust of wind picked up, and Isabel rubbed her hands over her arms. James stepped closer, putting his warm palms over her upper arms, and she had to admit that it did feel good. She'd been noticing his good looks lately, but now she was close enough to detect a hint of his cologne, too. This wasn't helping. If she was supposed to save face, standing here in the moonlight, noticing how good he smelled wasn't the answer.

And as if to clinch her complete loss of dignity, a tear slipped past her lashes and slid down her cheek. Before she could wipe it away, James did, brushing it from her face with the pad of his thumb.

She was about to say something stupid, she was sure, when he tipped her face upward with a finger under her chin and brought his lips down on hers. She was shocked at first, but he didn't pull back, and she realized after a moment that neither had she. Her lids fluttered shut and she leaned into those warm, strong arms.

For a moment it was gentle, chaste, even. And then, it was as if they forgot who they were, and why this was a bad idea, and they were just a man and woman in the moonlight, a cool wind swirling around them as they pressed closer together. She fit perfectly in his arms, and he felt solid against her—nothing like the teddy bear that Britney claimed him to be. No, he was a man in every sense, and as his lips moved over hers, it felt like coming home. Was that her loneliness talking, or was it just him?

James pulled back, and he smiled bashfully. "Should I not have done that?"

"Um." She swallowed and stepped back. "I think it was my fault, too." She certainly hadn't stopped him, and she'd been a very willing participant. She pulled out her keys. "I'd better get inside."

"Good night, Izzy."

Her nickname sounded good coming from him, and she wasn't sure she trusted herself to say anything. She'd do something dumber still and ask him in or something like that. No, she didn't need to do anything she'd regret. She needed to think. She needed to make sense of this evening.

She climbed the three steps to her front door and unlocked it. When she glanced back, James was still watching her.

"Good night," she said, and let herself in. She shut the door behind her and leaned against it in the darkness until she heard the growl of his truck's engine. Then she looked out the window and watched as the taillights made their way back to the main road.

What had just happened? Had she really just kissed James Hunter?

CHAPTER ELEVEN

JAMES SAT IN his living room for a long time that evening, watching TV on mute. He wasn't focusing on the television—his mind was back there in the moonlight with Isabel.

He'd most certainly crossed the line there. When George said that he expected him not to go breaking any hearts, he was pretty sure the old guy was thinking about that exact scenario, and Isabel had already warned him that George didn't keep his business and personal as separate as he pretended.

But she'd kissed him back. That knowledge gave him a rush of elation. He didn't know why he'd done it... It was a cocktail of things, like the fact that he'd hurt her by following her father's orders—he'd seen it in the tremor in her chin when she'd been trying to stare him down as if she didn't care. She *had* cared, and he had wounded her, and he couldn't be the guy who stabbed her that deeply. Add to that a cool summer night, the spattering of stars that had twinkled over-head, the cool breeze pushing them closer together for warmth and the glisten of moon-light in those dewy eyes of hers... He'd been standing alone in the dark with Isabel Bax-ter—wasn't that enough?

It had felt so right in the moment, and it had been the single stupidest thing he'd done so far.

He rubbed his hands over his face. He'd have to face her. That was the problem. If they'd shared a kiss in the moonlight and never had to see each other again, it would have been perfect. But they'd most certainly see each other again, and he'd have to see exactly how she really felt about him. He wasn't sure he was up for that. A moment of weakness didn't mean that she wouldn't completely regret it.

He wasn't that guy, the kind who stole kisses when the mood seemed right. That was another thing that was irritating him. He and Izzy had no future. Attraction—ab-solutely—but no future. So why had he jeop-ardized his job with George Baxter to steal a kiss with his daughter?

His phone buzzed, and he glanced down at it to see that his sister had sent him another email. He touched the screen, pulling it up so he could read it. It was a link to a job page for Haggerston.

"Hint taken, Jenny," he murmured with a wry smile.

She wanted a job. She wanted to contribute, be a part of something bigger than herself. He understood that feeling all too well. Maybe he could convince her to take a sabbatical from the job hunt—maybe to take up a hobby or something.

But the jolt back into reality brought with it a wave of guilt. Jenny was part of the package for any woman he made a life with, and he had no business twisting up people's emotions. He knew where he stood. He knew what he needed, and he resolutely refused to be the kind of man who jerked a woman around for his own entertainment.

Isabel was probably both tougher and more vulnerable than he was giving her credit for, but Jenny wasn't. What you saw was what you got with Jenny, and she looked to him to take care of her.

He could not kiss Isabel again.

Isabel got into her SUV and drove out to her father's house shortly after James left. Her heart was still pounding just a little faster after that kiss. It wasn't as if she hadn't been kissed before, but there had been something about the way he'd held her—so gently, so firmly—that she'd never experienced. How was it even fair that a kiss like that had come from the family lawyer?

She knew better than to mix business with pleasure. She'd learned that the hard way with Andrew, and if she had to break off a relationship with James, too, it would affect more than her heart—it would affect business. She could hear her father's opinion as if he was sitting right next to her: *Izzy, keep it separate. Don't let the man you date know anything about your money. Let him guess. Let him wonder. Just never let him know anything for a fact. And never mix romance with the legal team. Let a man do his job! Seriously, Izzy! Do I even have to tell you this?*

No, he didn't. And she'd never tell her father what had happened this evening. It wasn't his business, anyway. Her father had asked James to take her out, and it had gone a little further than her father intended. So this one was his fault, if someone had to be blamed.

Isabel pulled into the drive and followed

the curves around to the big, three-story house. The lights on the lower level were all off, but several lights glowed in the windows upstairs, so she knew that her father was still up.

The timing wasn't convenient, though.

She parked the car and turned off the engine, uncertain if she should disturb them or not. It wasn't like old times when it was just her father in that house, and she could come and go as she pleased. This was Britney's home now, too.

Isabel grimaced at the thought, not that her feelings mattered at all. It was what it was.

The porch light flicked on and the front door opened, revealing her father in his bathrobe. He shaded his eyes.

"What are you doing out there?" he barked.

"Deciding if I was too late to knock," she said, getting out of her vehicle and slamming the door behind her. "Am I?"

"Yes," he grumbled, but he stood back and gestured her in. "Come in, come in. What's going on?"

"I had dinner with James."

"Oh?" He turned his back so she couldn't see his face. He ambled into the sitting room, and they sank into their traditional spots—

her father in his armchair and Isabel on the couch. She leaned forward, resting her elbows on her knees.

"Don't ever try to set me up again, Dad."

"Who says I did?"

"I say you did!" she retorted. "Don't meddle, do you hear me?"

Her father didn't answer, and she knew better than to try to force him. Instead she added, "Maybe instead we could talk about his sister's house. You're very generous with my property."

At those words, her father froze. He shut his eyes, then he heaved a deep sigh.

"Yes, that," he said. "I should have mentioned it."

"You gave away my house?" she asked incredulously. It wasn't her house, exactly. The deed was still in her father's name, but when he purchased that particular house, he'd told her that it would be hers when she got old enough. That it was to be her home to do with as she pleased.

"I didn't give it away." He scrubbed a hand through his sparse hair. "I simply allowed the girls to live there rent-free. You were in New York, and it didn't look like you'd be coming back here anytime soon."

"You couldn't have handed over a different piece of property?" she asked. Her annoyance was petty, and she knew it, but there was more to this than a simple rental agreement.

"The others were rented already. And that one—" He cleared his throat. "Those young ladies needed to live in a safe part of town. I bought that house for you because of the location. Safety first."

"How long ago was this?" she asked.

"Three years. Back then, you didn't care what I was doing here. You didn't care about that house."

He was right. She'd been driving a Bentley, dating a funds manager for a major bank and not looking back. "I just wish you'd told me," she said.

"I should have." He nodded slowly. "That was about the time that I started dating Britney, and..."

She understood all too well. That had been an awkward time, and her father had hidden his new relationship for the better part of a year. When he asked Britney to marry him, he'd been forced to tell his daughter, and it had been ugly. Things had been said.

"Okay, well, apparently there are some

property taxes due, and the letter was sent to the house instead of to you."

"What?" He scowled. "Those idiots at city hall…"

"Probably some clerical error," she agreed. "I thought I'd let you know, because James was about to pay it himself."

"Pay my taxes?" he scoffed. "Ridiculous. I'll take care of it."

"That's what I told him." She eyed him cautiously, and silence stretched between them. Her father heaved a sigh and shot her an apologetic smile.

"I'm sorry I didn't tell you," he said at last.

"It's okay." She leaned back into the soft pillows of the sofa. "A lot has changed."

He nodded and grunted. "Life does that, Princess."

"You know what I miss?" she asked quietly.

"Hmm?"

"That painting of you and mom that used to hang over the mantel." She looked over at the modern monstrosity that beamed down on them. "Where is it?"

"In the attic. Do you want it?"

"I have no room for it," she admitted grudgingly.

"That's why you need a decent home," her

father said, shaking his head. "I have no idea why you decided to live in that...that doll-house."

Isabel laughed. "I like it."

"There's no room for anything."

"I like that, too."

Her father sighed. "I'll never understand you, Izzy. It's like you find the one thing that will drive me the craziest, and that's what you commit to." He waved his hand through the air in dismissal. "So are we okay now?"

Isabel nodded. "We're fine."

"Do you want to live in that house?" he asked. "I can relocate the renters—"

"No." She shook her head. "I'm fine where I am. Let them stay there."

Her father nodded, his flinty eyes locked on her. "You're sure?"

"Positive."

"Okay, well..." He pushed himself forward with a grunt. "It's late."

"Wait."

There was one more thing that had been nagging at Isabel, and she opened her purse and pulled out the photo of the baby that she'd found behind the picture of her parents. For some reason, she hadn't been able to forget that little, newborn face, and she wasn't sure why. She held out the picture.

"Whose baby is this?" she asked.

"What?" Her father took the picture between two stubby fingers, but when his gaze focused, his face turned ashen and he let his hand drop, the picture still pinched in his grip.

Isabel jumped to her feet, alarmed. Was he having a heart attack or something?

"Dad, are you okay?"

He nodded dumbly and handed back the photo. "Don't know who that is."

"You look sick. Should I call Britney?"

"No!" he barked.

"So you don't know who this baby is?" she pressed. "I just wondered. I mean, this is Mom. I recognize the necklace." She took the picture back. "Were you godparents to this baby or something?"

"Where did you find it?" he asked suspiciously.

"It was behind that picture of you and Mom that was in that silver frame. Remember? It came loose, and when I opened it, I found this picture behind it. I didn't know why Mom would hide it back there."

"Who says she hid it?" he retorted, anger flashing in his small eyes.

"Just a guess." Isabel frowned. "Dad, who is this baby?"

"I said I don't know," he snapped. "Do you think I'm lying?"

Frankly, she did. She'd never seen her father get so rattled as when he looked at that photo, but he wasn't about to tell her anything tonight.

"I just thought I'd ask." She sighed. "Okay, well, I guess I should get going."

Isabel tucked the photo back into her purse and headed for the door. She felt guilty, somehow. She'd caused something, and she couldn't even say what it was, but her father's reaction had scared her. This baby wasn't just familiar to her father—this baby mattered more deeply than she'd ever guessed. But whose was it? And how many more secrets was her father harboring?

"Thanks for coming by," her father said gruffly. "Take care."

"Dad, I—" Isabel turned back as she reached the door, but the words caught in her throat. Standing at the top of the stairs, Britney stood in a long, white nightgown, her hand cradling the bottom of her growing belly. She stood utterly still, staring down at them nervously.

"Hi, Britney," Isabel said. "I'm sorry to come by so late."

Britney didn't answer aloud, but she smiled wanly, and after a moment, Isabel pulled open the front door.

I've overstayed my welcome.

"Well, good night," she said quickly, and plunged out into the cool evening.

"Good night. Drive safe, Princess."

The door clicked shut behind her. She stood motionless for a moment on the porch, trying to sort through all of this new information, but nothing made sense. Nothing added up. Her father didn't normally give people free rent for years on end. That wasn't part of his nature. And that picture...

She heaved a sigh and trotted down the stairs and headed to her car. Only when she'd started her vehicle and begun to back up did the porch light flick off.

At the very least, her father had watched to make sure she got out safely. That was something.

CHAPTER TWELVE

ISABEL WOKE UP the next morning feeling restless. No one ever really stopped relying on their parents for love and support, but life wasn't carved in marble. Her father had a new wife now, and the tensions there didn't help her relationship with her father.

Did a childhood home ever stop being home?

It might have for her. That house might hold her memories, but the family inside was no longer hers. Not in the same way. Her father had divided loyalties, and as a grown woman, she could appreciate his position, but it still left her feeling mildly adrift.

It was time to make her own traditions. She'd always relied on her family and their position to give her a sense of identity and safety, but coming home again had blown that apart. Her father wasn't the same man she left behind. He wasn't the doting father and widower anymore. He was now a husband again, and his wife was about to have a baby. Isabel was no longer his world.

Maybe parents felt the same way when their children grew up, but that bittersweet heartbreak was part of the natural order of things. Wasn't it? Maybe not.

But in the midst of her melancholy was the memory of a kiss that had taken her breath away. Did James have feelings for her? Was she about to do the same thing to him that she'd done to his cousin—lead him on and then pull away? She shut her eyes and rubbed a hand over her face. It was time to start the day.

That morning, Isabel whipped up two batches of truffles—mint chocolate and hazelnut chocolate—to use as gifts for the owners and employees of various local businesses. It was good to let people know that her store was opening, and to give them a taste of her wares. She'd finally set a date, and that in itself felt good. This was happening. She'd already ordered boxes for her chocolates—the more ornate version with her logo embossed on the top would take another week to arrive, but she had a carton of simpler boxes that would do just fine for today.

After making a dozen boxes of truffles, four to a box, she locked up the store and headed down Main Street. The employees at the local businesses gladly accepted her sample boxes and eyed her business cards curiously.

"I'm opening in three weeks," she told them cheerily. "I'll be coming by with more samples…so tell your friends!"

If there was one thing she was sure about, people passed the word when there was free chocolate at stake.

After making her way up one side of Main Street and down the other, she had one box left, and her stomach was rumbling. She glanced at her watch, and it was noon on the dot. She'd bring this box to the bistro across the street from her shop, and stop in for lunch at the same time.

Carlo greeted her with a smile as she came inside, and he put his hand on the pile of menus.

"For…two?" he asked.

"For one. Thank you." She handed him her last box of chocolates. "I'm also handing out some samples. I'm opening a chocolate shop across the street. Opening day is in three weeks. I thought you might like to try some truffles on the house."

"Really?" Carlo peeked in the box. "Nice. Thanks. My girlfriend will love these." A blush rose in his cheeks. So the flirtatious waiter had a girlfriend. He smiled guiltily.

"Your secret is safe with me." She winked. "No worries."

He laughed self-consciously. "Let me find you a table, Miss Baxter."

Carlo led the way through the dining room, and on her way past a table, she bumped the person seated.

"Sorry about that," she said quickly, looking down. Her heart skipped a beat in surprise. "James?"

Heat flooded her cheeks. The last time they'd seen each other, they'd been kissing outside her little house. James looked equally surprised. His sister sat across from him, both with glasses of water in front of them, but their meals hadn't arrived yet.

"Isabel, hi." He motioned to a seat at their table. "Care to join us?"

"No, no." Isabel shook her head quickly. "Thanks, though. You've had me foisted upon you enough, I'd say."

She still wasn't sure what she thought

about that kiss, let alone what he thought, and she felt the flush of embarrassment.

James gave her a boyish grin. "I don't do anything I don't want to do. And I'm inviting you to eat with us."

She paused, turning his words over in her mind.

"Sit, sit," Jenny insisted, and Isabel realized there wasn't a graceful way to get out of this, and she'd have to face James eventually. At least this way his sister was here, which would protect her from having to talk about that kiss.

"It's nice to see you again, Jenny," Isabel said, shooting the younger woman a smile. Jenny beamed back.

"Can I take your order?" Carlo asked. "Unless you need time…"

"What did you order, James?" she asked.

"Soup and sandwich," he replied.

"That sounds perfect." She looked up at Carlo. "I'll have the same. Tomato soup and grilled cheese for the sandwich."

"Very good." Carlo vanished into the din of the dining room.

Isabel turned back to James and Jenny and found Jenny staring at her, eyes wide and mouth slightly open.

The scars.

"Jenny," James murmured, but Jenny didn't take the hint, her gaze still locked on Isabel's face.

"It's okay," Isabel said. "Are you noticing my scars, Jenny?"

"I saw them before, but now I'm closer," Jenny said in utter honesty. "Sorry."

"No, I don't mind." It was a half lie. She ordinarily did mind, but Jenny was different. There was no guile there. "I used to be pretty like you," she explained. "Now, well…"

"You're pretty still," Jenny said, shaking her head. "My brother thinks so, too."

James looked up, alarm in his eyes, and seeing him discomfited was oddly reassuring.

"Right, James?" Jenny pressed. "You said so before. You said that Isabel Baxter is still gorgeous, right?"

James winced, then nodded. *Gorgeous.* That wasn't a word that had described her in a long time. But now wasn't the time to melt under a compliment, and she fell back on her old ploy of pretending that the guy didn't feel anything more than passing interest in her.

"Thanks, James. That was nice of you."

Did he feel something? Was that kiss about

more than a moonlit night and some compassion?

"He never just says something," Jenny said earnestly. "He's a lawyer. He doesn't care what people think."

He seemed to care right then, and Isabel cast him an apologetic look. "So how are you doing, Jenny?" she asked, changing the subject.

"I got fired."

"I heard about that." Isabel winced. "Sorry."

"I'll get another job," Jenny replied. "James will help."

Carlo came back with their meals, and for a few minutes, everyone focused on their food. The soup and sandwich hit the spot, and Isabel sighed in contentment as she crunched into the buttery sandwich, stringy cheese stretching out between the toast and her mouth. Jenny was having a burger and fries, carefully dunking home-cut fries into a little bowl of catsup. James had minestrone soup and a beef sandwich on rye.

"This is so good," Isabel said after finishing half of her sandwich.

"Mmm," James agreed, his mouth full.

Carlo came by again and Jenny reached out and tapped his arm.

"Yes?" Carlo asked politely.

"May I speak to your manager?" Jenny asked. "I'd like a job."

"Sure." Carlo smiled and disappeared again.

"Jenny, this isn't a good idea," James said, swallowing his bite. "This place is pretty busy."

"That means they need people to work here," Jenny retorted. "And I need a job."

A few minutes later, the manager stopped at their table. Jenny sucked in a deep breath and addressed him, a dab of catsup on one cheek.

"Hello, my name is Jenny Hunter, and I'd like to apply for a job."

"We aren't hiring right now, I'm afraid," he said, a smile pasted to his face. "I'm sorry."

"But what about that sign?" Jenny asked, pointing, and Isabel followed her finger to a prominent sign at the front desk. Help Wanted: All Positions.

"Oh, uh—" The manager smiled again, his smile still not reaching his eyes. "I should take that down…"

"I can do things," Jenny insisted. "I can wash dishes and I can clear tables. I did that once at Ruby's Diner. And I'm really nice."

"We aren't hiring," he said more firmly. "Enjoy your meal."

He walked resolutely away, and Jenny's earlier bravado wilted. She picked up another fry, but she didn't eat it. She just held it in front of her face, tears welling up in her eyes.

"It's okay," James said gently. "This isn't a good place for you. You don't want to work for that guy, right?"

What did that manager even know about Jenny? He'd dismissed her on first sight. Isabel looked in disgust from the manager then back to Jenny, whose brother was trying to put a positive spin on her treatment.

"Do you want a job, Jenny?" Isabel asked softly.

"Yes, I really do. I want to make some money. And I'm good at things."

"I believe you," Isabel said.

Jenny turned to her brother. "I don't think I'm hungry anymore. Can we go now?"

James nodded and pulled a few bills from his wallet. He met Isabel's gaze. "This is on me. My treat."

His glance was filled with something tender and sad, akin to what she saw in him the night before when his lips had met hers. Was he remembering it, too? But it didn't matter—she couldn't do this.

"Jenny, wait—" Isabel had an idea, and while she hadn't thought it through, she couldn't just let Jenny walk away feeling as though she didn't matter, as though she had nothing to offer. Isabel was a little too familiar with that feeling lately. She couldn't let that manager crush this young woman.

Jenny turned back, her blue eyes still misting.

"I'll hire you," Isabel said. "I'm going to need a hand at the store when it opens. What do you say? Will you take the job?"

James looked about ready to speak, but Jenny's face lit up and she nodded excitedly.

"Yes! Yes, I'll work for you!" she squealed, then she dived down and hugged Isabel tightly. As Isabel lifted her gaze, she was surprised to see that James's expression was grim, the earlier tenderness evaporated. She'd assumed he'd be happy that she'd given his sister a chance. She shot him a questioning look.

"I've got to get back to the office," he said, glancing at his watch. "I've got a meeting in twenty minutes."

"Of course," Isabel said. "It was nice to see you both."

James gave her a curt nod and nudged his sister toward the door. That kiss had thrown off their balance. She didn't feel quite so confident with him anymore, and she hated that. With a sigh, she turned back to the food in front of her.

THAT EVENING, JAMES pulled up in front of Isabel's little house and turned off the engine. He sat there quietly for a moment, surveying the scene. In the distance, the jagged mountains were just visible against the dusky sky. The brightest of the stars twinkled through the blanketed sky, and a cool breeze whisked across the field, wild grasses bending and rippling in the dimness.

The last time he'd been here, he'd kissed her. He inwardly grimaced. He'd set himself up for rejection, but more than that, he'd started messing around with something that couldn't work. It was foolish and unprofessional, and he hadn't forgiven himself for it. But he wasn't here for that—he was here because of Jenny.

The Baxters had done enough for the Hunters. Isabel didn't need to hire his sister. Moreover, things would only get more complicated when she had to let Jenny go. Jenny needed the right job, and much as he found himself liking Isabel—more than liking her—he didn't think that this was the right fit, either.

I've got to stop this before it gets out of hand, he thought to himself. Ironically, he'd already let too much of his relationship with her get out of hand. That kiss had been his move. Her move had been to hire his sister. All too often people thought they were doing a good deed, when they were actually making everything else more difficult—like wealthy people traveling to developing countries to witness the poverty, take a few pictures and post them to the internet with the hashtag #feelingblessed. Some things just weren't helpful.

Like kissing his client's daughter. He was going to beat himself up for that for a while longer.

The house glowed from within, and the front window darkened as Isabel looked out. She'd seen him, so he opened his truck door and gave a wave.

The front door opened, and Isabel stood in the pool of warm light, crossing her arms over her chest against the evening chill. She wore a pair of fitted jeans and a pale blue tank top. Her feet were bare, and she shot him a warm smile, the scars along the side of her face masked in shadow.

"Hi," James called as he headed toward the door. "I'm sorry to come by so late, but I was hoping I could have a word with you."

"Sure." Her smile faltered. "Is everything okay?"

"Yeah, yeah…" He paused, not sure how to bring this up. She stepped back and ushered him. He smiled his thanks and stepped inside. It was different between them now—he could feel it. When he looked at her, he knew more than he had a right to know—like the way her hair smelled and the way she fit into his arms. He looked around for a place to sit and sank into a chair.

"How was your day?" he asked. The high ceiling made the space seem more open than it really was, and he glanced around, impressed with her decor.

"Good." She opened the little fridge under the counter. "Do you want something to drink?"

"No, I'm fine, thanks."

So they weren't going to address that kiss, were they? Maybe it was better that way.

She shut the fridge again and turned toward him. "So what's going on? Is this about my dad?"

"No." He must have made it seem like there was an emergency. "I'm sorry, I'm making this sound like it's more serious than it is. It's about my sister."

Isabel nodded quickly, and a blush rose in her cheeks. "She doesn't have to work for me. I only wanted to help. If she'd rather not—"

"No, she really wants to," James interjected. And that was the truth. Jenny had sent him three emails about how excited she was to have a new job, and called him twice. "That's the thing. I don't think you know what you're getting yourself into here. Jenny is sweet and a really great person, but she's gone through a lot of jobs here in Haggerston."

"Because she's misunderstood?" Isabel asked.

He smiled wanly. "Yes and no. She's definitely misunderstood, but it's more than that. She doesn't always make the appropriate decision. For example, she recently threw cheese at the head of a man who insulted her."

Isabel nodded slowly. "Okay."

"She doesn't do anything without reason. It always makes sense when I talk to her about it later, but customer service isn't easy. It requires a lot of patience."

"Definitely," she agreed.

"Good." He nodded quickly. The sooner this was over, the better. "So we're agreed, then."

"About what?"

"That working in your chocolate shop probably isn't the best solution for Jenny," he clarified. He had a sinking feeling that this wasn't going as planned.

Isabel blinked, then shook her head. "I didn't agree to that."

James smothered a sigh. To his knowledge, Isabel hadn't worked in customer service, either. She'd worked in marketing, but grass-level sales were a different experience altogether. Jenny aside, did she know what she was getting herself into with her business?

"Look, Isabel. You're a kind person—"

"Kindness has nothing to do with it. It's what's right. Jenny deserves a chance, and if people don't want cheese in their face, maybe they should treat others with respect."

"A noble sentiment, until you start losing sales," James pointed out.

She was silent for a moment, then shrugged weakly. "It hasn't happened yet. I'm willing to give her a chance."

"She's had chances. About a dozen." James gave her a tight smile. "I might sound too tough on her right now, but she doesn't need another chance. She needs the right fit. The last thing we need is for her to get fired. Again."

"What do you suggest?"

"That you take back the job offer." He shrugged. "It's better to do it now before she starts."

"And what reason would I give?" she asked.

"That you can't afford to hire anyone yet?" he suggested.

"But I can afford it, and I do need some-one."

"This is about sparing her feelings," James said.

"I'll tell you what." She sucked in a breath, narrowed her eyes in thought, and then met his gaze again. "If things don't work out, I'll call you. We'll find a way to end the arrangement without hurting her feelings."

It was a solution, he had to admit, but not the one he'd been hoping for. The Baxters were a powerful family, and Isabel didn't seem to recognize the awkwardness of it all. Was she really oblivious, or just being willfully so? Maybe this was her way of getting back a little bit of power after he'd kissed her.

"Can I level with you?" he asked.

"Of course."

"Your dad has already done a lot for us. He's provided a home for Jenny and her roommates to live in, and given me a great position. It's enough already. I don't like being beholden."

"Oh." She frowned and pushed her fingers into her jeans pockets. "I see."

The blush rose in her cheeks again, and she cleared her throat.

"It's a pride thing for me," he added.

"It wasn't about pride for me," she said quietly. "I thought we were…friends."

James inwardly grimaced. What was it about Isabel that she could slip right past his defenses? She was a Baxter, for crying out loud, and she had money and status backing her up. She had more privilege than anyone else in this town, and yet when he looked into those clear, brown eyes, he still felt like she needed him. Why couldn't he think straight when he was with her?

"Since we're being honest," Isabel added, "I just wanted to help out somehow. This is going to be a Haggerston business, and I want to employ locals. People here haven't fully forgiven me, but if I can provide some jobs, I'll be contributing."

"You don't owe me anything, Izzy," he said softly, the nickname flying out of his mouth before he could stop it. If she wanted to make up for Andrew or for anything in the past, she didn't need to do it. Not with him. He'd been wrong to cross that line with her, and in a way, he was trying to shuffle back.

"This company is going to be different. I'm not going to hurt Jenny's feelings. You have my word."

She wasn't backing down, and he wasn't sure what else he could say. "Fine."

"Yeah?" A smile lit up her face. "You trust me on this?"

No, he didn't. Not completely.

"Let me know if things don't work, okay? We'll sort something out."

"I promise."

James let out a pent-up breath and pushed himself to his feet. "I guess I should get going—"

She stepped closer to him, reaching to open the door just behind him, and the soft lavender fragrance of her perfume tugged him closer still. Again. He couldn't do this—he couldn't let himself kiss her a second time, knowing full well this would only hurt him if he did. She wasn't looking at him, though. Her gaze was turned toward something in her hand. Her long, silky lashes brushed her cheeks with each blink, and he found himself mesmerized. One cheek was soft and smooth, and the other was marred by puckered lines of scar tissue, but she was still stunning.

She'd always managed to rouse those feelings of manly protectiveness in the young men around town, but whenever he saw Isabel, he was reminded of Andrew, and that left him immune. Yet being in this close space with her was fueling some feelings that weren't in his best interest. She was his boss's daughter, and more than that, she was a Baxter. Things that burned a regular person didn't even singe a Baxter. He was most certainly playing with fire.

Isabel straightened, and when she looked up, he found their faces only inches apart. Her lips parted and she sucked in a breath of surprise.

"Oh…" she breathed.

"Not much space in here," he attempted to joke, but it fell flat as neither of them moved.

She was so close that he could have reached out and pulled her against him, run his fingers through her long, glossy hair. Her dark eyes met his, and he dropped his gaze down to her pink lips. He could kiss her again, regret it later, but allow himself this one last…

Bad idea, he told himself firmly, but the rest of him didn't seem to be listening. With a concerted effort, he tore his mind from dangerous territory.

"Well." He cleared his throat. "We've got to stop doing that."

"Thanks for coming." She took a step back, colliding with the edge of a table.

"Careful." James grinned and put a hand out to steady her. "I'd better get going."

"Yes, you should." She laughed and shook her head.

"Look, Izzy, about last night," he said, running a hand through his hair. "I'm sorry.

I overstepped. I made things really weird for us now, and—"

"It's okay," she said with a small shrug. "I don't do anything I don't want to do, either."

What did she mean by that? Had she wanted that kiss? Was there more to this than he'd thought? How much had he messed this up?

"Seeing as we're attracted to each other…" he began slowly.

"We should be careful," she finished the thought, and he felt a rush of relief. They were on the same page.

"Yeah," he agreed. "Probably for the best."

They were silent for a moment or two, and then James reached back and turned the doorknob, pushing it open.

"Have a good night, Isabel," he said quietly.

She waved wordlessly, and he stepped out into the night. As James trotted back toward his truck, a memory rose of his cousin sitting on the front steps of his house, scuffing his shoe against the ground. He could still see his cousin's grease-stained fingernails from working on his car, see the way he picked at a hangnail on his thumb.

"I'm leaving early," Andrew had announced.

"How early?"

"Right after my exams."

The news had been like a punch to the gut. "Why so soon?"

"I've got nothing to stay for."

"What about our road trip? We've been planning that since tenth grade. Come on, man. You can't bail on the road trip."

He'd been pleading at that point, and it wasn't entirely about the road trip. He'd sensed that something deeper, something more desperate was happening here, and he didn't know what it was or how to stop it. And in that moment of helpless certainty that this was wrong, he'd also been entirely certain that this was Isabel Baxter's fault.

"Sorry, man," Andrew had said. "I've got to get out of here. For good. We've got a few weeks still. I'm going to soak up all the shade I can before I go to boot camp." Andrew shot him a look, pleading for understanding. "That's what the boys over there say. Don't take the shade for granted."

Don't take anything for granted. James had taken that to heart. Life was short, happiness could be fleeting. People were fragile.

"And I'm playing with fire," he said to himself as he yanked open the door and hopped into the cab. Andrew hadn't been half as stupid as James had thought. Isabel had a way of making a man feel like the center of the world, if only for a few moments, and that could be intoxicating. Except James was no high school kid, and he knew better.

CHAPTER THIRTEEN

"ISABEL? ISABEL, ARE you here?"

Isabel looked up from the pot of milk chocolate she was tempering on the stove in her store kitchen. Was that who she thought it was? She closed her eyes and winced.

"In here!" she called.

Britney came into the kitchen, her Coach bag on one shoulder and pinched under her arm. She wore a cream-colored Chanel suit, her hair pulled up into a twist at the back of her head. She looked more mature in that outfit, Isabel realized. She liked it better. Britney looked around the kitchen, her lips pressed together into a prim line.

"So this is it?" Britney asked.

"Sure is." Isabel eyed her stepmother questioningly. "How did you get in?"

"It was open."

Isabel nodded. She must have forgotten to lock the door behind herself this morning. She wouldn't do that again. She stirred the chocolate slowly in the pot with a wide paddle, the lumps of chocolate slowly melting into the liquid.

"What are you doing?" Britney asked after a moment.

"Tempering some chocolate. I'm going to make some cream-filled chocolates with those molds over there on the counter."

Britney stepped to the side to look but didn't move any closer. She just nodded.

"What can I do for you?" Isabel asked. "Just wanted to see the place?"

"I was curious," Britney replied. "So are you sure it'll work?"

"You mean make money?" Isabel asked blandly.

"Yes, exactly." There was a flicker of something more intelligent in Britney's gaze, even though she seemed to be trying to hide it under a mask of bored indifference.

"That's the big question, isn't it?" Isabel replied with a small smile. "That's the thrill."

"Hmm." Britney's high heels tapped against the tiled floor as she ambled around the kitchen. She peered into a couple of cupboards, then turned back. "And if it fails?"

The question irritated Isabel. Was Britney afraid that Isabel would pump her father for more money? Was she already staking her claim on the Baxter fortune?

"I'll just have to take it one day at a time," Isabel said at last.

"I mean, you must have a plan B," Britney pressed. "Like, if this fails, then you'll… move back to New York?"

Isabel turned her attention back to the chocolate. It was nearly all melted now, and she turned off the heat, continuing to stir in slow, sweeping curves.

"Yes, that would be an option," she replied. "Why?"

"It only seems smart to know what you'll do," she replied with a faint shrug. "But if this business fails, then you'll have lost everything, am I right?"

Isabel's irritation flared. "Did no one ever tell you that talking about money is rude?" So was repeating the word *fail* three times in a minute.

"Not in the family, it isn't," Britney retorted, and Isabel bit her tongue against a sharp reply.

"Trust me, Britney," Isabel said, putting in some effort to remain calm. "I have my degree in business. I'm well aware of the risks, and I've got it under control."

"You see, the thing is," Britney said, dipping her finger into the pot, "if you lost all of that money in a business that didn't succeed, there wouldn't necessarily be another check to try again." She licked the chocolate off her finger. "Yummy."

"I'm not asking for more money," Isabel replied. "This is between me and my dad, so it really isn't your business, but I've never asked for money."

Not that her father had ever not handed it over, requested or not.

"But you might expect it," Britney replied. "I know I would."

Her comment hit a nerve because it wasn't entirely wrong. Isabel struggled to maintain her calm.

"Don't you think it's better to leave this to me and my father?" Isabel asked pointedly. "You're well taken care of. You shop. You travel. My dad gives you whatever you want."

"Actually, I don't," Britney replied, meeting Isabel's gaze for the first time. "I don't travel. I stay here in town with your father because he's my husband and I want to support him. And as for shopping, Carmella does more shopping than I've ever done. You don't know me as well as you think."

Isabel blinked in surprise. She hadn't expected that reply, and she felt the heat rising in her cheeks. Britney was much more intelligent than she liked to let on, and she was here for a reason.

"Why the sudden concern about money, Britney?"

"Because no barrel is bottomless," Britney replied quietly. "I'm having a baby, and when I do, there will be another heir."

"Of course." Isabel looked at Britney quizzically.

Britney narrowed her eyes. "When we got married, your father said he would change his will."

Isabel nodded. "Unless he cut me out completely, which I will never believe—"

"I'm not saying anything," Britney said quickly, her earlier bravado fading. "I'm just… I'm not saying anything." She turned back toward the door, hugging her bag in closer against her body. "Good luck with this. It looks like fun."

Britney's shoes tapped across the floor, and then the front door opened and shut, the little bell above it tinkling. Isabel stood in silence, the paddle motionless in her hand.

What was that? Britney had come for a reason, but she hadn't been willing to say anything outright. What exactly was in her father's will? And had Britney come to warn her about it?

She put down the paddle, moved the pot to a cold burner and went to lock the front door. She and Britney had never been fond of each other. It had started when Isabel heard of her father's engagement. She'd told him straight out not to marry her. Britney was young and silly. She would be a terrible match for him, and she was marrying him for his money. Her father had been offended and told Isabel to never speak like that again. There'd been nothing but tension between them all during the engagement, and frankly, Isabel had been surprised to be invited to the wedding.

The big day had been tense and strange. The guests had been talking behind their hands about George Baxter marrying an obvious gold digger. Britney was giddy and happy, her family was generally confused by the high-society reception, and the Baxter side of the guest list was at best amused by his choice of young bride. The expectations were different for men. They could marry young, penniless women based on looks alone, and no one cared. Britney wasn't expected to provide anything to the relationship—financially anyway. While the wealthier strata looked down on her poor breeding, their problem with her wasn't about her earning ability. Even wealthy women didn't need to earn anything if they could inherit. Marriage expectations were different for women who were born into money. They were expected to marry men who could add to their fortunes. In essence, her father could marry a pauper, but Isabel could not. At least not in her father's opinion.

Lately, Britney had seemed to be trying to forge some sort of relationship with Isabel, but there had been very little love lost between the two of them, and Isabel highly doubted that Britney was coming by the store to wish her well. In fact, she couldn't help but wonder if Britney was bent on claiming the entire Baxter fortune for herself and cutting Isabel out completely.

"Daddy wouldn't do that," she said aloud, clicking the lock into place.

And she believed it, but a tiny part of her wondered if Britney weren't even more manipulative than Isabel had given her credit for. George Baxter wouldn't be the first or the last man to be manipulated by a pretty, young wife.

Isabel's cell phone rang, and she picked it up as she ambled back into the kitchen. "Hello?"

"Hi, girl." Carmella's relaxed, happy voice greeted her. "What's new with you?"

"I just got the weirdest visit from Britney. How about you?"

"What?" Carmella asked. "What do you mean a weird visit?"

"It was all mysterious and fraught with warning." Isabel rolled her eyes. "If I didn't know better, I'd think she was trying to oust me from the family money."

"You need to get out," Carmella replied. "You're starting to sound paranoid. And I have the perfect solution. What are you doing this Saturday evening?"

"Nothing earth-shattering."

"I'm having a dinner party," Carmella said. "You have to come."

"Who will be there?" Isabel asked.

"Everyone, of course," her friend retorted. "You have to come. And if you don't bring a date, I've got someone for you to meet."

"Gee, I think I'm busy," Isabel joked.

"No, you can't be." Carmella dropped the banter from her tone. "I need you there. You know what it's like. I need one person in my corner who isn't going to badmouth me."

"Then why have a dinner party?" Isabel asked. "No dinner party is complete until the hostess has been thoroughly torn apart by her guests."

"Because it's sort of a welcome back for you."

The gesture was a sweet one, and Isabel sighed in resignation. It was all but impossible to refuse to attend your own "welcome back" dinner party.

"I'll come."

Maybe it would do her good to get out and socialize for a change. All this time alone was taking a toll on her, to the point that even Britney seemed like a secret agent.

But there was no time to wonder, because just then there was a knock on the door.

"Carmella, I've got to go," Isabel said. "I think that's my sign being delivered. I'll be at your dinner party, okay?"

Hanging up, she opened the door and clapped her hands in excitement at the sight of the long, narrow box being carried out of the back of a truck. Her sign for Baxter's Chocolates had arrived, and right behind the deliverymen stood a young man with a notebook.

She signed for the delivery and held the door open while two men carried it inside. The man with the notebook stood back, watching her patiently.

"Can I help you?" she asked.

"I'm here from the *Haggerston Chronicle*. I wanted to do a story on your business. Do you have a few minutes?"

Haggerston didn't have much for news, and it looked like she'd garnered some attention. It would be good for business—help get the word out. She stepped back and ushered him in.

A FEW DAYS had passed since James had seen Isabel, and he'd done his best to put her out of his mind. It hadn't been successful at all... James glanced at his watch. It was almost six, which meant that the receptionist would be heading home soon, leaving the lawyers to fend for themselves. He looked down at the will in front of him—the final draft.

I, George Baxter, being of sound mind and body, hereby make this Will and revoke all prior Wills and Codicils... My daughter, Isabel Baxter, having already received an agreed-upon portion of my estate, will receive nothing upon my death...

If he hadn't written it himself, James would never have believed his client capable of this. From a father who was so concerned about his daughter's happiness that he pressured his lawyer into asking her out just to make her feel better... Why would he cut her out of his will? And given that Mr. Baxter was so protective of his financial information that he refused to speak of it with his wife in the room, could Britney even make this happen?

None of it made sense, but Mr. Baxter had sat with him this morning and dictated his Last Will and Testament, and when James asked for an explanation for the sudden changes, Mr. Baxter hadn't given one. Nor did he have to. It looked like Isabel was going to experience a dose of real life—the kind of life everyone else had to live.

There were certain professions that gave a man a bird's-eye view into people's personal information: doctors, pastors, financial advisers, lawyers... Sometimes he wished that he didn't have this privileged view. In a large city, he might not have anything else to do with his clients, but in a place the size of Haggerston, it was, admittedly, more awkward.

His office phone rang, and he glanced at the number before he picked it up. It was reception.

"James Hunter."

"Mr. Hunter, Miss Isabel Baxter is here to see you."

James closed the file folder, his pulse speeding up. "Send her in. Thanks, Maggie." He stood and tucked the file back into place in the large cabinets that lined one wall. He'd missed her...much as he hated to admit that. He'd been keeping his distance purposefully, but it hadn't made it any easier on him.

His office door opened, revealing Isabel. She wore a red summer dress and matching red pumps. Her hair fell around her shoulders, and a purse was hitched up under her arm.

"Hi," he said with a smile. "How are you?"

"I'm well, thank you." Her tone was professional, and he looked at her quizzically. This wasn't a personal visit, as was obvious by that closed-off expression her face. She stepped inside and closed the door behind her. She moved to the visitor's chair across from his desk and sat down. He took a seat, too.

"Is everything okay?" he asked.

"I'm not sure." She met his gaze. "That's why I'm here."

"What happened?" he asked.

"I had a visit from Britney yesterday morning, and she—" Isabel stopped and frowned. "I can't even remember her exact words now, but she implied that I should be very careful with the money my father has given me, because it will likely be the last I see."

So Britney was warning her stepdaughter about the will? This was getting more perplexing by the minute.

"Hmm," he said softly, his mind whirling, attempting to reshuffle the information to make some sort of sense out of it.

"What do you mean, *hmm*?" she retorted. "Is it true?"

"I obviously can't discuss private information about a client—"

"Has he changed his will?" she pressed.

"I can't answer that."

"Does that mean yes?"

James rubbed his hands over his face. "Isabel, you know the position you're putting me in."

She nodded dismally. "I'm sorry. I don't mean to be inappropriate. I'm just—"

She was scared. She didn't need to finish the thought. Her expression said it all. Obviously, Britney had decided to give Isabel a heads-up about being cut from her father's will, but how much she'd said, he had no idea. He hadn't even known that Britney was aware of this. However, the fact remained that the check her father had written for her trust fund would likely be the last money she received from him.

Was it tough love? An attempt to teach her financial responsibility the hard way? James couldn't be sure what was motivating the sudden change of heart.

"Were you counting on your father supporting you further?" he asked quietly.

"I hadn't thought about that. Dad's always been there for me. Obviously, I hope to make this business self-sustaining." She sucked in a breath. "This isn't actually about the money, it's about…us. Me and my dad."

So she *was* still counting on her father's money. This wasn't good.

"Money equals love to the Baxters, James.

When my dad couldn't make it to school events, he bought me presents to make up for it. When he wanted to reward me for good grades, he sent me on a European vacation. When I graduated from Yale, he bought me a diamond necklace and matching earrings."

James remained silent. Isabel's gut instinct was right on target this time, and if she was counting on any more financial support from her father, despite her protestations to the contrary, she'd be smart to revisit her business plan. But how was he supposed to share that information with her without breaking client-attorney confidentiality?

"Are you asking me for legal advice?" he asked carefully.

Isabel looked at him in exasperation. "I thought we were friends!"

That had been his line, hadn't it? Friends... who had to be careful not to be left alone too long together in case it moved beyond that.

"We are," he replied. "But right now, I'm in my office and we're talking about some things that could cross lines, legally speaking. So I need to know if we're chatting as friends, or if I'm talking as your family's lawyer."

"All right." She straightened her shoulders.

"Let's start with strict professionalism. As the family lawyer, what is your advice?"

He smiled. Those were the exact words he needed to hear. "As your family's lawyer, I would advise you to revisit your business plan and make sure that you are able to financially support your business without any extra outside investors."

"Obviously, that's the plan, but—"

"Make it more than a plan. Make it happen." His tone was low. He didn't have time to mollycoddle her with this. "That's my advice."

"All right." She nodded, her expression slightly strangled.

"Good. Then next, I'd suggest that you go talk to your father."

"About what, exactly?"

"Whatever questions you might have," he replied. "I can't answer them for you. Your father is the only one who can."

"I doubt he will." She looked away from him, and James regarded her thoughtfully. She'd changed over the past few weeks. She was stronger, somehow. She was facing these challenges with more grace and determination than anyone had expected, himself included.

In a lot of people's opinions, Isabel might have this coming. She wouldn't get much pity from Haggerston when they found out about this turn of events, but James felt a stirring of sympathy. She'd been callous. She'd been protected. She'd thought she was better than most people in this town, but life had a way of balancing things, and that would be painful. While he couldn't exactly mourn for her drop down to the level everyone else lived on, he could understand how much this could hurt her.

"Are we talking as friends now?" James asked quietly.

"Okay." She turned toward him once more, her dark eyes filled with uncertainty and sadness. "Let's talk as friends."

"You're going to be fine," he said.

"How can you be sure?"

"Because you're smart, and you're strong and you're a Baxter."

The Baxters had always had a leg up, and he had a feeling that even a broke Baxter would still have an advantage around here. There was family reputation, after all, and people who had built up a fortune in the past knew how to do it again. Besides, who else would be as driven to get back her lost comforts?

"Possibly a disinherited Baxter," she replied with a bitter smile.

James shrugged. "I'm not confirming that, but I have to say—that wouldn't have stopped your father."

"I'm not my dad."

"You're one better. You're his daughter."

She was silent for a moment, and then she smiled wanly. "I've been invited to this dinner party. It's going to be for the privileged set of the county. My friend Carmella is hosting it."

"Sounds like fun," he said diplomatically. Actually, it sounded exhausting.

"Does it?" She shot him a quirky look. "These are the friends I've had since I was a kid. These are my clique, my social equals. It occurred to me that I might not be able to afford to keep up with them anymore if my father doesn't fund it. I mean, if I can't meet them in Greece in the spring, or even reciprocate dinner party invitations…"

"That's just regular life for the rest of us," he said wryly.

Color rose in her cheeks. "Fine. Yes, I get that."

Did she? Hopefully, George planned to generously fund his daughter's lifestyle between now and his eventual death, because if this was a sign of more changes to come, her life would be even more altered than she anticipated.

"Spoiled or not, I have a problem." She fixed him with a direct look.

"What's that?"

"If I don't dig up a date for this dinner party on Saturday night, not only will I be the one who lost her good looks, but I'll have to deal with Carmella's awkward attempts to set me up with men she thinks are low enough on the social ladder not to mind my face."

James winced. "Remind me why you're going to this."

"It's kind of in my honor. Would it be out of line for me to ask one tiny favor?"

James chuckled. He could see the writing on the wall. "You want me to be your date to deflect some of those 'good intentions'?"

A smile tickled the corners of her lips. "Would you?"

No. The correct answer here was a resounding *No*. This wasn't his problem, and going to dinner parties with people who looked down on her, and would only look down on her more once they found out her true financial situation, wasn't actually helping anyone. But he couldn't say that.

"Sure."

"You can always bill my father for the time." She shot him a grin. "I think he deserves it at this point."

James shook his head. "No, this one is for you."

He wanted to protect her, too. He wanted to fend off a few of the blows that were coming.

Pink rose in her cheeks. "I owe you one, James. You're a lifesaver."

She didn't owe him anything. In fact, he felt guilty for not being able to warn her properly about what was coming. He couldn't. He knew that, but a part of him had stopped being practical when it came to Isabel.

For all her spoiled upbringing and her previous self-centered ways, she didn't deserve all that was coming to her. In his humble opinion, this was just cruel. He couldn't fix it, though. He couldn't change it. He couldn't warn her. He was simply burdened with the knowledge.

CHAPTER FOURTEEN

"NOW POUR IT SLOWLY…slowly…slower!" Isabel looked over Jenny's shoulder as she poured melted chocolate into molds. Jenny's hands were quite steady for this meticulous work, and Isabel watched closely as Jenny stopped pouring, then moved to the next mold without spilling even a drop around the edges.

"You're good at this," Isabel said with a smile.

Jenny looked up, her eyes sparkling. "Really? I'm good?"

"You really are. After this, we're going to start on some caramels. You've got a talent. Just promise to keep my recipes a secret, and I'll keep teaching you."

Isabel had called James and asked if Jenny could come and help her today. The internet orders were steadily coming in, and she could no longer keep up with the workload alone. Outside, the construction workers were putting up her sign, and the grind of drills and thump of ladders against the building filtered into the kitchen.

It felt good to have someone to work with. She'd always had so many people around her that she'd believed she had lots of friends. In New York, she'd been introduced to the wealthy circles by her father's contacts, and she'd lived a life of dinner parties and air kisses. She'd worked a job in marketing that didn't pay a fantastic amount, but she could have supported herself if she'd needed to, albeit in a humbler fashion. Since her father had insisted upon footing the bill for her condo and car, she'd allowed a little extra so she could be presentable for social gatherings, too. This was good for her career, she'd told herself. These were the people who controlled New York's money.

Now with her changed circumstances, she didn't have anyone she could call to help her out in her business venture. New Yorkers would have forgotten her almost immediately since she wasn't the richest of the rich in the bigger pool. Haggerston friends weren't people she could really trust—they competed with each other too much to be trustworthy.

She didn't have many real friends at all, she realized.

"Good…good…" Isabel slid a mold away from Jenny and down the counter. "We'll let that sit so it can harden, but those look just perfect."

"I won't throw them at anyone," Jenny said, her expression deeply serious.

"I believe you," she said with a chuckle. "Don't worry about it, Jenny."

A smile split across Jenny's face, and Isabel realized belated that the young woman had been joking.

"Oh." She laughed. "Har, har." She honestly liked James's sister. She was good company in the kitchen. "Now, you have to remember to do exactly as I say, exactly when I say it. Some of these recipes depend on the perfect timing. Can you do that?"

Jenny nodded. "Yup."

"Good. Now, I've made some caramel, and we're going to cut it, roll it and then coat it in chocolate. It takes a steady hand. Let me show you."

Isabel went to the fridge and pulled out the caramel. Working with the caramel while it was chilled enough to be firm, but not cold enough to be solid, was the most important part of making the perfect sea-salt caramel. When one bit into the chocolate-covered caramel, it needed to be soft enough not to pull out fillings or get stuck on dental work, but still hold its shape.

She took a large knife and cut a piece off the cord of caramel.

"About this big," she said as she worked. "Then roll it."

She chopped off another piece and handed it over to Jenny. Jenny watched Isabel's movements, then slowly began to roll her piece of caramel between her palms.

"Then one little squish in the center to make the right shape, and—" Isabel held up the small oval of caramel. Jenny held up hers.

"Nice!" Isabel was impressed. Jenny was a quick study.

"Now, these are going to be sea-salt caramels. Have you tried them before?" Isabel asked.

Jenny shook her head.

"Well, you can try them today, if you want."

"You must eat a lot of chocolate." Jenny grinned.

"I do."

Not that she ever had in her old life. She'd

been so afraid of gaining weight that she'd counted her calories and drunk water to fill the ache in her gut. She had been size 2 or bust back then, checking her weight every morning in order to "stay on top of it." After the accident—after realizing that she could have died that day—she promised herself that she'd stop denying herself the simple pleasures in life. What did she want put on her tombstone? "Isabel Baxter was a size 2." What use was that to anyone?

As they worked together, the line of finished caramels grew longer, and then they started on a second row, then a third. The work felt good, her tension and energy fused into repetitive actions, chocolate after chocolate deposited on the parchment. She was making something solid, sweet and delicious—something concrete, instead of the size 2 clothing that she used to look to for validation.

"Jimmy said that people aren't nice to you," Jenny broke the silence, her hands still working.

Isabel shot her a curious look. "He did? When?"

"After you offered me the job. I asked him

about you. He said that people like to see really beautiful people come down."

Isabel smiled awkwardly. It was the truth, but it felt strange to hear how James talked about her to others. "What else did he say?"

"He said that they're stupid."

Isabel laughed, heat rising in her face. So he'd stood up for her. That was nice to know. James was turning into an unexpected ally.

"Is it true?" Jenny asked.

"Yes, it is," Isabel admitted. "You see, the thing is, I wasn't really very nice when I lived here before."

"You weren't?" Jenny stopped working, staring at her in surprise.

Isabel shrugged. "My father was wealthy, and I was considered very beautiful. I got my way a lot. No one ever said no to me."

"People say no to me all the time." Jenny picked up her next piece of caramel.

"And you're a very sweet person," Isabel said. "You know what it's like to not get your way and to have to work hard for something. I didn't know that. At least not then."

"So people were mean?"

"Oh, no," Isabel replied, dipping the caramel into the smooth chocolate. "Everyone was very nice to me. They were a little afraid of me, I think. It's now, after I have these scars, that people seem kind of happy to see me put in my place."

"I'm not." Jenny dipped her caramel next.

"Thanks." And she meant it. It felt good to have someone actually wish her well for a change.

"Do people look at you funny?" Jenny asked.

Isabel nodded. "All the time."

"Me, too." Sympathy warmed Jenny's tone. "They look at me kind of closely. Then look back at me again, after they pass. It's because I look different."

"I think you're lovely."

"Well, I think you are, too," Jenny replied. "But they still look, don't they?"

They had more in common than Isabel would have guessed, and she liked Jenny's company. There was no guile in Jenny, and that was something she wasn't used to.

Isabel grabbed a bottle of pink, large-crystal sea salt and sprinkled it in a wide wave over the chocolate. She didn't like to waste the salt because it was costly, but it wasn't right to skimp, either.

"If you're going to make sea-salted caramels, then you use enough salt," she said as she worked. After a moment, she stood back. "Beautiful. Try one, Jenny."

They each took a caramel between two fingers and popped them into their mouths. After some silent chewing, Isabel raised her eyebrows inquiringly.

"Well?" she asked, wiping her hands once more on a cloth.

"Yum." Jenny nodded enthusiastically. "So good."

"Great!" Isabel said. "That's what I want to hear. Now, we have fourteen internet orders for these. So, we're going to put these in the fridge to harden them, then we're going to box them up. Maybe you can start putting together the boxes for me. They're flattened and just need a little pop…"

In her mind's eye, after the store was open, customers would line up to choose their favorites or something new to try…but would that really happen? Would Haggerston come flooding into her store to try her wares, or would they sit back and watch her flounder, happy to see the spoiled little princess go down?

JAMES PARKED HIS truck in front of Isabel's shop and looked up at the newly installed sign. It looked like a monogram—a black swirling *B* against a cream-colored background. Underneath were the words *Baxter's Chocolates*. It was simple, elegant and refined, and he found himself smiling. She was better at this than he'd thought.

People would say that this was the kind of expertise that money could buy, but he knew better than that. This was a labor of love for Isabel, and she'd planned all of this herself. As he got out of his truck, he noticed a couple of women stop to look up at the sign, then shade their eyes to peer into the window. They murmured together, their words not reaching his ears, but he fully recognized the downturn of their lips.

Isabel Baxter wasn't forgiven yet.

James tried the front door and found it unlocked. Isabel had said that Jenny's shift would be finished at five, so she must have been ready for him. He pulled open the door and stepped inside.

The storefront was beautifully set up. The smell of wood varnish filled the air—not strong enough to be offensive, but the pieces were obviously newly finished. A large gilt-framed mirror dominated the wall behind the front desk, which still lacked a cash register.

The sideboard sat along the wall between two large windows. All the wooden pieces were the same color tone, yet they retained a look of distinctive elegance. There was a sense of charm and character already, even though there was obviously more to be done.

From the kitchen, voices filtered out to him.

"Okay, stir…keep stirring…harder. Use some muscle. Come on!" Isabel's tone was commanding, and he raised a brow. He'd heard of chefs being demanding and emotional, but chocolatiers, too?

"My arm hurts," Jenny said breathlessly. James paused, waiting for Isabel's tone to soften, but he didn't hear it.

"You'll build some muscle. Keep going."

This might be Isabel's dream, and if she wanted to push herself to the limit, that was her business. In fact, knowing what he knew, it was a good idea to pour all of her energy into this venture, but his sister was a different story.

He headed toward the kitchen and pushed open the swinging door. Jenny stood at the stove, sweat beading on her forehead, her sleeves pushed up above her elbows as she stirred a large pot. Her cheeks were flushed, and she glanced up toward her brother, then back to the pot.

"Is it melted?" Isabel asked, looking over Jenny's shoulder. "Okay, now pull it off the heat."

Jenny grimaced, then heaved the pot off the burner. It looked heavy.

"Stir, stir!" Isabel commanded. "Never stop stirring. I told you that."

"I know. Sorry." Jenny was breathless and focused on the pot. She bent over it, stirring again.

Was this what Isabel had been doing with Jenny all day—barking at her and making her work like a horse? Why wasn't Isabel stirring? Why make Jenny do the hard work? It looked like Isabel was taking advantage, and he didn't like her tone, either. Jenny didn't need to be ordered around. She was supposed to be helping out, not slaving away.

"Is all that really necessary?" James asked, his tone unimpressed.

Both women looked up, surprise registering on Isabel's face. Apparently, she hadn't heard the door. Irritation simmered to the surface.

"Yes," Isabel said simply. She glanced at Jenny. "Keep stirring."

"No, stop stirring," James ordered. "That's enough. Jenny, it's time to go."

Isabel took the paddle from Jenny's hands and continued to move the chocolate around, but she met his gaze easily, guilt-free.

"Jimmy, I'm working—" Jenny began.

"Let me take care of this," he said quickly. Jenny was trusting. She believed the best in everyone, but with a brother who was a lawyer, she wasn't going to be taken advantage of. He'd been standing up for her since they were children, and right now he was just plain annoyed. When Isabel offered Jenny a job, this was not what he had in mind. "Isabel, we need to talk."

"Absolutely," she replied. "If you come over here. This has to keep moving or it'll be ruined."

"Fine." He clenched his teeth in irritation and moved across the room. "What do you think you're doing? You're barking orders and making her stir until her arms are sore…"

"I'm teaching her to make chocolate." Isabel didn't look the least bit apologetic.

"I thought she was here to help you out with little jobs."

"Little jobs?" Isabel looked up at him incredulously. "There is nothing little about chocolate making. And she's good at it."

She was either choosing not to understand him, or trying to force him to say it out loud. Either way, he didn't like being manipulated.

"She's not going to be able to do everything you want her to." He lowered his voice. "Cut her some slack, would you?"

"No, I will not," Isabel shot back. "She's good at this. Really good. And she likes it. You go ahead and ask her once she's out of the store, and see what she says. Do you see those caramels over there?"

He glanced in the direction she pointed with her chin. There was a stack of candy boxes, and beside them, a pan of chocolate ovals, shimmering with what appeared to be a sugar topping.

"Sure."

"She made them," Isabel said. "And they're spectacular. Jenny has a real talent, so I'm not going to pretend that she's just here to sweep the floors. You're being too protective."

"Me?" Who did she think she was? She waltzed back into town with a trust fund and suddenly she knew more than he did about his own sister? "I've been taking care of her since we were kids. Who are you to tell me what I should be doing?"

Isabel slowed her stirring, then put down the paddle. She put her hands on her hips and tipped up her chin to meet his gaze. "You love her, and you don't want her to be hurt. But sometimes you have to let go a little bit if she's going to succeed."

"And maybe you need to ease off," he retorted.

"Jimmy?" He turned to see Jenny at his elbow.

"Hey, Jenny. Let me just talk to Isabel alone for a minute, okay?"

"No." Jenny scowled. "I like this job. And I don't want to get fired this time."

James raised an eyebrow at Isabel. Color rose in her face.

"Was I too hard on you, Jenny?" she asked.

"I can take it," Jenny said, but her voice wavered.

Isabel grimaced. "Look, Jenny, I'm sorry. I think your brother is right. I'll watch my tone from now on, okay? You don't have to learn everything all at once."

Jenny nodded mutely.

"You did really good work. Can you come back Monday? We have another couple of batches to make, and it will be good for you to see how it's done. I'll be nicer. I promise."

Jenny nodded exuberantly. "I'll be here. Thanks, Izzy."

Isabel smiled and moved the pot over to the counter. She turned her back, lining up several molds side by side. She didn't seem to be slowing down.

"I'll meet you at the truck," James said, and Jenny went about peeling off her hair net and apron. She hung them on a peg on the wall and shot James a grin before pushing through the swinging door.

"You were right. I was being too hard on her. We're both learning, and she really is good at this. There is a lot she can do," Isabel said seriously. "And candy making is one of them. I wouldn't trust her with this if I didn't think she could do it, and do it well. My name goes on these chocolates, and if any of them are just ordinary, there is no reason for my customers to come back. They can buy ordinary chocolates in the grocery store. She might be working hard, but she's got something to show for it, and she can be proud of herself. You wanted her to be-long somewhere—well, you don't really belong anywhere unless you've got something to contribute."

"So you're sorry but not sorry," he said drily.

"I'm sorry for my tone," she said. "But I'm serious about her talent."

James thought for a moment. Maybe Jenny really did have a talent. Would this last? Would this work out? And most important, would Jenny thrive in this environment? He wouldn't forgive himself if he made the wrong choice.

"Come here." Isabel ambled across the kitchen and plucked one of the chocolates from the pan.

He looked at her curiously.

"I said, come here." Her tone grew more commanding, and he smiled wryly and crossed the room. She stood next to the pan of chocolates, and she was forced to tip her head back to look him in the face, yet somehow she still didn't seem small.

"Open." She held the chocolate aloft in front of his face, eyeing him expectantly. After an awkward moment, he parted his lips and opened his mouth. Isabel popped the chocolate onto his tongue and waited as he chewed.

It wasn't sugar on top, it was salt, but the mingling flavors were amazing. The salt made the dark chocolate taste that much sweeter, and when the buttery caramel met his tongue, he nodded in appreciation.

"Mmm…" He chewed and finally swallowed. "Those are good!"

"Thank you, but save the compliments for your sister. She did most of the work on those. If that isn't something to be proud of, I don't know what is."

He found himself softening in spite of his best intentions, and he shrugged. "All right," he said ruefully. "Point made. Just don't work her too hard, okay?"

"I won't." She eyed him seriously. "I'll never make her work with customers, and I'll teach her everything I can. I'll also give her credit for being my assistant."

She seemed sincere, and the deal seemed fair.

"Okay," he reluctantly agreed. He glanced toward the pan of chocolates, his mouth already watering. "Can I have another one of those?"

Isabel chuckled. "After your first taste, Mr. Hunter, you pay just like everybody else."

CHAPTER FIFTEEN

ISABEL SLIPPED INTO her little black dress—
a knee-length frock with sheer sleeves that
looked fantastic with strappy stilettos. She
liked the sleeves because they covered her
scarred arm, and the length masked most
of the damage done to her leg. There was
a time when she used to look in the mirror
and criticize every square inch of her body.
She'd imagine fat where there wasn't any and
wish that her nose was just a little bit smaller.
Now, when she looked in the mirror, she saw
a healthy body, and she was grateful. Her
body somehow seemed more sacred now that
she could appreciate how very fragile it was.

As she stood in front of her mirror—getting ready for a dinner party that she wished
she could just skip—she wondered how
much James trusted her. He'd been awfully
protective of his sister the day before, and
while she'd reassured him about her inten-

tions, she'd seen something in him that surprised her.

He doesn't trust me. And that hurt. James probably knew her better than anyone at this point. What that said about her social life was downright pathetic, but it was the truth. And when the person who knew you best didn't trust you...

The newspaper reporter returned after James and Jenny left, just clarifying a few details. She'd done as she'd promised and named Jenny Harper as her assistant. Jenny deserved credit, and Isabel had been serious when she said she wanted her business to be different, better, more inclusive. Would anyone believe that of Isabel Baxter?

James's truck rumbled to a stop outside, and Isabel stepped into her heels and checked her lipstick in the mirror one last time. Then she opened the door and stepped outside just as James was getting out of his truck. He froze when he saw her, then smiled awkwardly.

"You look great," he said.

"Thanks. You, too."

He wore a pair of black dress pants and black shirt, open at the neck. Silver cuff links shone at his wrists. He headed around the truck and opened the passenger door for her.

"I appreciate your coming to this," she said as she scooted into the seat.

James came around the other side and slid into the seat next to her. "No problem." He turned the key, and the engine rumbled to life. "So, tell me a little bit about these people."

Isabel thought back to the group of people who would be at Carmella's party. This was the group she'd been tight with back in high school, and she'd spoken to a few of them on the phone since she'd come back, but she hadn't met up with them in person.

"Do you remember Carmella Rawlins from high school?" she asked.

He nodded. "Cheerleader, right?"

"That's her. She married a ranching tycoon named Brad Biggins a couple of years ago. It was the wedding of the century around here."

"Yeah, I think I remember that. What does she do now?"

Isabel smiled wryly. "She married Brad. She's doing a lot of shopping."

"Okay." He laughed softly. "It's the life, I guess. So who else will be there?"

"They'll have invited Greg Cranken. His

father owns the Cranken Beef empire, and he's single."

"So he's the intended setup?" A smile twitched at the corner of James's lips, and he turned to look behind him as he backed out of the drive and onto the gravel road once more.

"Afraid so. The rest are probably all from the same group. A couple of them went to school with us, but the others were from other parts of Montana. Beef, cattle and land. That's where the money is out here, right?"

"True enough." His tone was low.

"Carmella wasn't from a privileged family, but she was gorgeous. She was the Miss Montana runner-up."

"You were Miss Montana, weren't you?"

Isabel felt the heat rise in her cheeks. "I was."

Her beauty queen days were well behind her, and she was glad about that. The pageants had been intensely competitive, and behind the scenes the girls could be savage. She'd been proud of her crown, but not always proud of what it took to get it.

They drove in silence for a few minutes, the lowering sun making Isabel squint.

"Did you know these people at all?" Isabel asked after a moment.

James cast her a wry look. "Did you know me?"

She felt her face flush again. Why did he have to keep reminding her that she didn't remember him?

"I knew who they were," he conceded after a moment of awkward silence.

It was more than any of them could say about James Hunter. Looking back on her high school days, her circle of friends had been small and elite. Her father hadn't wanted to send her to private school. He said that she was welcome to move out when she was eighteen, but before that, she was living under his roof. She'd been secretly relieved, and since she was at the top of the food chain at Haggerston High, she'd been happy. The rest of the school didn't seem important back then. It was all about friendships—she and her group would be together forever. They'd sworn to it. It seemed ridiculous now.

"Have you seen any of them recently?" he asked.

"I saw everyone at Carmella's wedding."

Carmella's wedding had been beautiful— held on her father-in-law's sprawling estate.

No expense had been spared, and for the first time since high school the whole gang had been back together again. The first couple of evenings had been pleasant enough, but then the old irritations began to rub. Isabel had told off another bridesmaid for not being supportive enough of Carmella's demands. She couldn't remember her exact words, but the other woman had crumpled into tears and ran off. She'd had a strange talent for cutting right to the quick back then. Carmella had been the quintessential bridezilla. Brad had gone off and gotten so drunk the night before the wedding that his eyes were bloodshot for his vows. By the end of the night, both Brad and Carmella were drunk and stumbled off to their limo, leaving the last of the wedding party and the heartiest of family to finish the celebration without them. It was then that Greg asked Isabel to dance and she'd agreed. Why not? She'd recently broken up with another boyfriend and wanted to boost her ego. During that awkward, fumbling dance, Greg had tried to cop a feel.

"What do you think you're doing, Greg?" She'd felt the laughter bubbling up before she could stop it. "This is a pity dance. Don't you get that?"

I was awful. At the time she hadn't realized it because they'd all been equally awful, but she wasn't proud of who she'd been at that wedding.

"You're nervous," James said, pulling her back to the present.

"No…" She laughed self-consciously. "Okay, a bit. It's been a while."

"Are you sure you want me with you?" he asked with a wry grin. "The family lawyer and all… It might not be the impression you want to give."

"What?" She shook her head. "Of course I want you along. You're the only person who seems to see anything good in me."

"No, Jenny is pretty taken with you, too."

She shot him a questioning look. *Too?*

"I mean—" He cleared his throat. "You know what I mean."

She laughed and rolled her eyes. "I wish I'd known you better in high school. You're very sweet."

The drive didn't take long, and within a half hour, they'd pulled up in front of Carmella's house—a modern, one-level affair that sprawled out over manicured grounds. Windows went from floor to roof, lit up from within and revealing wooden rafters and shining light fixtures. Several cars were already parked on the wide tarmac, and James pulled into a space next to a white Mercedes.

This felt comfortable, somehow. She had been used to nice things—expensive cars, large homes, lavish vacations. In a way, this felt like coming home—coming back to the life she'd led. Yet with that affluent lifestyle came pressure, too. Nothing ever came without strings attached, and as her gaze flowed over the pond, the cascading waterfall, the stone walkways and the wide, dark front door, that familiar heaviness settled back onto her shoulders.

It was funny. Sitting in this truck, looking at the luxury she'd always expected to have, made her wishes for a business of her own feel so much less possible. Privilege—at least the kind that came in this county—was narrower than most people knew. And perhaps that was why they were all so awful to each other—because they knew just how trapped they really were.

"Nice place," James murmured, then he pushed open his door. "Ready?"

THEIR HOSTESS, CARMELLA BIGGINS, was tall and lithe with a slightly prominent nose and soulful eyes. She gushed and chatted with Isabel, giving James a quick once-over with a practiced eye. James had the feeling he'd just been evaluated and priced on the spot.

"I'm so glad you made it," Carmella was saying. She lowered her voice and leaned closer, just under James's hearing.

"This is James." Isabel turned and shot him a brilliant smile. "And yes, he counts as a date."

Carmella didn't look entirely convinced, but she shrugged her milky-white shoulders and smiled in his direction.

"Nice to meet you, James. What are you into?"

"Into?" James mouthed at Isabel.

"He's a lawyer," Isabel replied, giving him the translation in her answer. She turned to her friend. "Now, exactly how scathing has everyone been so far?"

"Oh, they're all still on good behavior." Carmella slid an arm through Isabel's and led her out of the entryway and toward the sound of muffled voices. "Let's try to keep it that way."

James wasn't entirely sure if Carmella was looking for support or if she was issuing a veiled warning to Isabel, but the taller woman didn't stop to see where her words landed, and she ushered them into a brightly lit sitting room.

The room was broad, two glittering chandeliers hanging from the rustic rafters. The couches and chairs that were arranged around the room were a mixture of leather and hand-polished wood, but the carpets were elegant Persian rugs, woven with gold and scarlet, giving the effect of something royal mingled with down-home charm.

A few people lifted their gaze as they entered, and after a moment, all eyes were on them. Expressions ranged from surprise to wan smiles, and then the wide smiles and nods kicked in—the chosen reaction to cover the initial one. He was used to watching for these things in a courtroom, but tonight, it hit him in the gut.

So these are Isabel's friends.

"I hope you don't mind if I steal Izzy for a bit," Carmella said over her shoulder, tugging Isabel after her. He wasn't really being consulted, and Isabel allowed herself to be led away to the first gaggle of guests. They greeted her with gushing and kiss-kissing, and James looked away. At the moment, he wished he hadn't come. She didn't really need him here, and he wondered why she'd invited him along at all. If Carmella had set her mind on finding Isabel a wealthy husband, he highly doubted that his presence would deter her.

"So you're with Isabel, are you?"

James turned to see a shorter man sauntering up to him. He was balding, narrow through the shoulders and wider at the hips. His sport jacket was forgiving, and expensive. The cut was precise.

"Sort of," James said. "I'm a friend."

"Ah." The man looked mildly amused. "I'm Cranken. Greg Cranken." He said it like James Bond would, and James laughed, but then stopped when he realized the man was entirely serious.

"Nice to meet you." He covered his earlier mirth by shaking his hand. "I'm James Hunter."

Greg nodded and lifted a glass of champagne. "She doesn't look too bad, does she?"

Greg wasn't looking at James. His eyes were trained on Isabel, now across the room.

"Everyone changes," James said as diplomatically as possible.

"Not that much," Greg muttered. "But she's now in my league. That's something."

He glanced over at James. "You still aren't in hers." He laughed to himself and took a sip from his glass. "No offense."

"None taken." James recognized the name as the man Isabel's friends would attempt to set her up with, and he wondered if the match was even likely. He found the little man distasteful on first meeting, and he couldn't imagine that he would improve over time.

"So, seriously, how bad is it?" Greg rose up onto his toes, narrowing his eyes. "I need to know before I go over."

James didn't answer, and when Greg glanced over at him, James shook his head. "Did any of you ever like her?"

"Like her?" Greg widened his eyes in surprise. "We wouldn't be here if we didn't like her. This is a welcome-back party."

"Ah."

Greg didn't seem to catch the sarcasm in James's reply. She'd brought him along for good reason, it seemed. If these people were her friends, what did she need with enemies? He was used to some pretty intense competition from law school, but this wasn't a group of competing law students—this was supposed to be a relaxed gathering of friends for a little dinner and catch-up. Apparently, a friendly dinner party meant something entirely different to him than it did to the Greg Crankens and Carmella Bigginses of the world.

"Oh, well..." Greg drained his glass and set it behind him without looking. "Don't take me too seriously. Did you know her before—" He winced. "How does one refer to that in polite company?"

"Yes," James said simply. "I knew of her, at least."

"Then you know why I might be a tad bit ornery. She was gorgeous—completely and wildly beyond the likes of me—and I was the Quasimodo of the group. She never looked at me twice, even if I were to trip over her foot. It's ironic, at the very least."

James could actually understand that— partially, at least. He'd been in the same boat. He hadn't even registered on her radar enough to warrant her looking in his direction...until she needed a favor. And then he'd been forgotten again just as efficiently. He'd been invisible to the likes of Isabel Baxter, but it hadn't bothered him. He'd simply accepted that he ran in different circles. Andrew, of course, had been more hopeful...

"You want to know what I heard?" Greg

leaned closer, and the smell of alcohol was strong on his breath. "She never should have been Miss Montana."

James frowned. "Says who?"

"There was a girl who was prettier and more talented, but our Izzy was smarter."

Was Greg referring to Carmella—the runner up? James narrowed his eyes, wondering what the man was getting at, but he didn't ask. These kinds of conversations with slightly intoxicated people were generally a bad idea, but somehow he couldn't quite make himself walk away.

"Smarter…" Greg repeated.

"Yeah, she's pretty smart," James agreed nonchalantly.

"No, you don't get it." Greg chuckled. "She knew how to get sympathy. She claimed to work with war amputees. But she never did. Okay, their gardener had lost a hand in the war, and apparently, she'd spoken with him, but her work—" he put air quotes around the word *work* "—was highly exaggerated. He was the one who worked—for her family. And it was the sympathy vote that won it for her."

"You think she campaigned for a sym-

pathy vote?" James asked, not entirely convinced that this bitter story was based in fact.

"That's not the only time," Greg retorted.
"She used blind puppies for another beauty
pageant. They're all born blind, by the way."
He chuckled. "She knows how to work the
sympathy card. She's smart. I like that. A
good woman wins at all costs. I could use a
girl like her on Team Cranken."

James had never suspected what life must
have been like for Isabel. He'd imagined—
as most people did—that she simply breezed
through her days, looking down on everyone
else who had less. But this atmosphere was
like a lion's den, and he thought he could
see the forces that had created Isabel Baxter.
She was kinder than this group—gentler. She
didn't seem to have their instinct to crush the
competition. If Isabel had these people to
rely on in her formative years, he could only
imagine the courage it would take for her to
open up and be genuine—with anyone. He
didn't like the way Greg was talking about
her. Someone needed to stand up for Izzy.

"She's not in the beauty pageants anymore," he countered. "She's opening a store,
actually."

"That's a real thing?" Greg's eyebrows

shot up. "I thought that was just a wicked rumor."

"No, it's real. Everyone deserves a fresh start."

Greg huffed something halfway between a laugh and a snort. "Well, mark my words, she'll have a sympathy card up her sleeve somewhere. Maybe she'll play up her own injuries. Whatever she does, it'll work. She's got the touch."

A sympathy card—like a woman with Down syndrome working in the kitchen? He didn't like the possibilities, and he shoved the thought away.

"Okay, she's coming this way." Greg nudged James and drained another flute of champagne. "Give me some space."

"What?" James demanded.

"Oh, don't be like that." Greg rolled his eyes. "I think we both know that you don't have the resources for the Baxters. Now get lost."

James shot him an icy look but stood his ground.

Isabel had worked her way around the room, and she fluttered a wave in James's direction as she headed back. When her gaze fell on Greg, her smile faltered, but she didn't change course. Her black dress was feminine and clung in all the right places, but it still left an awful lot to the imagination. Even so, James didn't like the way Greg leered at her. He had an urge to remind him that her face was up about ten inches.

"Sorry to abandon you like that," Isabel said as she came over. She gave Greg an uncomfortable look and turned away from him slightly. "Did you survive?"

"Oh, I'm tougher than you think," James said with a dry laugh. That was a pointed message to Greg, if the other man cared to take it. James took her by the elbow and steered her away. The smaller man glared in their direction, obviously not used to having his peevish demands thwarted. James felt a surge of satisfaction. If he did nothing else tonight, he'd thoroughly annoy that little troll.

"By the way," James said, leaning down so only she could hear him, "that Greg guy is no friend of yours."

Isabel glanced back. "Really? What did he say?"

"Never mind. It doesn't matter."

James's cell phone vibrated, and he pulled

it from his pocket. He had a text from Mr. Baxter:

Come by the house. I have some documents for you to take care of.

That was nebulous. Mr. Baxter was never one to explain, and he expected a prompt response. James paused for a moment, weighing his options. This party was a school of sharks, and he couldn't say that he was completely comfortable leaving Isabel alone with Greg Cranken.

"What is it?" Isabel asked.

"Your dad wants me to swing by the house."

"Oh, feel free to go," she said with a slight shake of her head. "I don't mind."

"Yeah, but I kind of do," he replied, keeping his voice low. "These are your friends?"

She nodded. "Why?"

"I hate to say it, but I don't think these people like you."

Was that harsh? Probably, but how else was he supposed to phrase it?

"Oh, you mean Greg." She looked back over her shoulder. Greg had another glass in hand and was chatting with two women.

Greg looked in their direction, his expression sour.

"Yeah, Greg."

"He's always been like that. Don't worry about him." She appeared entirely unconcerned. "He's just…it would take me a month to explain him to you."

James glanced at his watch. "I'll tell your father that I'll go by in the morning."

"Are you honestly worried about me?" she asked with a low laugh. "I'm a big girl, you know." Despite her words, she deflated slightly as she glanced around the room.

She *was* an adult. He knew he was being too protective. These were her friends, after all, and this party was in her honor. Who was he to her, anyway?

"You know what," she said after a moment. "Let's go."

It was James's turn to balk. "What do you mean?" he asked. "I don't want to cut short your fun. Apparently this is a welcome-back party. Maybe there's cake."

She shook her head. "Do you ever just get tired of it all?"

"The social shark pool?" he asked with a wry smile.

"Yes, the shark pool."

"Sometimes," he agreed, and truthfully, that had been a factor in his decision to settle down in Haggerston after law school. He liked the idea of community and family. He liked being able to count on people, not constantly watch for the knife in his back.

"Don't get me wrong," she murmured into his ear. "I'm still a shark. Just a wounded one, and I can sense them circling."

"You aren't like them," he said with a shake of his head. "Not from what I can see."

"It's a choice," she replied, sadness in her dark eyes. "I know how to hurt every single one of them—Greg included. I could crush them all with a snip here and a withering look there. But I don't want to play these games anymore. Not only am I no longer the most beautiful woman in the room, which is a major loss to my arsenal, but it takes too much bile. You have to let yourself marinate in it in order to be sharp enough to cut. Does that make any sense?"

"Yeah."

But looking into her face and seeing her emotions sparkling in her eyes, he admired her for that choice. Vulnerability in the face of all of this—that was bravery.

Isabel started toward Carmella, presumably to make her excuses, and James typed a response to his boss:

Be there in twenty minutes.

CHAPTER SIXTEEN

THE DRIVE TO the Baxter residence was oddly quiet. Isabel seemed to be caught up in her own thoughts, staring out the window at the twilit fields. James glanced toward her once more as he turned onto Mr. Baxter's road. Some cows stood still, sleeping on their feet, and a sliver of a moon rose over them. The fields, which were so green in the daylight, looked gray in the dusk, as if the plains were soaked in darkness. A silvery splash of moonlight shone off fence posts as they rumbled past.

Greg's comments about Isabel being smart enough to use sympathy to sway people nagged at James. Would she use Jenny for her own benefit? Isabel had admitted tonight that she could still be a shark.

Jenny was vulnerable because she wanted to please people so badly. She wanted to be liked. She wanted to fit in. But she wasn't stupid, either, and eventually she would sense that Isabel didn't really like her—if that were the case—and that would hurt Jenny deeply. Jenny went through life with her heart open to the world—she didn't have the defenses that other people took for granted. For Jenny, it would just hurt more.

"So that Greg guy—" James glanced toward Isabel. She looked up, her dark eyes gleaming in the low light, and for a moment, he almost forgot what he was going to say.

"What about him?"

"He was telling me about how you won Miss Montana."

She smiled, the scars along her cheek tugging slightly. "My glory days."

"So how did you win?" He laughed uncomfortably. "I mean, obviously you were gorgeous—"

"It isn't all about looks," she said with a shake of her head. "It's about heart, too, you know."

"That's what Greg said." Sort of. If he'd wadded it up and reformed it. "He said that you were working with war amputees?"

She nodded. "I needed to find a cause. Every girl needs a cause if she's going to get anywhere in the competition."

"A cause?"

She shot him a wry smile. "Something to show that you care about more than your own face. Beauty isn't only skin-deep, you know."

He chuckled. "So I've heard. So you chose war amputees?"

"Well, we had a gardener who was a Vietnam vet, and he'd lost one hand above the wrist. He could still do all the work—he was really inventive that way—and I used to watch him, wondering what I would do if I only had one hand."

"So he was a friend?" James pressed.

"A friend? No, he was an employee."

James's stomach sank. This was sounding a little too close to Greg's version of things.

"But you knew him?"

"Not really. I'd watched him. I mean, he was the gardener, after all."

She'd picked a cause and used it for her own purposes. James listened in silence as she talked about how her father had asked the gardener if she could interview him, and how she had come face-to-face with the casualties of war for the first time in her young life.

"What is he doing now?" James asked.

"Who? Greg?"

"No, the gardener. I mean, after you'd gotten to know him and all of that, did you stay in contact?"

Isabel was silent for a moment. "I don't know. He moved on to another job at some point. I don't remember. Maybe he retired? He was an old man already. My dad might recall."

"So this man wasn't really a personal thing, just…a cause." He inwardly winced at his barbed tone.

"That's not really fair." She glanced toward him uneasily, her earlier candor evaporating. "I was eighteen. What kinds of causes was I supposed to have personal investment in?" She eyed him speculatively. "Those are some mighty big expectations to have for a small-town girl with a wealthy father. No, I didn't get cozy with the employees. I was the boss's daughter. I tried to see something beyond my own nose, though, and apparently, it resonated with people at the competition. Is that so terrible?"

Was it fair of him to judge her for playing by the rules of the game? How was an eighteen-year-old girl supposed to have any perspective when it came to causes and world issues? She was a kid—a privileged kid who had never had to face any hardship. He couldn't rightly blame her for some questionable judgment.

"What did Greg say, exactly?" Isabel said after a moment.

"It doesn't matter." He didn't want to repeat Greg's criticisms.

"It really does." She fixed him with a direct stare. "Because you're not telling me everything, and I have a feeling I'm getting slammed behind my back."

"Beautiful people always get slammed behind their backs," he said, attempting a joke, but the humor appeared to bounce off of her.

"What did he say?" Her tone stayed level, and James sighed.

"He said that you have a history of using the sympathy card to win," he said bluntly.

"That's part of the competition," she replied with a shake of her head. "Evening wear, swimsuit, world peace and something that sets you aside from the pack—an ability to sympathize with someone less fortunate that you."

"Yeah, I get it," he said softly.

"Do you really?" she retorted. "Because I'd hate to have you wondering if I'm a complete hypocrite, using people for my own devices."

"I didn't say that." He shook his head. "I was just wondering what the story was, that's all."

"Why?" She eyed him appraisingly. "Are you worried about Jenny?"

James was silent. He wasn't sure how to address that last statement, and he couldn't lie to her, either. He was most definitely concerned about Jenny.

"That's it, isn't it?" she asked, surprise tingeing her tone.

He glanced back at her. "It had crossed my mind. Jenny is sensitive—"

"What kind of person would I be to use her?" Her voice cracked and she looked away, her dark hair falling to cover her face.

"Don't cry," James said.

"Cry?" She turned toward him again, anger snapping in her gaze but her eyes dry. "I'm not crying. Do you think I'm a woman who sheds tears to manipulate men, too?"

This conversation was getting wildly out of control, and he winced. "I didn't mean it like that."

"Look, I'm not using Jenny. Did I feel sorry for her after she was treated like a second-class citizen in that restaurant? You bet I did, and when a decent person sees someone treated badly, they do their best to make it right. Feeling badly for someone and then not doing anything about it is, frankly, useless."

He had to agree, and he was beginning to wonder if he'd just really put his foot in it. "I guess a beauty competition and real life are two different things."

"What about you?" she pressed. "Have you ever tried a case that you didn't feel personally connected to? Did you ever defend a client with an argument that you didn't fully believe in?"

James sighed. Of course he had. That was what law school was all about—learning how to fight for your client and trust the system to balance it all out. It was his legal obligation to give his client every ounce of his expertise. Anything less than that would be unfair.

"I really thought you were different," she said, bitterness entering her tone.

"Hey," James said, stung. "You know, it doesn't really matter what people say about you. What matters is what is true."

"So I shouldn't take it so hard when my supposed friends trash me?" she retorted.

"Don't think I'm one of the people trashing you," he corrected her.

She remained silent as they pulled into

the drive that led up to the house. It was lit up from within on the first floor, and one window on the third floor glowed dimly. He parked in a pool of light and turned toward Isabel.

"I'm always going to be looking out for Jenny," he said, trying to piece together his thoughts. When it came to forming a legal argument, he could do it in his sleep, but this was about his own personal feelings, and those didn't come together quite so easily or so gracefully. He swallowed. "I'm her legal guardian. I'm all she's got, and I'll be looking after her for the rest of our lives. I worry about her. It's not easy for her, and I'm that brick wall between her and a very unfair world. I take that role pretty seriously."

She nodded. "Fair enough."

"I'm not meaning to take this out on you, and I do appreciate how you're trying to help her, but just—" He heaved a sigh. "I don't know how to sugarcoat this… Just be careful. Sometimes things flow along so easily, and they might flow right over Jenny before you notice."

"I told you before that I would be careful, and that hasn't changed."

He could tell that she wasn't thrilled with

him right now, but when it came to Jenny, he couldn't take chances. His sister got knocked around enough, and he knew her well enough to see that this wasn't just a part-time job for her. This was something deeper, something that mattered more to her. After tonight, he was convinced that Isabel was tougher than she looked. Jenny wasn't. She needed her big brother to make sure that she didn't get caught up in the Baxter machinery, because if there was one thing he knew for a fact, it was that the Baxters got what they wanted. Every time.

ISABEL TROTTED UP the front steps to her father's house after James. Her heels tapped lightly against the wood, and she brushed a dark tendril away from her face. So much for all her effort to get dressed up tonight—she'd lasted all of forty minutes at Carmella's party. And now, apparently James thought worse of her after meeting her friends. That stung. This whole town seemed to be enjoying her downfall just a little too much, and she'd thought James could see past all of that. Maybe she'd expected too much.

Carmella would be miffed at her early escape, and she'd have to make it up to her somehow. With chocolate? It was worth a try. Her problem with James wouldn't be so easily resolved.

James glanced back at her uneasily, and she realized belatedly that her father wasn't expecting her—he was expecting his lawyer. Never in her life had she ever worried that her presence might be a disappointment to her father, but things were changing around here, and for a split second, she did worry.

James knocked on the front door, and after a moment, her father opened it. He wore his usual khaki pants and a salmon-colored polo shirt, open at the neck so that his gray chest hair tufted out. His eyes widened in surprise when his gaze fell on her.

"Hello, James," her father said. "And Izzy. What brings you by?"

"We were together when you texted me," James explained, and her father turned to look at James with an arched brow. She could sense the questions beneath that look, and she had to curb the urge to roll her eyes. Was this going to be the new norm around here—show up at her father's house for a chilly welcome?

"I took him along to Carmella's dinner party," Isabel explained. "Not that it matters. Daddy, do you always call on James at this hour?"

She'd meant the comment to be a joke to break that layer of ice, but her father didn't smile. He just stepped back and let them in. Britney was nowhere to be seen, and the house smelled faintly of coffee and toast.

"I'll just wait in the kitchen—" Isabel said. Obviously, her father hadn't expected her, and she knew how private he was about business.

"No, no… You might as well come with us," her father replied with a sigh. "I had wanted to go over all of this with James first, but it does concern you."

Isabel shot her father a look of surprise, but he'd already turned away and was ambling toward the living room. She looked at James, and he shrugged.

"What concerns me?" Isabel pressed. She followed her father, and James took up the rear. "And what's with all the mystery lately?"

"Discretion is not mystery," her father retorted. "It's how ordinary people deal with personal matters."

"How personal?" she asked.

Her father muttered something unintelligible and shook his head. "Izzy, you are too much like your mother."

He said it often, sometimes as a remonstrance and sometimes with tenderness. Today it was the former, but she'd never let her father's gruffness or ornery temperament put her off. He turned his back on them and went to the couch where he had a few documents spread out over the cushions. He had his ways.

"This." Her father turned and passed the document to James. "This is a deed. I want it put into my daughter's name."

James nodded and glanced down at it. "This is—"

"Yes, the house I promised her from the beginning."

Isabel looked over James's shoulder at the document.

"The house where Jenny lives?" Isabel interjected.

"I promised you that house when you were twelve," her father replied with a shrug. "A promise is a promise."

James nodded, albeit a bit more stiffly than before. So what did this mean, exactly? Why give her a house that was already occupied? Isabel couldn't imagine what James must be thinking.

"Dad, if you don't mind, why not give me another property?"

"Because I'm giving you this one." His expression turned stubborn. "Didn't we talk about this already?"

"Not this…" She crossed her arms. "And why now?"

Her father blinked. "Why not now?"

She hated it when he got like this. Her father was a wealthy and intelligent man who felt no obligation to explain his behavior to anyone, let alone his daughter. He would dance around in circles all night if that's what it took, but he wouldn't give an ounce more information than he'd already decided upon.

"Look, Princess." Her father lowered his voice and stepped forward. He put his hands on her shoulders and gave her a little shake. "I've let you down an awful lot. This is my attempt to make something right."

She was too surprised to speak, and before she knew it, her father was escorting them back to the front door. "James, you can take care of the paperwork, I'm sure. In fact, can you bring it back to me tonight?"

"I could—that's overtime, though, sir."

"Yes, yes. Just get it done. I'll sleep better. Izzy, you look beautiful, as always."

"Dad—"

"Izzy." His tone grew firmer. "Let me do this. It's important to me." His eyes misted for a moment, then he cleared his throat and looked down. "Well, good night."

"Dad—"

"Good night, Izzy."

She wasn't entirely sure of what had just happened, except that she'd been summarily dismissed, and as she and James walked back to his truck, her thoughts were whirling.

"What was that?" she asked once they were in the vehicle once more.

James glanced over at her. "He's giving you a house."

"No…" She shook her head. "Why now? What's the urgency here? I went by to talk to him about the taxes, and I did mention that he'd promised me the house years ago, but you have to believe me that I didn't want *this*."

"It's okay." His voice was low and soft.

"No, it isn't," she retorted. "My issue with the house was that he hadn't told me about anything. It's always like this—he's always the puppet master."

James started the engine and pulled out into the drive, the tires crunching against the gravel.

"Maybe he's trying to make it up to you," he suggested.

Isabel wasn't entirely convinced of that. It mattered to her father, she could see that much, but why? She wished she knew. But there was one thing she was certain of: the family business would never be hers while he was alive. That was one thing he wouldn't share.

"I can refuse the gift, can't I?" she asked after a moment of silence.

"You could," James said. "But I wouldn't recommend it. What if this is all you get?"

He'd voiced her own fears bubbling deep beneath the surface. What if this was her inheritance? After being raised to expect only the best, to appreciate quality and luxury?

"My father isn't about to disinherit me." She pulled a hand through her hair, tugging it away from her face. "I'm his only child... for now. Why would you say that?"

"I'm not saying that he will," James said quickly. "I'm talking as your lawyer here. You need to look out for your own future. Your father is remarried with a baby on the way, and he might consider you already taken care of." He glanced at her, and she thought she saw a warning in his eyes.

"So you think I should take the house?" she clarified.

"Yes. Keep it in your name. It's paid for, and you will need it eventually. Let your father do this for you."

"I know this sounds rather spoiled, but I want a different house."

"This is the one he's offering," he said. "Take it."

It felt wrong. All of it felt wrong. Her father was shifting the balance of power ever so slightly—enough to make a difference in ways she hadn't anticipated. She was about to own the house that her father had used to do a favor for James. This was putting Isabel very solidly in the middle of their personal arrangement.

"Fine." She sighed. "You know something more about this than I do."

"I'm your father's lawyer. I always know something more than you do. It can't be helped."

He had a point there. "What happened to my dad?" she asked quietly. The question wasn't really meant for him. Too much was changing. Her father was no longer the delightfully grouchy Daddy who solved her problems. He was different, more serious. He saw her differently now, too.

James didn't answer, and they drove on in companionable silence for a few more minutes. She couldn't help but resent her father for this. Up until his point, Isabel was simply the Baxter daughter and James was the lawyer. Now, she'd be the charitable landlord for his sister. It gave her power. It made her more than just plain Izzy.

"I don't want to be Jenny's landlord," she said quietly. How was she supposed to explain all of this?

"Why not?"

"It changes things," she replied. "Between us."

He smiled over at her. "How so?"

"You know it does. Don't make me break it down."

He laughed softly, the sound low and comforting. "Nothing's changed. You'll always be Isabel Baxter. I've never forgotten that, you know."

His words stung, and she felt as if her heart suddenly contracted, pulling away from the pain. He'd never forgotten.

Well, she had. For a little while, at least.

Maybe it was better to know it now—she was Isabel Baxter, his boss's daughter. They'd always been on different playing fields, and that wasn't about to change. Somehow, though, that reality hurt more than she'd expected it to. She wasn't going to be Izzy anymore, was she?

She would always be Isabel Baxter of the Meagher County Baxters. A name with a vise grip.

CHAPTER SEVENTEEN

ISABEL AWOKE TO a blister on her little toe from her strappy shoes. She could feel it rubbing against the sheet, but that wasn't what woke her. It wasn't yet morning—the sky was still black. She twisted around to look at the clock—it was 2:00 a.m. She blinked in the darkness, wondering what had awoken her, but it didn't really matter. She'd been having restless dreams anyway after the party and the visit to her father's place.

"I need to sleep," she muttered to herself. The next day would be misery if she couldn't get at least a few more hours, but her mind was awake, and she knew she was probably up for the day.

Carmella's party hadn't been a surprise. She knew she wouldn't fit in with those people anymore, which was why she'd been avoiding them. It was her father who had her stumped. He was hiding something—

she could feel it. Had he been trying to point out to James that she was out of his league?

She had wanted to shake off this life she'd been born into, to try something brand-new. Haggerston would never forget where she came from, and even James had kept a solid handle on her position in this town. Her scars didn't change who she was, and an ordinary existence wasn't in the cards for her, so maybe it was time to accept it. She was the same Isabel Baxter she'd been before the accident; she just had to dig a little deeper to find that core that didn't require men's attention. She used to scoff at their silly little crushes, but she'd relied on them at the same time. Take away the male adoration, and she was still the same woman, but less encumbered, and far wiser. She had what it took to navigate life on her own terms, and she didn't need men to do her dirty work for her. That was freeing.

James's reaction had hurt her the most. It was their connection. She and James respected each other. There weren't any games between them, no flirtatious power struggle. James had seen her for who she was, and he'd still come out of it liking her—kissing her even. But he still hadn't trusted her. And that lack of trust hurt. He was the only true friend she had right now—the only person in her life not trying to manipulate her, punish her or get something from her. She'd learned to trust him, but that hadn't gone both ways, and she felt like she'd failed somehow. She hadn't given as much as she'd received. She'd messed this up.

If he'd seen the real her, then why couldn't he trust her? But perhaps he had a point. She knew how to arrange things for herself, arrange *people* for herself, and if she couldn't manage it, her father certainly could. If James wanted to join her in that carefully arranged life, it would be quite comfortable for the both of them. Except that he didn't want to slide into her Baxter-made cocoon. He wanted his own life, his own way, and she didn't know how to be a part of that. She cared for James, but it was distinctly possible that she wasn't *good* for him.

She tried to bat that aside, but it didn't move away so easily, the disappointment settling into her chest like a sodden rag.

"Don't be silly," she told herself aloud, sitting up.

Isabel Baxter had never been a woman to mourn over a man for long. Mind you, in the past, there had always been a lineup of replacements waiting. She smiled wryly at the memory. Regardless, lineup or no lineup, a man had never slowed her down before, and she wasn't about to start now.

Her cell phone lit up a split second before it started to ring, and she picked it up, squinting at the number. It was Britney. What could she possibly want in the middle of the night?

"Hi, Britney," she said, picking up. "What's going on?"

And as Britney began to speak, Isabel froze.

JAMES ROLLED OVER, groggily waking up from a fitful dream. The sheets were tangled around his legs, and a pillow lay on the floor beside the bed. A breeze fluttered the curtain next to his open window, and the clock's red numbers glowed out the time: 3:07 a.m. His dream had been indistinct—a jumble of anxious feelings and random images. These were the dreams he seldom remembered, except for those first bleary moments after waking, the kind that made coffee an absolute necessity throughout the day. He'd gone to bed late—having drawn up the documents Mr. Baxter requested, and then gone back for a signature. It was irritating, and he'd documented the overtime with precision. The old man deserved it—middle of the night transfers of property pushed the limits of his patience.

His cell phone buzzed on the bedside table, and his hand shot out and slammed on top of it. He blindly pushed the button to pick up the call and brought it to his ear.

"Yeah…" he mumbled into the phone.

"James? It's Izzy." There were tears in her voice, and James shook himself fully awake.

"Izzy? What's wrong? Are you okay?" He sat up, a barrage of possibilities slamming into his sleep-sogged brain. Was she hurt? Was she stuck somewhere needing a ride? He rubbed his eyes and looked at the clock—the time was as ungodly as it felt.

"I'm at the county hospital. It's my dad."

"Is he hurt?" he asked quickly. "What's happened?"

"He's—" She let out a shaky breath. "They said that he had a heart attack. Britney called an ambulance, but by the time they got him here… It doesn't look good."

"Oh, God…" He pulled a hand through his tousled hair, then swung his legs over the side of the bed. "Okay, I'm on my way. I'll be there soon, okay?"

"I'm sorry to wake you up." There were tears in her voice again. "I didn't know who else... I mean... I probably should have called Carmella, but I didn't want to wake her up, and—"

"Hey." He softened his voice. "I'm on my way, okay? I'm glad you called me. I'm here for you."

He wasn't sure if his words were enough, but they'd have to be until he could get down there. Hanging up the phone, he grabbed a T-shirt and a pair of jeans. He was moving on auto-pilot, his mind spinning. Mr. Baxter's new will effectively cut Isabel out, and if he'd had plans to make that up to his daughter somehow...

"He's not dead," he muttered to himself. People had heart attacks all the time and recovered. This was simply a medical emergency, and the older man was right where he belonged.

He pulled his T-shirt over his head, then grabbed his wallet and shoved it into a back pocket. Within a matter of minutes, he was in his truck and driving down the empty streets. As he drove, his thoughts finally had a chance to catch up with his body. Isabel had called him—and that touched him. He'd met her friends, and he knew exactly why she hadn't called any of them. She needed support right now—her defenses were down. As she'd said, they were sharks and there was blood in the water.

Not that he could fix anything. Not that he could really do anything as the family lawyer. This was the job for doctors and nurses, but Isabel would need someone by her side, too. She'd need someone to tell her that it would be all right, to get her some coffee. That's what he could offer tonight—a shoulder for her to lean on. And a steady flow of coffee.

The hospital was located in the next town over, and it took half an hour before he parked and headed in the sliding front doors. The waiting room was nearly empty. A young man in dusty jeans and cowboy boots sat on a chair cradling an arm, a tired young woman beside him. A nurse called him, and he stood up to follow her.

This was the quietest he'd ever seen the emergency room. Not that he'd been here often, but at this time of night, it would have to be a serious emergency to get someone to slog all the way out to the hospital. He looked around and spotted the triage window.

"Hi," he said, dipping his head down to see the nurse behind. "A friend of mine was admitted tonight with a heart attack. George Baxter. I'm a friend of the family."

Announcing that he was a lawyer didn't always get the best results. Especially in a hospital.

"Yes, of course." She tapped something on her computer. "I don't see—"

"James?"

He looked up to see Isabel standing down the hallway. Her dark hair was mussed and her eyes were big and red-rimmed in her pale face. She crossed her arms over her chest as if protecting herself from falling apart. She looked smaller, somehow, thinner.

"Thanks," he said to the nurse and headed in Isabel's direction. She stood immobile and waited for him to get to her, then her face crumpled.

"Hey…" he murmured, and he wrapped his arms around her and pulled her solidly against his chest. She fit under his chin nicely, and he held her there while she shook with sobs. "Hey…" He wasn't sure what else to say, so he kept repeating the word softly into her hair. She wrapped her arms around his waist and balled his shirt into her fists. He leaned forward, holding her close. He couldn't fix this, but he could be that brick wall for her. It was what he was good at. Finally, she sucked in a shuddery breath and pulled away. She wiped at the wet spot she left behind on the front of his T-shirt.

"Sorry," she whispered.

"I'll dry," he said. "Are you okay? Where is your dad right now?"

She shook her head. "He—um—he's gone."

"What?" The words hit him like a sucker punch to the gut.

"He…" Tears slipped down her cheeks. "He didn't make it. The doctor told us right after I hung up with you. They said there was just too much damage to his heart."

"Oh, Izzy." He didn't have anything that could make this better, and he felt a lump rising in his own throat. George Baxter had been a force to be reckoned with, and he'd earned James's respect. He'd been a good man, albeit flawed, and while he knew Izzy would feel this more than he did, it still was a personal loss.

"How can that happen?" she asked, looking pleadingly up into his face. "I don't get it. He was fine. Last I saw him—last *we* saw him—he wasn't sick. He was just fine."

The last James had seen him, he'd been signing the papers in his house coat—perfectly healthy.

"Heart attacks can be like that," he said woodenly. What was he supposed to say? "I could look into the hospital if you think there was malpractice or—"

"No." She shook her head. "I didn't mean that. I mean, how can someone be there one minute, and then just die when you need them most?"

"I don't know."

Idiot. She doesn't need a lawyer.

She also didn't need platitudes and she didn't need philosophies about the meaning of life. She needed to be held. She needed to cry. She needed her dad, but he wasn't here.

"And all that tension between us lately—" She swallowed hard. "I shouldn't have made such a big deal about his marriage…"

"He knew you loved him," James assured her. "He knew that without a doubt."

She looked back down the hall. "Britney is down there," she said. "They have a room for us to sit in for a bit."

He knew the room well. It was a grieving

room set aside by the hospital where families could come to grips with the hard news they often got in emergency rooms.

"Do you want a coffee?" he asked softly.

"Um." She blinked. "Yes, I think I do."

"Good. Who else is here? I'll get some coffee for all of you and I'll meet you back at the room."

"Britney, her mom, that's it…" She wiped the tears from her face.

"Okay." He leaned down and kissed her forehead. "I'll be back soon, okay?"

She nodded. "Thank you, James. You're a really good friend."

A good friend. He wasn't sure why those words stung a bit. Andrew would probably have understood that sentiment all too well. Isabel had a way of making every guy in the friend zone feel like he was missing out. But that's what she needed right now, and that's what he'd be. She didn't need to thank him. He simply couldn't leave her to face this on her own.

What were friends for?

CHAPTER EIGHTEEN

ISABEL AWOKE THE next morning exhausted and weak. The only thing that pulled her out of bed was the meeting to read her father's will at James's office. Would he have left her the company, after all? Would his last gift to her be a chance to be a part of Baxter Land Holdings? Somehow she doubted that. He'd died unexpectedly. There was no lingering illness giving him the opportunity to change his mind about anything. When he'd died, he'd been convinced he'd live to ninety-five.

Isabel had requested the meeting for first thing in the morning—not because she was so eager to hear the will, but because she hadn't wanted to be alone and this seemed like an excellent excuse to be with someone. To be with James. So she pulled on a pair of jeans and a baggy blouse, tugged her hair back in a ponytail to hide that she hadn't washed it, pushed an oversize pair of sunglasses onto her face and headed out the door.

Ten minutes later, she climbed the staircase to the second floor of the downtown Haggerston office building and opened the door to the law firm. The receptionist looked up from her desk and smiled reassuringly.

"Hello, Miss Baxter," she said kindly. "Are you here for Mr. Hunter?"

"Yes." Her voice was hoarse from crying, and she didn't trust herself to say more than that.

"Just go on in. He's there."

She found herself looking forward to being next to James again. He was so strong, so sure of everything, that he was a comfort at a time like this. Her father had chosen his lawyer well. And wasn't it like a Baxter to rely on their legal representation during the hardest times of their lives? It was both ironic and sad.

James's door stood ajar, and she stopped in the doorway. James sat at his desk. He looked tired and grim. He looked up.

"Hi," he said, his voice low. He stood and met her on the other side of the desk. "How are you holding up?"

She nodded. "I'm okay."

He took her hand in his broad, warm grasp, but before he could speak again, Britney's voice traveled down the hall as the receptionist greeted her. James cleared his throat and gave her hand a squeeze. The younger woman appeared in the doorway. She looked as haggard as Isabel did, and Isabel felt sorry for her. She might not like Britney much, but there was no denying that her stepmother was grieving.

"Come on in and have a seat," James said, moving to the door and closing it. "You are the only two people in Mr. Baxter's will, so we can start."

Only the two of them? There would be uncles and cousins who would be royally annoyed with that. But still, it didn't add up.

Britney was silent, and she sank into one of the waiting chairs, sitting down with a hand behind her to feel for the chair and her belly sticking out. She didn't look at Isabel, and she dabbed at a red nose with a sodden tissue.

"You've both had a big loss," James said quietly. "George asked me to read the will first, and then to do a little explaining afterward. Is that okay with you?"

Britney nodded, and Isabel sat rigidly upright, waiting. It didn't matter what she preferred. James would do things the way her father had outlined. James started reading, and the will was full of legalese and florid language.

I, George Baxter, being of sound mind and body, hereby make this Will and revoke all prior Wills and Codicils...

Finally, they got to the part that sounded more like her father's voice. James cleared his throat and glanced toward Isabel.

"My daughter, Isabel Baxter, having already received an agreed-upon portion of my estate, will receive nothing upon my death."

Isabel stiffened. She'd been cut out of the will? The shock hummed around her, filling the room, filling her ears. How could he do this to her? How he could raise her to expect wealth and status, and then simply cut the string and let her fall? What kind of father—

"She will have the house at 180 Knottington Lane, the money set aside in her trust fund, which has already been transferred to her, and whatever items in the family house that she might like for her own personal memories. That is all."

James looked sadly at Isabel, and when she

made a move to rise, he added, "Izzy. Wait. Trust me, this is worth it, okay?"

She hoped it would be, because sitting here next to the woman who had taken everything from her was pure agony. Britney must have done it—she'd convinced her aging husband that his daughter didn't deserve any more financial support and had gotten the money for herself. Isabel wanted to get out of here, to process this alone—

"To my wife, Britney, I leave the house and furniture, except for the items my daughter chooses for memory's sake. My life insurance is to be used to raise my unborn child.

"My company, Baxter Land Holdings, of which I am the sole owner, will be sold and liquidated in order to pay off any and all creditors."

James fell silent, and he placed the papers back on his desk and smoothed them with his palm. Isabel looked over at Britney and found a confused frown on the younger woman's face. The house—he'd left Britney only the house. Wasn't her father worth much, much more than a couple of houses? What about the rest of his fortune, the other real estate? If the business was sold, it would be worth…millions, wouldn't it?

"That's it?" Isabel asked uncertainly.

"That's all that's in his will, but he did ask me to explain," James said. "Isabel, when your father cut you from the will, he was trying to protect you from the debt he'd acquired over the years through his company. The market wasn't kind to him, and he hadn't wanted you to know how rocky things were, so he kept up appearances. That was expensive. The rental homes he'd acquired will be sold to pay off his debts, as well. He knew he was sick. I didn't realize it was this bad, but considering how he started putting his affairs in order, he must have had an inkling."

"He knew he was dying?" she asked.

"I'm assuming so." James shook his head. "I can't confirm that, though."

Silence descended onto the room, and Isabel's mind spun.

"Are you saying that my father was losing money instead of making it?" Isabel clarified.

"Your father had already lost most of his fortune," James replied. "I just went over the numbers with his accountant. I'm sure you could do the same, too. He owed a good many people a lot of money, and when his company is liquidated as he requested, there will be very little, if any, money left over."

"He was broke?" Britney spoke for the first time, her voice torn and weary. "Why didn't he tell me this?"

"He had his pride, I suppose," James replied. "I'm very sorry, ladies. He managed to protect a little bit for each of you, and that was the best he could do."

Isabel looked over at Britney, and they exchanged a long look. Britney's eyes were wide, and she opened her mouth as if to speak, then shut it again. Britney hadn't gotten a windfall of money, after all. Had there really been no plotting?

"So what was all that secretive warning about me not getting anything else?" Isabel demanded. "You knew something."

"I knew he wasn't going to give you any more than he already had. I didn't know there wasn't anything else to give." Her voice was barely a whisper. "I had no idea."

"So you thought you had the money all to yourself," Isabel retorted.

Britney's silence was answer enough. She'd married a man old enough to be her father, and ended up with nothing more than a house in the end. Isabel wondered if it had been worth it for her. If Britney had married for money as Isabel suspected, then she'd just put in a whole lot of work for very little payout. At least she was young enough to marry some other rich guy and maybe have better luck.

"Isabel," Britney said, her voice choked. "Come anytime to choose the things you'd like to have to remember your dad."

"Thank you."

Civility was the only thing that would get Isabel through this. She didn't feel the least bit thankful or kindly disposed toward her father's wife. As far as Isabel was concerned, Britney had gotten what was coming to her... and maybe a little more, since she'd gotten the family house and some life insurance for the baby.

Britney nodded quickly and levered herself to her feet. "Thank you, Jimmy. If you don't mind, I'm going to head home now..."

"Of course." James stood and went around to open the door for her. He shook her hand, and she left. Isabel slowly stood, her mind whirling.

"James, I can't keep you on retainer for the

family any longer, obviously—I don't think Britney will be able to afford it, either, considering."

"That's okay. I understand."

Isabel bent to pick up her bag, and she could feel James's dark gaze on her.

"Izzy," he said.

She put her purse on her shoulder and looked toward the handsome lawyer. "Yes?"

"Can I offer one last bit of advice?"

"Please."

"Britney isn't a bad person. She lost him, too. Maybe you two could help each other through this."

Isabel put her hand on the doorknob. That was asking too much. Britney had lost a sugar daddy—she'd lost a father. Big difference.

"No." She could hear her father in her own voice. "Thank you for everything, James."

Why did this goodbye feel so final? But everything was different now. Her father was gone. The money was gone. She would no longer have any reason to inconvenience James, either. She was no longer someone's daughter, and she was no longer an heiress. Everything had changed in a day.

"If you need anything…even just to talk. Call me, okay?"

"Okay." Tears welled in her eyes again, and she escaped before they fell.

CHAPTER NINETEEN

THE NEXT DAY, Isabel crouched over a cardboard box in her father's attic. She'd come to gather those few items from the house her father had promised her. Britney wouldn't have any use for these things—they were from the family before Britney, and while this house was legally Britney's now, she'd always be the interloper here. Somehow, now that her father had passed, Isabel's parents' memory—the two of them together—seemed stronger, and Isabel wondered if Britney felt it. Probably not.

The attic was dim, a dirty window letting in a little natural light, but Isabel was relying on a hanging bulb overhead to see. She glanced back. Britney's head emerged through the opening in the attic floor.

"Are you almost done up here?" Britney asked.

The attic was filled with mementos from Isabel's childhood—items she remembered from days gone by. Her mother's box of year-books was still up here, her father's clothes from the eighties that he refused to toss out, Isabel's old high chair, her first bike…

She didn't have room in her home to bring it all back with her, and for the first time since arriving, her tiny, immaculate space wasn't enough. She felt the need to gather all these memories in one place, cradle them, keep them together. There was no one left to share the memories with her. Both her parents were gone now, and it was up to her to keep those memories of their family life alive somewhere…proof that they'd been something, the three of them.

Britney climbed all the way up and came to the streaky window. She looked outside, the natural light that reflected off her face revealing puffy eyes and colorless cheeks.

"He used to love the garden," Britney said after a moment.

Isabel's mother had created that garden, and it was only after she died that George started spending time in it. It was his way of remembering Stella, working the soil that his late wife had loved. Isabel used to watch him garden. There was a landscaping company that came by and took care of the bulk of the work, but he'd still putter and pull up a weed here and there. He'd stand there in the cool of a summer morning eating fresh peas out of their pods. Isabel remembered the sight of his steaming coffee mug sitting on top of an overturned bucket while he stood in his bathrobe and a pair of clogs, his back to the house so that she couldn't see his face. Had he known that she'd watched those private moments? Maybe not. That he'd continued his silent vigil even after his marriage was comforting somehow.

But Isabel wouldn't share that—and it wasn't out of sympathy, either.

"What will you do now?" she asked.

"I don't know." Britney ran her hand over her belly. "This wasn't exactly the plan."

Of course it wasn't. But how long would it have taken for Britney to realize that lounging around a house and trying to be helpful to a man who didn't want a woman's help wasn't going to fulfill her?

"Did you want to work...ever?" Isabel asked.

"No." Britney shrugged weakly and shot Isabel a small smile. "I wanted babies, kids. I wanted to be a mom. He liked that idea, too."

So if her father had lived, there would have

been a whole new generation of Baxter siblings to go bankrupt together. Her father always had liked the idea of a woman at home with the kids. Not that there was anything wrong with that life. Her mother had loved it, and it was the future he'd had in mind for Isabel, too.

"Did you know that I'm having a girl?" Britney turned to face Isabel, and her expression was serious, sad—the most honest that Isabel had ever seen her. She'd dropped the "little girl" act and finally looked like a grown woman, an equal. Isabel wasn't sure if she was annoyed or intimidated. Maybe a little of both.

"No," Isabel admitted.

"We just found out." Tears welled in Britney's eyes. "Your dad was thrilled. He said girls were wonderful, because he'd always be Daddy. He said with a little girl, they never outgrew that."

Yet, for being thrilled, he hadn't told Isabel. He'd been her "Daddy," and he'd pushed her right out of the nest. Was this baby her father's second chance? Or did he still have hopes of making them one big, happy family after all?

"He liked his secrets." Bitterness tinged

Britney's tone. "If he'd told me about the money problems…"

"You'd have done what?" Isabel asked icily. "Gotten a job?"

Britney's eyes flashed. "Been able to comfort him. I wasn't here for the money, Isabel. I loved your father, whether you believe that or not." They were silent for a few beats, and then Britney added, her voice quavering, "You're like him in the worst ways, you know."

So now her true feelings were coming out.

"I thought you said you loved him," Isabel retorted.

"I did. I do. But everyone has flaws, and your father could be heartless. Don't get me wrong—he could be generous to a fault when he wanted to. He'd do anything for me. Anything. He loved me like no one ever has, and he could accept me for my faults, too. When he loved, it was like the sun shining down. But his shade was a very cold place. I could accept him for his faults, because I was in his sunshine. But when he couldn't personally identify with someone, they were like scenery to him. Empathy didn't even occur to him. People were there to get him his way."

"And I treat people like scenery?" Isabel

demanded. "What do you know about my relationships?"

"You treat *me* like scenery!" Britney's voice rose, and Isabel blinked, surprised at the directness of her outburst.

A retort came to mind, something about Britney being not much better than youthful scenery around here, but she bit it back. This was the shark in her coming out. Her father's death wasn't Britney's fault, and she was going to try to hurt his widow for no other reason than because she was feeling hurt herself. Isabel sighed. "What did you want from me?"

"To be friends." Britney swallowed hard. "I don't have many left."

"With all the money—" Isabel stopped. There wasn't any money. It was hard to remember that. She started again. "What about your friends around town?"

"The ones who stayed didn't have anything in common with me anymore," Britney said. "I was married to a man twice their age, and I wasn't willing to go partying anymore. Your dad was my life, and they didn't get it. Even Carmella didn't really understand. Since you loved him, too, I thought you might."

Isabel hadn't realized that. Mind you, she hadn't stopped to think about it, either. It hadn't occurred to her.

"I suppose I could have been...kinder." Isabel sighed.

They faced each other without speaking for minute or so, then Isabel pulled an old curtain off a picture nearby. It was the portrait of her parents. Her father looked young, and her mother was slim and beautiful. Her father sat, her mother behind him, a hand on his shoulder. This was how she remembered her parents—united, happy, attractive.

Of all the items in this attic, this one couldn't stay here. It was the one thing that pulled their family back together again.

"I'm taking this," Isabel said.

"Okay." Britney's eyes were pinned to the painting, then she looked away.

"I'll get a storage locker somewhere and come get the rest of this stuff after the funeral," Isabel added. "I'm sure you don't want it."

"No, it's yours," Britney said with a nod. "I'll see you at the funeral."

Where they would say goodbye to the man they'd both loved, and who had lied to them both. Yet, he'd still wanted to make something out of them—the Baxter family 2.0. Except that this blended family was no Brady Bunch.

JAMES STOOD AT the graveside of George Baxter. The day was warm—too warm for his black suit, and a trickle of sweat meandered down his spine. Isabel wore the same knee-length black dress from the party, lace covering her arms and peeking over the edge of the underskirt to tickle her knees. She looked appropriate, somber, modest. She hadn't worn makeup—or if she had, it had all been wiped off by now. She swiped at a tear on her scarred cheek, but she didn't look at James even once. She stood with her ankles together and her gaze directed at the suspended coffin.

James was listening to the minister intone some words about heaven and a life away from sickness, sadness and pain. He read a few familiar Bible passages, and James allowed the words to flow over him. He'd never been a terribly religious man, but he believed well enough to find comfort in the ritual. Did Isabel? He wished he knew.

May George find some peace...

It was half prayer, half wish. The old man

hadn't been at peace for as long as James had known him. He was always pent up, wound up, ready to conquer…until he'd been undone by something as common as a heart attack. It seemed wrong somehow that George Baxter should go down in such an ordinary way. He was the sort of man who should have been gored by a bull or something more in line with his boulder-like personality. But that was life for you—no one ever seeming to get the poetic ending they deserved.

The last funeral James had attended had been his cousin's, and Andrew had gotten a slightly more heroic end to his life, but it was too early. Andrew had deserved more living first.

Don't take the shade for granted… Wasn't that what Andrew had told him? Life was short. It could be over in an instant, as he and George had found out.

George Baxter's funeral was stately and stoic, much like the man. The whole town turned out for the funeral service at the church, or just about. Jenny had wanted to come, too—Mr. Baxter had provided her a home, after all—but James had convinced her to stay home with her roommates. He needed to say his goodbyes with some privacy. George had been a client, but he'd somehow slid closer than that, and this death had hit him more personally than he anticipated.

The church service had been packed to overflowing, people standing along the walls and huddled into the hot, sweaty foyer. The minister had said some kind words about a man who loved his community and left a mark upon this sod, or something like that. It was a little overdone, but appropriate, considering the man it honored. Isabel and Britney had sat at the front of the church in the first pew—several feet apart. James knew his place, or at the least the place he felt most comfortable, and he'd stayed toward the back, his forehead moist with sweat.

His client was dead. Job complete, right? Except nothing felt complete about George's life and family.

James hadn't gone to view the body. Britney and Isabel had looked generally overwhelmed by all the people filing past them, speaking a few words, shaking hands. He wasn't going to add to that. Besides, he didn't belong in the throng. His relationship to both George and his daughter had been unique.

But standing here, several feet away from

Isabel—Britney being opposite them across the grave, flanked by her parents—he wondered if she even wanted anything more from him. Maybe his usefulness was at an end. That wouldn't surprise him, either.

When the minister said his last prayer, that was the cue for people to disband and leave. Isabel dabbed her nose with a tissue, came over to where James stood and gave him a small smile.

"Thanks for being here, James," she said.

"How are you holding up?" he asked. She looked petite and younger with her lack of makeup. She wiped her nose once more and tucked the tissue away. He found himself yearning to touch her, slip an arm around her. He restrained himself. That wasn't where this relationship was going.

"Not too badly, all things considered." She tucked her hand into the crook of his arm, and he pressed her hand against his side—the closest he could come to holding her. "Walk with me? I want to avoid condolences for a bit. It's really tiring."

"Sure."

They moved together across the graveyard, bright June sunlight toasting his shoulders through his suit jacket, and he realized how relieved he was to be this close to her. That wasn't smart—she wasn't the kind of woman he needed—but somehow Isabel still had a way of softening him against his better judgment.

"I have a favor to ask," Isabel asked after a moment.

He sighed. There it was. She didn't want his physical comfort, she wanted him to do something for her.

"What do you need?" he asked.

She seemed to sense the reticence in his tone, because she blushed slightly. "I'll pay you for your time, of course. It's just…" She pulled her hand out of the crook of his arm and opened her purse. She pulled out a small photo and passed it to him. "I found that behind a picture of my parents together that my mom had really cherished. That's her holding the baby. I just need to know who the baby is."

James took the picture by one corner and looked closer.

"Why does it matter?" he asked.

"It might not," she said quietly. "I know that. It's just that when I asked my father about it, he got so guarded. He kept so many secrets, and I want to know who this child is, and why my father cared so much. And if my mother tucked it away like that…"

This was personal, obviously. And she was right about George and his secrets. He thought women were to be protected, and men should shoulder the burdens. While James agreed that men shouldn't heave unnecessary burdens onto the women they loved, he believed it should go both ways. He didn't want a woman to idolize; he wanted a woman to share his life, his worries, his goals. He wanted a partner, not a trophy.

"I would pay you," Isabel repeated. "I'm not asking for something for free."

No, she wasn't, but she did want something from him besides his company. That shouldn't bother him, but somehow it did, because he'd felt relieved at just being next to her, her hand pressed against his arm.

"Okay," he said. "I'll look into it."

He asked a few more details about where her parents had lived during their marriage. Apparently, they'd landed in Haggerston only just before Isabel was born. He had somewhere to start, at least. Isabel suspected the baby was maybe a cousin or a godchild. But he agreed that her mother's attempt to protect and hide the photo was interesting. And if she had someone else in her family, it would be good for Isabel to find them. As it was, she had a stepmother and an unborn sibling.

"Thank you." Isabel's eyes misted again, and she met his gaze. "I really mean it, James. Thank you. You've been so…so…" She swallowed hard. "I don't know what I'd have done without you."

"It's okay," he said. "We're friends, aren't we?"

She nodded. "Most definitely."

He was smarter than Andrew in this respect. He'd accept friendship and leave the rest alone—no matter how much he wanted more right now. Those were feelings, and he knew better than to be led by them, especially with Isabel Baxter. But he was reluctantly grateful, too, because she'd given him something to do for her, an excuse to see her again. He wasn't quite ready to say goodbye, even though he knew it was coming. Isabel was special. She could make a favor feel like his idea. And as long as he could keep that line carefully drawn, that could be his own personal vice. For now. A man didn't build his life on being a woman's hero. Life was too complicated for that.

CHAPTER TWENTY

THE NEXT FEW days after the funeral, Isabel sorted through a few more items from her childhood home—crafts she'd made as a little girl, a framed photo of her from her beauty queen days that her father had kept on his dresser… Funny that a man's life—and her own relationship with him—could be encapsulated in such innocuous items. She'd spent a good deal of time in tears, and then she'd looked at the calendar and realized that she had only a couple of days before her official store opening. She could have taken a week off, even more, but she didn't want to. Sitting alone with her grief only made it worse. Besides, she was doing this in memory of her father.

George Baxter had been hungry for success, but more than that, he'd thrived on the challenge of starting up a new business. That his last venture had failed just before his death was even more heartbreaking because

Isabel knew how much his ability to make something self-sustaining meant to him. She shared that drive. He might not have thought that this store could be a success, but she disagreed. And just like the rest of their relationship, she'd prove him wrong.

The morning her store was set to open, Isabel crouched in front of the chalk sandwich board and put her attention back into her grand opening announcement. Her boxed chocolates would all be two-for-one, today only. There would be free samples, the first tray of which were already arranged and waiting inside the kitchen. The sign was almost done—just a few more strokes and it would be about as good as she could make it.

There was a tap on the glass, and Isabel looked up to see Jenny smiling through the window. Isabel got up to let her in.

"Hi, Jenny," she said with a smile. "Come on in. Am I glad to see you."

She shut the door behind her and crouched in front of the sign once more.

"I'm sorry about your dad," Jenny said, twisting her hands in front of her. "He was nice to me. He let me stay in my house. Do I have to move now?"

She was worried—Jenny didn't hide her

feelings well. It was written all over her face, and she licked her lips, waiting for Isabel to answer.

"What?" Isabel pushed herself to her feet. "No, Jenny. You don't have to go anywhere."

"But it's your house now, right?" Jenny pressed. "James says—"

"Never mind that." Isabel tried to smile reassuringly. "I do own the house now, but that doesn't change anything for you. I have a home of my own, remember? It's okay."

Jenny relaxed slightly and dropped her hands to her sides. "Okay. So I can tell James I don't have to move in with him?"

Isabel laughed softly. "You get to keep your privacy, Jenny."

"When do we open?" Jenny asked.

Isabel looked at her watch. "In forty minutes. I'm just going to get this sign outside, and then I'll help you in the kitchen. We need to have all the samples on trays and ready to go. I have one tray finished. Do you think you could start on another one? I'm making each tray a selection of different truffles and cream chocolates."

Jenny nodded. "You bet." She hooked a thumb over her shoulder. "Are you going to let her in?"

"Who?"

Isabel looked over to the window to see Britney standing by the glass, her hand shaded over her eyes to look inside. She wore a black pantsuit, her hair pulled into a bun at the back of her head and a pair of oversize sunglasses perched on top of her head. Isabel met her gaze through the window, and they stared at each other somberly. It had been an emotional week, and she had no idea what Britney wanted now.

Isabel opened the door a few inches and looked out. "Hi, Britney. What can I do for you?"

"I—" Britney let out a long breath. "I came to see if you needed a hand."

Isabel blinked. "You what?"

"I came to help," Britney repeated. "This being opening day and all."

Isabel regarded Britney in frank surprise. What was the catch? More important, did she even want Britney here today? This was a day about her own dreams, not about Britney Baxter.

"I thought you didn't approve," Isabel countered.

"No, I said your dad didn't approve." Britney smiled wanly. "There's a difference.

And even though he didn't like your business plan, I think he would have wanted us to be…friends."

Isabel stepped back and opened the door the rest of the way. "Come in." She angled her head.

"Unless you have enough help already," Britney said. "And you don't have to pay me."

Isabel had Jenny, but Jenny was most comfortable in the back of the store away from customers, and one more person handing out samples while she rang up purchases would actually be a big help. She thought for a moment, then nodded in acquiescence.

"I'm good at that." Britney pointed at the sandwich board. "I took a few art classes. Do you want me to spruce it up a little?"

Isabel looked from the chalk in her hand to Britney in surprise. "Sure." She passed the chalk over. "Thanks."

Britney flashed her a smile that lit up her young face. "I just need a stool or something to sit on." She rubbed her belly. "Or else I won't be able to get up again."

Isabel pulled a low stool out from behind the counter. "Will this do?"

Britney settled herself in front of the sandwich board, and her slender hands began to move swiftly, switching colors of chalk as deftly as any artist.

Isabel looked at her watch once more. She was ten minutes closer to opening, and her stomach fluttered in anticipation.

This was hers. She'd dreamed about a chocolate shop for years, and she'd never really thought that it would be a possibility—at least not with her father's blessing. He'd always been the financer of her dreams, and he'd financed this one, too. He just wouldn't be around to see her actually succeed. Yet today with the summer sunshine streaming into her shop, her boxed chocolates arranged on the shelves, the smell of sweet chocolate mingling with the scent of fresh paint, she felt more confident in her own abilities than she ever had before.

Baxter's Chocolates wasn't opening because of her beautiful smile or her stunning looks. Baxter's Chocolates wasn't opening because her father's friends were humoring her or because her father was bankrolling it like a hobby. This shop was opening because of her own vision and hard work, and that was a feeling she'd never experienced before.

"Britney," Isabel said quietly, and the younger woman looked up.

"Why are you here...really."

Britney was silent for a moment, and she turned back to the board, chalk scraping softly as she worked. Then she paused and looked up once more.

"You asked me if I ever wanted to do anything else in my life," she said, eyes fixed on the work in front of her. "And I did. I wanted babies and to raise my kids, but I also wanted to help your dad out...in the business."

Isabel eyed her stepmother in surprise. She'd wanted to be involved in the family business, too? If Isabel had learned this earlier, she might have been angry, even seen her as competition. But now, she recognized something familiar in Britney—a Baxter ambition.

"Did you tell him?" Isabel asked.

"No." Britney glanced up, pink tingeing her cheeks. "I was working up to it. He kept kicking me out of the room whenever he talked business, so I didn't think the time was right."

No, it probably hadn't been.

"He wouldn't let me in, either," Isabel said. "If it makes you feel any better."

"He would have," Britney said. "If he'd had a business left to run, I think he would have."

Britney's guess was as good as hers right now, but the facts remained that there wasn't a Baxter Land Holdings left to build, but there was a Baxter's Chocolates.

"Well, one day at a time," Isabel said, and sucked in a breath. "Let's get that sign out. We have thirty minutes until we open."

She had Jenny in the back, her stepmother pitching in, and it looked like today might actually work out... The only thing missing to make it perfect was her father's approval.

She'd be grateful that she had the support of the women in her life—perhaps the most surprising support possible. Maybe Britney wasn't the enemy she'd imagined.

IT TOOK A FEW phone calls and several favors called in, but when James got the information from the state records office, he stared at the email in a state of shock.

...I'm sending some faxes of the originals, as well. If there is anything else I can do for you...

"This isn't good," he muttered. It seemed like his job was to deliver bad news lately. He double-checked the dates, the names, all the pertinent information. He'd searched through baptismal records first and come up with nothing. Then he took a shot at hospitals in the towns where Isabel's parents had lived, looking for births to a mother named Stella Baxter. And bingo—it had almost been too easy.

"Yeah, it's right…" He sighed and pushed himself up from his chair. This was the sort of thing he couldn't fire off in a text message. Isabel deserved to hear this in person.

Grabbing his suit jacket, James angled his steps out of his office and down the air-conditioned hall. The receptionist sat at her desk, squinting at her computer screen.

"Maggie, I'll be out for a little while. If there's anything pressing, text me."

"Will do, Mr. Hunter." She smiled up from her desk. "Oh, these faxes just came for you—"

She spun around and grabbed some papers, then passed them over. James glanced at them. They were the scans from Montana's state records. He nodded his thanks and headed out of the office.

As he walked down Main Street toward Nicholson Avenue, his mind was spinning. Of course, he wanted to see Isabel—he wanted the excuse to drop by. He would have found a reason, even if this hadn't come up, but she wasn't going to like what he had to say. She'd said that she thought the baby might be a cousin or a godchild. She wasn't expecting a brother.

She's opening her store today. The timing was miserable, and twice, he almost turned back, determined to leave this for a better time, but when would that be? Her father had passed away, her hopes of running the family business had been crushed, the family money evaporated, and what was left she had to share with her late father's wife…but this was something he could give her—a small piece of information, a meager explanation. And then he was going to have to take an emotional step back.

He couldn't be Isabel's rescuer. She'd be fine—she was a Baxter, after all. Business sense was in their blood. And for all his client's lack of faith in his daughter's money-making abilities, James disagreed. Isabel was smarter than she looked, and hungrier for this than anyone else imagined. She'd succeed, if only to prove her point. She might be a wounded shark, but as she said, she was still a shark.

James stopped at the front of the store and looked through the window. Isabel stood with her back to him, sorting through some papers on the counter beside the cash register. He tapped on the glass, and she turned.

My God, she was beautiful. The scars didn't take that away from her—if anything they made her more relatable. She was stunning, but she was on a mortal level now. Somehow, he didn't think she'd stay there for long. Isabel wasn't the "normal life" type. She'd build something more for herself.

"Hi, James." She smiled, pulling open the door. "Ten minutes until I open."

"Maybe this could wait—" He nodded to his sister and Britney, who were arranging some platters of chocolates.

"What is it?" Isabel asked. "Is it about the picture?"

"I found out who the baby is, but it's probably better to let you focus on your opening day first. I'm sorry, I shouldn't have—"

"James, I'm perfectly capable of dealing with more than one thing at once." She shot him an annoyed look. "What did you find?"

"Your parents lived in Billings before moving to Haggerston, right?" he asked.

"Yes. They came here just before I was born."

"Well, I checked out the public birth records," he said, then paused. "Did your mother ever mention a pregnancy before she had you?"

Isabel shook her head, but the color drained from her cheeks, and she put a hand back onto the counter. "Do I have a sibling?"

James nodded. "Well, you would have. There was a baby boy born two years before you—" He looked down at the certificate in his hand. "—to George and Stella Baxter at the Saint Vincent Hospital in Billings, Montana. He was born on September 6 at one fifteen in the morning."

When he felt uncomfortable with feelings, James dug down into facts and figures. He knew his own tendency to hide in the minutiae, and he shot Isabel an apologetic look.

"I'm sorry," he concluded.

"I have a brother out there somewhere?" she breathed. "Why? How? I don't understand—"

"He passed away," James explained. "He was only three days old when he died. The death certificate says that he was born with severe birth defects, and I suppose he just couldn't make it."

Isabel took the papers from his hands and looked down at them, her lips moving silently as her eyes scanned the words. She shook her head slowly.

"Tyler Baxter," she said, lifting her gaze to meet his. "His name was Tyler. I don't understand… Why did they hide him? Why wouldn't Dad say anything—" She swallowed hard, the papers falling to the counter beside her.

"I don't know," James said quietly. "But the information was available in public records for anyone who cared to look."

"I was their only child." Her voice grew strong again. "I was their one and only child. That's what they told me. They said they longed for a baby, and when my mother discovered she was pregnant with me, I was an answer to her prayers. She was never able to have any more children, and I was it."

"Maybe they thought you wouldn't be able to handle it."

"Why not?" she retorted. "How would it have changed anything to tell me?"

"Maybe they couldn't cope with it," he

suggested quietly. Grief did strange things to people.

Isabel nodded, and tears welled up in her eyes. "Do you have the picture?"

James pulled the photo from his pocket and passed it over. She looked down at the picture and smoothed a finger gently over its surface.

"Thank you, James." Her voice was low and choked. "This is—" She sucked in a breath. "Thank you."

"Look, Izzy, I—" James wasn't sure how to say what he was feeling. "If you need anything—"

What was he hoping she'd say? He knew he needed to back off, but here he was, putting himself forward again. She just looked so vulnerable standing there, shocked by this news and rocked by the loss of her father. He didn't know what he was hoping she'd ask for, but he knew he'd give it—whatever it was she wanted. That was the power she'd always held over men, but for him it wasn't because she was beautiful, it was because she was *her*. He'd fallen for her—against all his better judgment—and he'd have to deal with his emotional fallout alone.

"I'm fine." She nodded curtly. "I'm fine."

She sounded like she was trying to convince herself more than him. "I have a store to open. Thank you for this, James. Just give me an invoice, and I'll pay you."

What she was feeling with all of this, he could only guess. But she wasn't looking to him for comfort.

"This one was on the house," he said.

"That's sweet." She wiped a tear from her cheek that had slipped past her defenses. "But I'll pay you, James. You don't owe me anything."

And maybe he didn't. Was he just another fool reading more into Isabel Baxter's smiles and touches than he should?

"Take care, Izzy."

As he turned away, he made the choice to keep walking. It was time for him to back off. She might be a Baxter without a fortune, but she was still a Baxter, and he knew what that meant. She was his sister's boss and landlord. That balance of power was always tipped ever so slightly in her favor.

She'd be just fine. Baxters landed on their feet.

CHAPTER TWENTY-ONE

ISABEL STOOD BACK, watching as the last customer ambled out of the store, a Baxter's Chocolates bag swinging at his side. That logo—the stylized letter *B*—felt heavy with meaning now that her father was gone. This was all they had left of the Baxter empire, and ironically it was a tiny start-up of which her father hadn't approved. Baxter Land Holdings Inc. was being disbanded. It wouldn't be anything more than some old letterhead now. A lifetime of work, all for nothing. But Baxter's Chocolates bore their name, too, and it was fueled by the same passion to succeed…although perhaps this Baxter would balance her life a little more successfully. Would that logo—the Baxter's Chocolates sign—mean something for the generations to come?

"It's good, right?" Jenny asked jubilantly, coming out of the kitchen.

"It's very good, Jenny." Isabel grinned,

and she realized that this was the first real smile since her dad's passing, and she had a feeling he'd understand it.

Isabel grabbed a box of bags and started to refill the cubby under the till. The bell over the door tinkled, and she looked up to see the photographer from a few days ago come in. He was a man in his forties with a belly and a camera over one shoulder.

"Good afternoon, ladies," he said. "I wanted to take a few pictures for the paper. Would you mind?"

"You're writing about my store for the paper again?" Isabel asked.

"You're the talk of the town, Miss Baxter," he replied. "I'm sorry about your father, too. He was a good man."

"Thank you." She accepted the condolences with a nod. "I appreciate that."

"With your permission, I'd like to get a group shot," he said.

"Sure." The exposure was good for business—free advertising. She was tired but grateful that the town was taking an interest in her store, after all. Without the support of Haggerston, this business would most certainly fail.

"If we could get you all together," he said,

glancing around the store. "Over here, with the windows behind me would be perfect."

"Sure," Isabel said, and she gestured for Britney and Jenny to join her. They had worked just as hard as she had today. They stood in front of the counter, Isabel in the center. Behind them was the Baxter's Chocolates sign.

The photographer took a couple of shots, then checked the results on his view screen.

"What a beautiful group," he said with a smile. "If those faces don't sell chocolates, I don't know what will."

He was trying to be friendly, and a couple of years ago she might have enjoyed the flattery and attention, even thought it her due. But those years were behind her. She didn't want to be complimented on her looks—this was something she'd worked for, not something she'd been born with.

"One more," the photographer said. "Smile this time—beautiful! Yes!"

Isabel smiled for the camera, and she could feel the scars tugging at the side of her face. She didn't feel ugly anymore. The scars were becoming a more natural part of her, and she didn't feel the urge to turn to the side, to hide the damage. She'd survived a lot in the past year, and she'd survive even more, but she wanted to do more than get through. She wanted to thrive.

After a few more photos and some pleasantries, the photographer headed off with a small box of samples. Isabel hadn't expected herself and Britney to make such a good team today. Their dynamic was different without her father between them. Without the "Georgies" and the machinations, they actually did get along, and Britney had proved to be an exceptional saleswoman. She could sell chocolates to anyone, it turned out, and she'd barely had to try. If Isabel had Britney's help in the store—but dare she go that far?

"What's the matter?" Britney asked.

"Hmm?" Isabel glanced over to find Britney eyeing her.

"That photographer annoyed you," Britney said, and Isabel was surprised at her acuity.

"I thought I hid that better." Isabel smiled wanly. "Yeah, he did. It's the compliments that get to me. 'Aren't we pretty.' 'Aren't we lovely.' 'These smiling faces…'" She sighed. "You know what, Britney? I don't want to be called beautiful. I want to be called 'ma'am.'"

Britney gave her a peculiar look. Maybe she couldn't appreciate that yet. Britney still had her looks. But Isabel didn't need the re-assurances that she was still attractive. She wanted to build this store into a chain, then into an online chocolate empire. She wanted a head office in Billings, a team of accountants, and when someone approached her for a photo, she didn't want to be called "you ladies," she wanted to be called "Ms. Baxter, ma'am." It wasn't about money or social status—it was about having earned the right to their respect. When people came to her, she didn't want them to be patting her on the head with patronizing compliments. She wanted them coming with a résumé in hand, asking her to hire them.

"I'm serious," Isabel said. "My dad didn't think I had what it took to make a business thrive, but I think I do. And with the right people, I can grow this business into something we can be proud of."

"This felt good," Britney said quietly. "I miss George so much…but this was nice. I have a feeling he'd approve."

Isabel nodded. She had the same feeling. He'd gotten his wish, after all, and the two Baxter women were bonding. Britney ran a hand over her belly, and Isabel was suddenly reminded that they wouldn't be the two

Baxter women for much longer. A new Baxter girl was coming soon, and maybe, just maybe, they could grow this business into something that would show her what women could do when they put their minds to it.

"You're grieving and you're pregnant," Isabel said. "You shouldn't push yourself right now. But when you're ready, if you want to be part of a Baxter business, we could sort something out."

Her father had been the businessman, providing for the ones he loved. He'd wanted to leave behind a thriving business that could fuel the family for generations, but he hadn't managed it. However, he had raised a daughter who'd watched his every move, and he'd sent that daughter to Yale. He might not have left them a fortune or a salvageable business, but he'd left something more important—a legacy.

Britney would need some support for the next while, and so would their little girl. Someone had to step into George Baxter's shoes. Someone had to bring the Baxter name back to its earlier glory.

This is for you, Dad.

CHAPTER TWENTY-TWO

THE NEXT EVENING, James sat across from his sister at her kitchen table. Jenny's roommates were watching a reality show in the living room, the tinny voices filtering across the hall. Their evenings were always so happy and celebratory, and he knew that Jenny would miss this house. This arrangement had been good for her—for both of them. She'd really blossomed since she'd had some space to herself, and he'd enjoyed having his own privacy, too. But with George gone, the balance of power was different, and it felt wrong.

"I know you like it here, but things change. That's part of life. Luckily you've got me, and I'm too stubborn to change." He tried to cajole her with a smile.

"I don't have to leave here, though," Jenny countered, not willing to be mollified. "Isabel says I can stay."

"Look, Jenny..." He tried to control his

frustration. "Living here in Haggerston means I don't get paid as much as I would in the city. It isn't easy to pay for your rent, my mortgage, taxes, food, gas… It adds up. And even if I found a way to make it all work, things are different now with Mr. Baxter gone."

"But Isabel says I can stay!" Jenny shook her head irritably. "You can ask her. She said so yesterday."

"She says that now," James said. How could he explain this to her in a way she'd accept? "But this is all she's got, Jenny. Her dad didn't leave her much else. I think she wants to let you stay, but eventually, she won't have much choice."

Besides, he hated this—being beholden to her. He could take care of his sister himself, and he didn't need charity from Izzy in order to do so. He sincerely wished that George had left Izzy a different house and allowed this one to be swallowed up in the disbanding of Baxter Land Holdings Inc. It would have been simpler that way, black-and-white. Jenny would still have had to move, but at least he wouldn't be the bad guy.

"Where would we go?" Jenny demanded.

"Well, you'd come to live with me again,"

James said. "And your roommates would find something else, too. But that would be between their families and Isabel."

"I don't want to live with you, Jimmy." She used the air quotes around "with you." She was mad.

"I'm not such a bad roommate," he joked. "I don't have big parties. I make coffee when I get up. I'm pretty clean, too."

"You get up too late to make my coffee," she replied with annoyance. "I have a job now."

She was just throwing up barriers now, and he felt sorry for her. She hated change, and as far as she could see, he was the one messing up a good situation.

"Jenny, it isn't about the coffee. Things change, and we have to roll with it. But you can rely on me to always be here, okay?"

"When do I have to move?" she asked quietly.

"I don't know yet, but I don't want you to worry about it." He knew that was easier said than done. Jenny was a worrier by nature, but she did better with a little warning. "Let's talk about something else. How are you enjoying your job?"

"I'm good at it." She met his gaze solemnly. "I make good chocolate."

"That's great. Maybe you could make some for me." He smiled hopefully.

"No, sorry." She shook her head. "I can only make it for the store. It's Isabel's recipe."

"Oh, I see." She wasn't going to forgive him that easily.

"But you could buy some, and then you'd know that I helped to make it," she conceded.

"I'll do that." He squinted at her. "You seem happy lately."

"I am!" She nodded quickly. "Isabel says I'm really good in the kitchen. She says I don't have to help customers if I don't want to."

"Do you really want to be kept in the kitchen?" he asked.

"Oh, I can go out and help people choose chocolate if I want to," she said. "I just don't want to."

"Fair enough." As much as he'd worried about this before, he had to admit that the job did seem like a good fit for Jenny, after all. His sister seemed more confident, somehow, more sure of herself.

"Other people don't think I'm very good at things," Jenny said. "They think I can just do something small and that's it. But Isabel thinks I'm good at making chocolate. She wouldn't let Britney in the kitchen. She said that I did everything perfectly."

"Yeah?" He was curious to ask more about Isabel and Britney's dynamic, but he didn't want to put Jenny in the middle.

"She says that I could even become a chef one day if I wanted to. She says that it takes a special kind of person to make candy, and that I'm that kind of person."

"A sweet person?" James teased.

"Oh, stop it," Jenny replied. "I'm being serious."

"Okay, sorry."

"Isabel says that even if her store doesn't last too long, I could get a job in a bakery or something, but she says that she hopes I'll stay working for her, because she doesn't know how she'd do everything without me to help her."

"She said that she was worried about the store?" James asked quickly.

"I don't know. Maybe."

James sighed. He refused to accept Izzy's charity, and Izzy refused to accept his emotional support. He missed her—more than he should. More than he wanted to. He wanted to keep her at arm's length, but give him time alone with her, and he always ended up a whole lot closer. She'd been creeping into his dreams at night, where he'd pull her into his arms and kiss those pink lips... But those were dreams and this was reality.

"How come you're sad, Jimmy?" Jenny asked softly.

"Because I'm disappointed about something," he said. "It's okay. It's nothing to do with you."

"I'm in the newspaper," Jenny said with a hopeful smile. She pushed the *Haggerston Chronicle* toward him across the table. "And I look good."

James looked down at the picture on the third page—Isabel, Britney and Jenny standing in the store, smiling into the camera with the Baxter's Chocolates sign behind them. The headline above said Isabel Baxter Opens Local Chocolate Store. Nothing terribly descriptive there.

"You do look good," he said with a grin. "Very pretty."

"Isabel says it's better to be called 'ma'am,'" Jenny replied archly.

He had the sneaking suspicion that Jenny had just set him for that, and he chuckled.

His gaze skimmed over the article beneath, and he stopped at a direct quote from Isabel.

"I'm not doing this alone. I have help. A company is nothing without skilled employees, and what you've heard is right—one of my chocolatiers-in-training is a young woman with Down syndrome. Baxter's Chocolates is about inclusiveness and respect. We'd be nothing without this community, and that includes people with disabilities."

It was smooth—well constructed. She'd thought out this response in advance. And there it was—the machinations he'd been waiting for. Jenny wasn't a cause to be trotted out for newspapers. She wasn't a box to be ticked. If Isabel was looking for a sympathy card, she'd have to find someone else, because while Jenny didn't see it yet, she'd be devastated if she discovered that Isabel had used her. Jenny didn't know how to swim with sharks.

"Jenny, I'm going to head out," James said, standing up. "You mind if I keep this paper?"

"It's my only one," Jenny said. "You have to bring it back."

"I promise." He forced a smile, anger pulsing through him. He knew that the anger was covering something more tender—something that ached like betrayal—but he wasn't about to go poking around at his feelings.

Isabel Baxter had crossed a line, and he was in no mood to step lightly. It was time they got a few things straight.

ISABEL HAD JUST gotten home from her second day of business, and she stood outside her tiny house, bathed in the warm light that flooded out the windows. The sun had slipped behind the jagged mountains, leaving the sky washed in coral pink and orange. This used to be her favorite time of day when she visited her dad—standing with him in the garden at sunset, listening to the whir of insects and watching the darkening twilight. Why did it still feel like that was a possibility?

She could hear the truck's engine before it turned into her drive, headlights bouncing along the gravel drive toward her. She crossed her arms, a cool breeze bringing up the goose bumps. She recognized it was James as he parked, and she turned toward the truck as he got out. He held a folded newspaper in his hand, and he didn't speak.

"Hi," she said with a small smile.

"Are you okay?" he asked after a pause.

She must have looked as melancholy as she felt.

"It's a hard time of day to be alone," she said.

He nodded. "I get that. How was the grand opening?"

"Excellent. Didn't Jenny tell you?" She'd seen him when he picked Jenny up, just a wave through the window, nothing more. That distance had stung, reminding her that their earlier closeness had been purely professional. Warm looks and sweet words all part of the job. And the kiss? Maybe that had just been a mistake.

"Yeah, she did..." He cleared his throat. "Speaking of Jenny—"

She paused, waiting. Did Jenny want to quit? Was her brother going to negotiate a raise?

"Is she okay?" Isabel asked.

"She's fine," he said. "Me—not so much." He passed her the folded newspaper, and she looked down at the picture of herself, Jenny and Britney standing in the store together. She had a copy of the article inside, and she was pleased with it. This kind of advertising was ideal.

"What's the matter?" she asked, looking up. "Did you not want Jenny in the picture? The photographer was there to take pictures of all of us. She wasn't pressured, I assure you."

"It isn't the picture." Tension rippled along his jawline. "It's your quote."

"I know what I said." She handed the paper back. "What's the problem with it?"

"Why did you hire Jenny?" he asked, and she frowned. That wasn't what she'd been expecting.

"You know why I hired Jenny. She needed a job, and I thought she might be a good fit for my store," she replied. "And I was right. She's excellent. What's the problem, James?"

"One of my employees is a woman with Down syndrome," he paraphrased. "Baxter's Chocolates is about inclusiveness and respect."

Her words in his mouth sounded hollow and mildly self-serving, but that hadn't been the way she'd intended them. That hadn't been the way the article had spun them, either.

"Are you seriously suggesting that I hired Jenny to make myself look good for a local newspaper article?" she demanded.

"No." The word was clipped, angry. "But I am suggesting that you used her for your own ends. You didn't have to do that to her, Izzy. You could have just smiled for the camera and let Jenny be Jenny."

"Is she upset?" Isabel asked, worry building up inside her. If she'd offended Jenny, she would have to apologize and make it right. That hadn't been her intention at all.

"No!" James ran a hand through his hair. "No, I'm the one who's mad!"

"I don't think you have a right," she shot back, her own anger rising. Who did he think he was? "When I hired your sister, I didn't sign any confidentiality agreements. Jenny isn't a dirty secret to hide. The photographer asked me about rumors that I was hiring employees with disabilities. I simply answered him and told him where I stood. Baxter's Chocolates is mine, it's my work, my vision. My personal views on the valuable contribution of my employees are mine to share whenever I please!"

"Then maybe Jenny is working for the wrong person," he retorted.

"Are you seriously going to make her quit because I stood up for her in print?" Isabel demanded.

"This reminds me too much of your gardener," James said. "You used him to look sympathetic to get the beauty queen crown."

"I was eighteen!" Isabel threw her hands in the air in exasperation. "I thought I explained this to you! How on earth was I supposed to have any experience with human pain at that age? I was young, I was sheltered and I did my best to broaden my views. I'm no longer a teenager, and you can stop throwing that in my face."

"It isn't that," James said, and he swallowed hard, then looked away.

"Then what?" she demanded. "What is it? Because I don't understand why I'm suddenly the bad guy here!"

"It's Andrew!" James turned to face her, his eyes flashing. "Do you even remember him?"

"Of course I remember him!" She shook her head. She was embarrassed about how she'd handled things with Andrew, but what that had to do with James's sister, she had no idea.

"You used him," James said. "You needed a tutor, he had a crush on you, and you used him."

"That isn't true," she snapped. "I needed

a tutor, I offered to pay him and he refused payment. We got to know each other and I really liked him—" Emotion choked off her voice.

"You had a funny way of showing it," James said. "Because you wouldn't tell anyone you liked him, or that you were dating him. He told me all about it, and he'd fallen in love with you. He told me that I didn't know the real you…"

And she'd dumped him. She remembered that all too well. She felt her cheeks heat, and she hoped James couldn't see that in this dim light.

"Okay, I was cruel." She shook her head. "I'm sorry. I could have handled that better."

"Do you notice that he didn't come to the prom?" James pressed. "Because he wasn't there. He left early for boot camp, and he never came back."

"He left early because of me?" she asked in disbelief. Somehow, she'd never really considered that her cruelty would have left such a lasting mark on the young man. She'd assumed that he'd brush it off, maybe be angry with her, but she never once dreamed that she'd broken his heart…

"He did," James said. "He was an eigh-

teen-year-old kid, too, and he was humili-
ated. You told him that you cared about him,
and the minute he let that slip and word got
out, you called him a liar and walked away."

She was stunned. "James, I'm so sorry…"

"Yeah." He heaved a sigh.

"I don't know what to say—" She brushed
a tear from her cheek. "I was young, stupid
and thoughtless. If I could take it back…"

"I'm not blaming you for his death," James
said, his voice tight with emotion. "That was
the war, not you. I'm just saying that you
have a track record for using people and toss-
ing them aside."

"James, I'm not using your sister." She
looked up into his face, wishing there was
some way she could make him believe her.
"And I'm not using you."

"I couldn't blame you for using me if you
were," he said, his tone dropping low. He ran
a finger down her cheek. "I've been the idiot
putting myself in your path…hoping for… I
don't even know what."

"I didn't know," she whispered.

"It's okay." He sucked in a deep breath.
"I'm no smarter than Andrew was. I knew
what I was doing, I knew you were a shark,
and I still let myself fall in love with you."

His words echoed through her mind.

"You love me?"

He slid a hand behind her neck, nestled it deep into her hair and tugged her closer until his lips hovered over hers.

"Yeah," he whispered gruffly.

His lips brushed hers, and when she lifted her face to his, his mouth covered hers in a warm, bittersweet kiss. She leaned into his strong arms, and when he pulled back, he gave her a sad smile.

"Sorry," he murmured.

"I've fallen for you, too," she admitted softly.

"We need to stop this now," he said, releasing her.

"Do we?" she asked. "Why?"

"Because it can't work," he said, and the sadness in his eyes showed how hard this was for him to say. "I can't fool around, Izzy. I've got Jenny to consider, and I'm not the kind of man who can keep his heart guarded forever. Look how successful I was with you."

"But why is Jenny a problem?" she pressed.

"Because she's my sister, and I have to take care of her. I need a woman who can do that with me—not grudgingly, but willingly. I need a woman to shoulder all those difficulties with me."

"And I'm not that woman," she whispered, the realization hitting her in the gut. He didn't think she could handle the hard stuff. He was a realistic man who knew that life was difficult, and he just didn't trust her to have his back.

"Besides, you might not have a fortune now, but you're still a Baxter."

"Meaning what?" She frowned. "A Baxter without money, without her looks, still isn't an ordinary person?"

"Izzy," he said quietly. "You still have all the power. You always did. You own the house my sister lives in, and you provide her with a job. One of these days, you'll need a lawyer, and you'll hire me. You're George Baxter, in a prettier form."

Her father had never recognized their similarities, and now all those parallels were being thrown into her face.

"I am just like my father," she said, her voice shaking with emotion. "And I'll build that store into something the entire state looks at with respect. And I won't apologize for being my father's daughter."

"Nor should you." He sighed. "I'm sorry. I'm saying it all wrong. You are a formidable woman, and I'm not sure that I'll ever completely stop loving you. But I'm the kind of guy who needs a woman at my side—equals, partners. I'm no good at pedestals."

And Isabel realized he was right. She might be ordinary in her bank account and her lack of an estate, and she might be ordinary in her loneliness at sunset, but her father had very carefully made sure she had power over the handsome lawyer. Giving her that house had cemented that position, and she hadn't even noticed it, because she was so used to being on top. Most men seemed to like the idea of either taking care of her or looking up at her, but James was the one, heartbreaking exception.

"You have no idea how badly I wish it could work," he said, a catch in his voice.

"I know." She nodded, tears welling in her eyes. "Me, too."

James bent and kissed her forehead, then turned back to the truck. "Izzy, I'm moving Jenny into my place. It's better that way."

She didn't answer, and he didn't wait for her to. He started the truck again and slowly pulled out. James wasn't a man who could be led on a leash, and she realized that she didn't want to. With his last gift to her, her father had set her up as a Baxter woman with some clout, and he'd effectively put her up on a pedestal—the loneliest place in the world.

When James's truck pulled out onto the main road, Isabel gave up fighting her tears. She'd fallen in love with a man who wouldn't play the Baxter game, and she didn't know any other way to be.

CHAPTER TWENTY-THREE

THE NEXT EVENING, Isabel sat on the couch in her father's living room. His chair sat empty, the ridiculous orange chair mocking her from across the room. None of it seemed to matter quite so much now, and she looked over at Britney, who sat across the couch from her.

"My parents want me to move back in with them," Britney said. "But I said no."

Isabel looked at the younger woman in surprise. "You don't want the extra help?"

"Not really." Britney smiled sadly. "I want to raise my daughter in her father's house."

Isabel nodded. "It's a good place to grow up."

"My family thought I was crazy to marry your dad, too," she said. "They thought I was throwing my life away on an old man."

"I'm sorry I wasn't more supportive," Isabel said.

"It's okay, I get it." Britney rubbed her hand over her belly. "I'm scared, though. For all the flak I got for marrying George, I'm now on my own."

"No, you aren't."

"How do you figure?" Britney cast her a bland look. "Should I move back into my parents' house?"

"We Baxter women aren't pushovers," Isabel replied. "We might have acted the part at some time or other, but deep down we're strong. We're smart. We have what it takes to really make something."

"We?" Britney asked.

"We're both Baxters, Britney. And I meant it when I said that you could be a part of it."

Britney shifted her position and smiled that gentle, secretive smile that mothers had. "Do you want to feel the baby kick? She's pretty active in there."

"Okay…" Isabel put a hand out tentatively, and Britney put it onto her stomach. At first she felt nothing, then there was a little tap, then another. She grinned. "I felt that!"

"Yeah…" Britney laughed softly. "I feel that all the time now." She was quiet for a moment. "Isabel, I always wished I could be more like you."

"No, you don't…" Isabel shook her head.

"You were strong, beautiful, confident," Britney countered.

"I wasn't confident, I was mean," Isabel replied quietly. "I used people. I thought I was better than others. You don't want your daughter to be like I was. Raise her to be like you, and to be proud of who she is."

Isabel looked around the room. This was no longer her childhood home—it would be another little girl's childhood home. Her sister would grow up a new breed of Baxter—a kinder generation of women who were tough enough to succeed on their own, and confident enough to retract the claws.

She didn't want to live her life on a pedestal anymore. She knew exactly what she needed to do. She pulled out her cell phone and typed in a text: James, would you meet me at the diner at 8? I have some business to discuss.

JAMES SAT IN a back booth of the diner, a ceramic mug of coffee in front of him, two empty creamer packets lying on the table. He glanced out the window into the twilit evening, his own haggard reflection clearer than the outdoors. He looked rough—he felt rougher. Somehow, this business arrangement had gotten very personal.

What was it with Isabel and her clandestine meetings? Not that he minded. He missed her. He'd felt a hollow ache inside ever since their talk last night, and while he knew that she couldn't be the woman for him, he still longed for her. She'd inherited her father's penchant for odd hours, and he'd shared his cousin's ability to fall for the one woman capable of breaking his heart.

But he couldn't blame Isabel for this—he'd done it to himself. She hadn't lured him in, or manipulated anything—she'd just been a bare, honest version of herself, and that was all it had taken.

The door to the diner opened, and the bell overhead tinkled. He glanced over his shoulder to see Isabel coming in. She wore a pair of blue jeans and a billowy pink blouse that brought out the rosiness in her cheeks. She had a manila envelope under one arm, and when she spotted James, she moved in his direction.

"Hi." James stood and kissed her cheek before they both sat down. He'd have to stop that—the physical contact—but he couldn't help himself one last time.

"Thanks for meeting up," she said, and a smile tickled the corner of her lips. "I was halfway here before I realized that ordinary people don't do their business after hours...or have their lawyer's personal phone number."

He chuckled. "Baxter to the core. It's okay. What can I do for you?"

She placed the envelope on the table and pushed it toward him. "This is the deed to the house your sister is living in."

James raised an eyebrow. "Is there a problem? I checked for liens or anything like that. You should be in the clear."

"I want to sign it over to Jenny."

James stared at her. "You what?"

"I'm serious, James." The smile dropped from her lips. "I want to sign this house over to Jenny."

"That's a very bad idea," he countered. "I told your father—"

"My father is gone!" Her voice trembled. "I know what he was doing when he gave me that house, James. He was setting me up like a Baxter, giving me some clout, raising me just a little higher to give me that leg up—" her voice softened "—over you."

"Isabel, you don't need to sign away your property for me," he said.

"Who said this is for you?" she demanded. "This is for *me*. My dad raised a shark, and I don't want to be that woman anymore. I've chosen a different life, and I might not ever be ordinary—I'm okay with that. But I can't be a shark."

"Izzy…"

"No." She pushed the envelope closer to him. "I want Jenny to have that stability. I know you think you're the only one who cares about her future and her happiness, but you aren't. I care, too. I'd love for her to keep working with me, but if she loses interest or decides she wants to do something else, I don't want her to feel like she has to keep working at my shop in order to please me. I want that house in her name—no strings attached. The thing is, I've figured out why my dad took Jenny under his wing like that—it was in honor of my brother. My dad really cared about Jenny, and so do I."

"But it's all you got from your dad," he said.

"No, it isn't," she countered. "I got the seed money for my business, a Yale education and the Baxter genes that thrive on that entrepreneurial challenge. I'm going to be just fine. I can build this business, and I can build others after it if I need to. I've got that tiny house of mine, and it suits me to a T. I'm not suffering in the least, James. Now, are you going to do the legal part of this, or do I have to go find that baby-faced lawyer?"

James shook his head. She wasn't going to listen to him, and he suspected that if he turned her down, she'd do just what she threatened and find Eugene. "Why are you so stubborn?"

"I'm a Baxter." She grinned. "And I'm tired of the pedestal. I'm going to earn what I get, and I'll deserve it when I get there. But I'm starting out on a level playing field, and with a clear conscience."

"You don't owe us anything," James reminded her.

"I owe myself," she said, and he could hear the emotion in her voice. "Will you take care of this?"

"Yeah…" He reached out and put his hand over hers. She turned her palm over, intertwining her cool fingers with his. His heart pounded in his chest, and he swallowed hard. She was giving it up—the power, the house, any hold she might have over him and Jenny. She was giving it away. Shoulder to shoulder… wasn't that what he wanted?

She pulled her hand out of his and wiped the tear away. "I'd better go."

"Izzy, wait—" He couldn't leave it like this, couldn't let her walk away. "I'm sorry. I wasn't fair to you. I was afraid that you'd be the kind of woman who would resent how much I have to do in order to take care of my sister. But I was wrong about you."

"Very wrong." A small smile came to her lips. "And I like to hear you say it."

"That I'm wrong?" He laughed softly. "Well, there you have it."

"Thank you." Her gaze softened. "It means a lot to hear that from you."

James scooped up her hand in his and tugged her closer. She didn't resist, and she stood so close that he could rest his forehead against hers.

"I don't come from money," he said quietly. "I'm not a powerful man who can rescue you and give you everything your heart desires. I can't promise you an easy life, but I'm asking—" He swallowed. "I'm asking you to stand by my side, to face the world with me. I'm asking you to be the woman who makes me stronger, the woman who keeps me honest with myself."

"A life with you?" she asked softly.

"Yeah." He moved a tendril of hair away from her face, and she looked up at him. "Would you take care of Jenny with me? Would you build a life with me? Maybe have a few kids with me, too?"

"I'd help take care of Jenny even if you didn't want me," she whispered.

"Want you?" he asked. "Isabel Baxter, I want to marry you."

She nodded, and he felt a weight lift off his chest. Had she really agreed? He hadn't been sure he'd ask until the words came out of his mouth, and once they did he knew he wanted this more than anything else in the world. "Is that a yes?"

"Yes, James," she said, moving into his arms. "I'll marry you."

James pulled her against him, sliding his arms around her slender waist, and dipped his head down, catching her lips with his. She felt warm in his hands and tasted sweet on his lips. Her breath tickled his face, and when he finally pulled back, her eyes were glittering again.

Around them, three waitresses and a couple of truckers broke into a spattering of applause.

"The ring won't be what you're used to—"

he began, and she put a finger on his lips, silencing him.

"The ring will be perfect," she said. "And the wedding will be small, and the honeymoon—"

"Will be very sweet," he said with a low laugh.

"Actually, I was going to say that it'll have to be quite short, because with the store just opened, and—"

James laughed and smothered the last of her words with a kiss. She melted into his arms and sighed softly against his lips.

"Baxter to the core," he murmured lovingly. "We'll sort it out together."

* * * * *

LARGER-PRINT BOOKS!

GET 2 FREE LARGER-PRINT NOVELS PLUS 2 FREE MYSTERY GIFTS

Love Inspired®

Larger-print novels are now available...

YES! Please send me 2 FREE LARGER-PRINT Love Inspired® novels and my 2 FREE mystery gifts (gifts are worth about $10). After receiving them, if I don't wish to receive any more books, I can return the shipping statement marked "cancel." If I don't cancel, I will receive 6 brand-new novels every month and be billed just $5.49 per book in the U.S. or $5.99 per book in Canada. That's a savings of at least 19% off the cover price. It's quite a bargain! Shipping and handling is just 50¢ per book in the U.S. and 75¢ per book in Canada.* I understand that accepting the 2 free books and gifts places me under no obligation to buy anything. I can always return a shipment and cancel at any time. Even if I never buy another book, the two free books and gifts are mine to keep forever.

122/322 IDN GH6D

Name	(PLEASE PRINT)	
Address		Apt. #
City	State/Prov.	Zip/Postal Code

Signature (if under 18, a parent or guardian must sign)

Mail to the **Reader Service**:
IN U.S.A.: P.O. Box 1867, Buffalo, NY 14240-1867
IN CANADA: P.O. Box 609, Fort Erie, Ontario L2A 5X3

**Are you a current subscriber to Love Inspired® books and want to receive the larger-print edition?
Call 1-800-873-8635 or visit www.ReaderService.com.**

* Terms and prices subject to change without notice. Prices do not include applicable taxes. Sales tax applicable in N.Y. Canadian residents will be charged applicable taxes. Offer not valid in Quebec. This offer is limited to one order per household. Not valid to current subscribers to Love Inspired Larger-Print books. All orders subject to credit approval. Credit or debit balances in a customer's account(s) may be offset by any other outstanding balance owed by or to the customer. Please allow 4 to 6 weeks for delivery. Offer available while quantities last.

Your Privacy—The Reader Service is committed to protecting your privacy. Our Privacy Policy is available online at www.ReaderService.com or upon request from the Reader Service.

We make a portion of our mailing list available to reputable third parties that offer products we believe may interest you. If you prefer that we not exchange your name with third parties, or if you wish to clarify or modify your communication preferences, please visit us at www.ReaderService.com/consumerchoice or write to us at Reader Service Preference Service, P.O. Box 9062, Buffalo, NY 14240-9062. Include your complete name and address.

LILP15

LARGER-PRINT BOOKS!

GET 2 FREE LARGER-PRINT NOVELS PLUS 2 FREE MYSTERY GIFTS

Love Inspired®
SUSPENSE
RIVETING INSPIRATIONAL ROMANCE

Larger-print novels are now available...

LISLP15

LARGER-PRINT BOOKS!
GET 2 FREE LARGER-PRINT NOVELS PLUS
2 FREE GIFTS!

HARLEQUIN®

super romance®

More Story...More Romance